What the critics are saying…

"*Dirty Pictures* from Elisa Adams is just the latest in a long line of erotic fiction. She has already made a niche for herself in paranormal erotic romance, and has finally dipped her toes into more mainstream erotica. She's made a splash! "~ *Marissa for Novelspot Romance Reviews*

"This tale is deeply erotic and at the same time very moving. Ms. Adams does a great job with every aspect of the telling. The romance is poignant and the sex is extremely hot, HOT! This one is going in my permanent file! "~ *Thia McClain for The Romance Reader's Connection*

"*Dirty Pictures* is a fun, feisty, fantastic trip through the rocky road of a relationship! Ms. Adams has created some wonderful characters both main and secondary that are all fully drawn and full of fun!" ~ *Julie Esparza for Just Erotic Romance Reviews*

"I highly recommend this book and can't wait to see what Elisa Adams comes up with next." ~ *Angel Brewer for The Romance Studio*

Elisa Adams

Dirty
PICTURES

ELLORA'S CAVE
ROMANTICA PUBLISHING

DIRTY PICTURES
An Ellora's Cave Publication, May 2005

Ellora's Cave Publishing, Inc.
1337 Commerce Drive, Suite #13
Stow, Ohio 44224

ISBN #1419951858

Edited by: *Martha Punches*
Cover art by: *Syneca*

Warning:

The following material contains graphic sexual content meant for mature readers. *Dirty Pictures* has been rated *S-ensuous* by a minimum of three independent reviewers.

Ellora's Cave Publishing offers three levels of Romantica™ reading entertainment: S (S-ensuous), E (E-rotic), and X (X-treme).

S-*ensuous* love scenes are explicit and leave nothing to the imagination.

E-*rotic* love scenes are explicit, leave nothing to the imagination, and are high in volume per the overall word count. In addition, some E-rated titles might contain fantasy material that some readers find objectionable, such as bondage, submission, same sex encounters, forced seductions, etc. E-rated titles are the most graphic titles we carry; it is common, for instance, for an author to use words such as "fucking", "cock", "pussy", etc., within their work of literature.

X-*treme* titles differ from E-rated titles only in plot premise and storyline execution. Unlike E-rated titles, stories designated with the letter X tend to contain controversial subject matter not for the faint of heart.

Also by Elisa Adams:

Dark Promises: Demonic Obsession

Dream Stalker

In Moonlight

Just Another Night

Dark Promises: Midnight

Dark Promises: Shift of Fate

In Darkness

Dark Promises: Flesh and Blood

Eden's Curse

Dirty Pictures

Prologue
A Word of Warning from Lily

Before you read this story, I want to say something in my own defense. I'm impulsive. I sometimes make not-so-smart choices, but who doesn't? Life can get a little boring if you don't do something to liven it up once in a while.

Where was I? Oh, yeah. My story. This is what happened to me when I posed nude for a magazine. No, not what happened during the photo shoot. I'm talking about the aftermath, when everyone in the small town where I live found out about it. Get your mind out of the gutter.

When I look back at it all, I realize that, when this whole fiasco happened, I was long past due to stir up some trouble. I hadn't offended my family in months. Coming from a girl who grew up with the nickname Lily Don't, this is a huge improvement. Trust me. Yes, posing for the magazine was an impulsive decision, but even today I stand by my choice. No matter what my reasons were, I'm not ashamed of what I did — especially when it got me something I'd wanted for a *long* time. What, you ask? You'll just have to wait to find out. For now, I'm going to keep it a secret. I'd rather let you be surprised.

This is not your typical memoir, I confess, but I'm nobody special. I don't have any heroic, Nobel-Prize-worthy events that shaped my life, but I did learn a lot about my family and friends — and about myself. I can't tell you the names have been changed to protect the innocent — or guilty, as the case may be — because that would be a lie. This is all how it happened, the good, the bad, and the utterly mortifying.

Don't worry. It all works out in the end. And it's *good*. So read on, enjoy.

And don't say I didn't warn you.

Chapter One

If she had known what an uproar posing nude for a nationally known men's magazine would cause, Lily would have chosen a magazine with a smaller circulation. She leaned against her partly-open front door, her hands gripping the doorknob so she didn't fall over and bash her face off the cement steps, her body swaying forward and back as the door moved on its hinges. She stifled a yawn, fighting to keep her eyes open while her brother Jake ranted and raved and waved the latest issue of *Seduced* magazine in her face.

"What the hell were you *thinking*?" He smacked the magazine on the doorframe hard enough to crease the pages. His eyes bugged out, his face reddened with rage, and she might have found it comical had he not dragged her out of bed at six in the morning. "Do you realize what a mess you've gotten yourself into this time? And what are you doing answering the door in something so...so...*revealing* anyway? I could have been anybody, and you might have found yourself in trouble."

She glanced down at her ratty, washed-a-hundred-times, extra-large *Metallica* concert T-shirt and stifled a chuckle. "Oh, yeah. I dress like this just to seduce all the men in the neighborhood. Good thing I have you to watch out for me, Jake, since I apparently have no mind of my own and wouldn't be able to defend myself in any situation." Her annoyance at the interruption in her much-needed sleep left a tinny taste in her mouth. Or maybe that was just morning breath. Either way, she needed to go brush her teeth.

She leaned back a little too far and nearly lost her balance. The cool metal surface of the front door hit her in the chin as she yanked on the knob to keep herself from falling. She rubbed the spot with the heel of her hand.

Caffeine.

She needed caffeine, and lots of it, if Jake expected her to concentrate on his sermon. He might as well have been barking like a dog. It all sounded the same before her morning dose of java.

"Stop with the smart mouth. This is serious," he said, or rather, ordered.

She rolled her eyes. Serious for whom? Was the world going to come to an end because he'd seen his sister nude in a magazine? *For crying out loud.*

She snagged the magazine from his fingers and flipped it closed. How did he manage to get a hold of it, anyway? Jake the Saint, with a copy of *Seduced* magazine? It didn't fit. Her eyes widened when she saw the white subscription label in his name on the glossy front cover — along with the post office box he used for his business mail. She smiled — or the closest thing she could manage this early in the morning. It probably looked more like a smirk, but hey, that worked, too. "Shame on you, Jake. Does your wife know about this?"

He opened his mouth, gaping at her like some demented beached fish struggling for breath. After a few seconds of uncharacteristic speechlessness, he snatched the magazine back, rolled it up, and shoved it into his back pocket. A burst of laughter escaped her.

"Didn't think so. Are you through yet? You're going to wake the neighbors." He'd been droning on and on at her since she opened the door five minutes ago. Knowing Jake, he'd be able to go on for another sixty or seventy if she let him. Maybe being only semi-coherent wasn't such a bad thing, after all. She stifled another yawn as she squinted into the bright sun, scanning the street for any of her nosy neighbors. None yet. That was always a good sign. "I'd invite you in for coffee, but since I'd be too tempted to pour the entire pot over your head, that might not be such a wise idea. If you don't have anything worthwhile to say, can you please leave so I can get ready for work?"

Birds chirped in the silence that followed. Heat bugs buzzed already, signaling another scorcher of a day.

"No, I'm not through. I still have a lot more to say, and you're going to shut your mouth and listen."

Too bad he recovered his voice. She'd been about to forgive him for his little outburst. She shook her head in disappointment. "I think not, Oh Great Asshole. You can talk all you want, but I'm finished listening."

He started to speak again, but she didn't hear a word he said. She was too busy slamming the door in his face.

Brothers.

Men.

She made it to the kitchen when she heard the door open again. *Shit.* Having Jake as her landlord definitely had its drawbacks. What did a girl have to do around here to get some privacy? Change the locks?

He appeared in the kitchen door, looking ready to kill. She rolled her eyes.

"Lily Jane, stop right there," he told her when she tried to brush past him out of the room.

Of all the nerve. She turned to glare at him, her hands on her hips. "What now?"

He blinked, apparently taken aback for a second that she gave him the floor. Did he really expect her to fight? The more she argued, the longer it would take to get rid of the guy. After a few seconds of excruciating silence, he cleared his throat. "This was really irresponsible of you."

Irresponsible? Ha! He just didn't like the fact that his baby sister had grown into a woman. If he'd had his way, she would have stayed twelve for the rest of her life. "Making money isn't irresponsible, Jakey. How do you think I paid the rent last month?"

He sputtered and coughed, finally throwing his hands up in the air and shaking his head. "Fine. You want to be difficult about this, go ahead. Just don't expect me to be there for you the next time you need me."

She raised an eyebrow. "And when exactly have I needed you?"

"Well..." His eyes rolled ceiling-ward. After a minute, he looked back at her and frowned. "What are you staring at?"

"I'm trying to see if smoke is coming out of your ears. Don't think too hard. You might hurt yourself." She patted his cheek. "Go home, Jake. I don't want to be late for work because of some stupid, misplaced tirade. I'm a grown woman. There's nothing wrong with showing a little skin."

Anger flared in his eyes. She bit the inside of her lip. Stupid, stupid, stupid. Why did she have to go and say something to set him off, just when he'd started to calm down? She really needed to learn to control her impulses. Reprimand built in Jake's eyes again as he crossed his arms over his chest. *Think fast, Lil. Deal with this before he explodes.* She wrinkled her nose. What a mess that would be. "Look, Jake. You're right, okay? I shouldn't have posed for those pictures. I'll *never* do it again. Does that make you feel better?"

"It would, but I don't believe you." He narrowed his eyes at her. "You don't really think that."

Duh. "Of course I do." *Now get the hell out of my house so I can get out of my nightgown and take a shower.* "You get going to work now before you're late. I'll talk to you soon."

Yeah, like when the Hell figure skating team won a gold medal.

"Fine. I'll go. But we're not done talking about this yet." He stomped back to the front door and let himself out, closing it hard enough to shake the mirror that hung on the wall next to it.

"Real mature, Jake," she muttered. He could talk until he turned blue, but she didn't have to listen. She walked down the hall to the living room and stood by the front window to watch him drive away down the street. Were all men such domineering jerks, or only the ones in her life? There had to be some good ones out there. At least one or two.

Yeah, right. A woman was much better off with a trashy novel and a showerhead with a massage setting. Luckily, she had both.

After downing a quick cup of coffee, she wandered back into her bedroom to make the bed and dress for work. When had it become a terrible thing to show her body to the world? She hadn't committed mass murder. What was Jake so worried about, anyway? At least she didn't star in porn movies like a girl they'd gone to high school with. But did anyone mention *her* name? *No.* They all pretended she didn't exist—which would have been preferable to *this* treatment.

She stripped and stood naked in front of the full-length mirror hanging on her closet door. Those stupid pictures had Jake in a snit. She sighed and shook her head at her reflection, still not understanding why he made such a big deal out of it all. Women did this all the time—if they didn't have women willing to pose without clothing, they had no magazines to sell to horny guys looking for something to masturbate—

Oh.

Maybe that was part of the problem. Funny, but she hadn't thought about that when she'd been in the studio with the very professional—female—photographer.

Her cousin Crystal, a die-hard feminist, would probably react the same way Jake did, but for different reasons. Crystal thought anything relating to the adult industry was a blatant exploitation of women. Lily laughed at the thought. Her views on the subject were just the opposite. She saw it as more of an exploitation of men—they were the ones who drooled over the magazines and videos, the ones who spent small fortunes on the various products. Their high libidos drove them to it. People publishing the magazines and making the movies knew that— and used it to their advantage to become very rich.

She smoothed her hand down her stomach, flat and toned due to her job as a yoga instructor. She kept in shape, but she worked hard for it. She took care of herself, so why not show it off? She didn't fool herself into thinking she'd stay in this kind of shape forever. At twenty-seven, it wouldn't be long before things started to go downhill. If a person only had the body of a twenty-year-old during their twenties, what did making the most of it hurt?

She didn't even look like the same woman now, standing all goose-pimply from the air-conditioner and pasty pale in front of the mirror. They'd put her in full-body makeup to make her fair skin look tan and made her press her arms to the undersides of her breasts to make her C cups look like Ds. She didn't even want to get started on her hair. They'd used some kind of rinse that had given her mousy-brown hair an unnatural, but not unwelcome, sheen—and then they'd ruined the look by teasing the roots an inch off her head. It had taken her a week to get all the hairspray out. Add to that the soft lighting in the studio and the immense amounts of airbrushing they did to those kinds of photos and—voila!—instant slut puppy.

She looked at it as an experience, something to look back on when she was old and gray with her breasts sagging to her knees—a story to laugh about with the grandchildren. Okay, maybe not the grandchildren, but she and her future husband could have a good chuckle over it. If she ever found a man who interested her for more than a week. That was a big if. Huge. *Enormous.*

Most of the men in Monotony, er... *Tranquility*, New Hampshire, were stuck in the dark ages. *Me man. I provide. You woman. You stay home and do laundry.*

As if. She had better things to do with her time than cater to the every whim of some old-fashioned jerk.

Like scrub toilets.

With a laugh, she walked away from her reflection and put on her work clothes, light pink yoga pants and a matching tank top. She pulled her hair back into a loose ponytail and swiped a light coat of shiny lip-gloss over her lips. She never bothered with more makeup than that. She'd inherited her father's full eyelashes, and mascara made her look like she had tarantulas dangling from her eyelids. Not a pretty sight.

She picked up her watch, checking the time before fastening the Velcro strap around her wrist. Seven a.m. Still two hours before her first class started. She'd have to thank Jake for his early morning wakeup call. His misplaced sermon had actually done some good. She had time to indulge in her favorite pastime—watching her neighbor stretch out from his run—without having to rush to get out the door.

She hurried to the bedroom window and glanced out across the street just in time to see him round the corner. Her breath caught in her throat as he slowed to a stop in front of his house and propped one foot on the front steps. She couldn't help the small sigh that escaped her lips. The guy was pure physical perfection. He stood about six feet tall, with the long, lean muscles of a long-distance runner. He ran every morning in nothing but a pair of black ultra-short nylon shorts that pulled taut over his rear when he bent over to stretch, giving her a nice view of that fabulously toned ass—and prompting her friend Janet to nickname him Mr. Fine Ass. And the nickname fit. Boy, did it *ever*.

In the two months since he'd moved into the house across the street, he'd said maybe a total of twenty words to her. But it was enough for her to know that his voice matched the rest of him. Hot. Scorching. Sexy.

With her luck, probably gay.

Evan was his name. Evan Acardi. No, he hadn't told her. She'd sneaked a peek at his mail one day. He couldn't very well take top billing in her fantasies if she didn't have a name to put in the credits.

He switched legs and she sighed again. She would have swooned if it hadn't been so terribly outdated. Why did she think she needed coffee in the morning? Waking up to Evan was so much more appealing. The phone on the table next to her rang. She fumbled for the receiver, bringing it to her ear without taking her eyes off her neighbor's perfect form. "Hello?"

"Is he doing it again?"

"Uh-huh," she answered Janet, momentarily caught up in the way Evan stretched his arms over his head. "God, this guy is incredible."

His hair was dark, almost black. Despite the short cut, the locks still curled softly as if in rebellion. A sprinkling of hair the same color peppered his chest, arms, and legs. His bronzed skin tone and defined features hinted at Hispanic heritage. His dark, espresso-colored eyes made her shiver right down to the soles of her canvas mules. He never smiled, keeping a dark and brooding expression on his face that brought to mind nights of hot, steamy sex. It was as if someone had tapped into her every sexual fantasy, created the perfect man, and dropped him into the house across the street.

Too bad he didn't even notice she was alive.

"He's definitely not from around here. If the men around here looked half that good, they wouldn't be single." Janet laughed. "Has he been there long?"

"Just a few minutes."

"Good. I'll be right there."

Lily blinked. Not a good idea. "Don't you think he's going to get suspicious if you show up three days a week at the same time he's finishing his run?"

"Are you kidding? He's a guy, hon. I'm sure he basks in all the attention."

What was this? Cable TV? "I've got to get to work soon." Lily tucked a strand of damp hair that had escaped the ponytail behind her ear and fanned her face. Maybe she needed a cold shower before work. Evan probably showered after his stretching. That thought brought to mind an even more appealing visual.

"It's only seven. You have *hours*." Janet sighed. "Besides, I have another reason for visiting this morning."

"What's that?"

"You haven't seen the morning paper yet, have you?"

"No. Why?" A wave of suspicion rolled over her, prickling the hair on the back of her neck. It almost ruined her mood. *Almost.* But then Mr. Fine Ass bent forward and touched his toes and she felt better.

"You'll see. I'm almost there. Wipe the drool off your chin and come answer the door, okay?" Janet disconnected the call and Lily dropped the receiver back on the cradle—or at least she thought she did. With her gaze still glued to the most perfect body she'd ever seen, she couldn't be a hundred percent sure.

A few seconds later Janet's little red Honda Civic pulled into the driveway. Lily broke her gaze away from the buns she wanted to cup in her palms and rushed through the house to the front door. She swung it open just as Janet got out of her car and hurried up the front walk. "Inside, Lily. *Now.* I don't want to miss any of this."

Janet pushed past Lily and ran to the living room window before Lily even had the door closed. "Nice to see you, too," Lily muttered. She slid the door shut and followed Janet across the tile floor. She scooted up beside her friend and peered outside just as *he* finished his stretches and shook his body out.

"Wow," Janet said on a sigh. "He's something else. Wish I had one of those in my front yard. I'd never go out again."

"He doesn't hang around outside in next to nothing all day, you know. I'm pretty sure he has a job."

Janet didn't remove her face from where she had it pressed up against the window when she answered. "Job? Not if he was mine. I'd keep him chained in the bedroom and only let him out…well, never."

Lily laughed. After a couple days, the poor guy would probably gnaw off his own arm to get free. Janet could be a little…intense. Besides, Evan didn't strike her as Janet's type. She preferred them intellectually challenged. It made the chaining to her bed experience a little easier if they didn't have the wit to fight back.

"What did you have to show me?" she asked, trying to drag Janet from the window. Janet brushed Lily's hands aside and pressed her nose to the glass. Lily winced. That would leave a streak.

"Hold on. Hold on," Janet said. "He hasn't gone inside yet."

He turned toward them just then, and Lily's heart stopped. His gaze met hers across the thirty or so feet that separated them, and his eyes darkened. A corner of his mouth quirked in a half smile that broadcast loud and clear that he knew they'd been watching. He'd probably known it all along. "Shit. He sees us. Get down." She pulled Janet down to the floor and they collapsed in a fit of giggles.

"Why do I feel like I'm back in the fourth grade?" Janet asked, shaking her head. "So what if he sees us. Maybe he'll look into my eyes and fall madly in love and demand I run away with him."

"Yeah, right. And I'm going to be the next Miss America."

Janet stopped laughing and shrugged. "Hey, it could happen."

"Not in this lifetime. Hands off, tramp girl." Because he's *my* fantasy man.

Janet huffed, pretending to be offended. "Well, I *never*...okay, maybe I'm a *little* trampy, but I swear it's just for show. A girl's got to do something to liven up this boring place."

She glanced at Janet's outfit—skin-tight white jeans and a bright yellow cropped T-shirt with a neckline that plunged almost to her knees. "You certainly dressed the part."

"No harm in trying to entice the guy with my body, is there?" Janet laughed. "Unless you want him. You get first dibs. He's your neighbor and all."

Lily pushed herself off the floor and ran her hands down her thighs. She held a hand out to help Janet up. "Nah. He's great to look at, but he doesn't look like he'd be much fun. He's not the type of man I'm looking for. I don't know anything about him."

Janet gaped, dramatically clutching her chest. "What do you mean? How can he *not* be the man of your fantasies? And what do you need to know about him? Sex with a stranger is the best kind."

Fantasy and reality...two very separate entities. She knew better than to get them confused. She could dream about *him* all she wanted, and honestly, that was enough. It would have to be, because no matter how much the guy interested her, he saw her as only a step above a speck of dirt on the sidewalk. "Okay. Enough fooling around. I do have to work today, you know. What is it you felt the need to rush over here and show me?"

Janet rolled her eyes and pursed her lips. "Oh, yeah. *That.*" She struggled to get her fingers inside the pocket of her way-too-tight jeans, finally managing to pull out what looked like a folded piece of newsprint. She thrust it in Lily's direction. "The editorial in this morning's paper. Read it and weep."

Lily unfolded the piece of paper and glanced down at the headline. *Local Girl Contributes to Decline of Morals in Modern Society.* Her gaze skimmed the byline and she bit back a growl of frustration. *Toby Hartford.* Read it and weep? Ha! More like read it and commit murder. Fuming, she plowed on.

"'A local woman has disappointed family and friends in Tranquility by posing nude for a nationally-known men's magazine,'" she murmured, her anger ratcheting up another notch with every word. "'Lily Baxter, twenty-seven, of Harmon Road is featured as the centerfold model in the current issue of *Seduced* magazine, in a move that has shocked an entire town.' Oh, give me a break!"

Lily bit the inside of her cheek to keep from screaming. Who did Toby think he was, printing this crap for everyone in town to read? "I'll kill him. That's *it.* This is the *last straw*! Why can't he just let it go? And what gives him the right to publish my address?"

Janet took the newspaper clipping back and shoved it into the pocket of her jeans. "You dumped him a few months ago. You know how long Toby holds a grudge."

"So he has to put me down in front of the whole town? Because he's *mad* at me? What the hell was he thinking? He is *so* dead. I hope he has a burial plot picked out. He's going to need it when I get through with him."

What was it with men? You dump them because they're lousy in bed, and they've got to go and get all high and mighty with morality in the local paper. Toby had such a Napoleon complex, of sorts. He wasn't all that short, but his...*member* was. He felt the need to compensate by being a supreme asshole. "Maybe I should write a letter to the editor. Then I can tell everyone in town about the nickname I have for him. Stumpy."

Janet doubled over laughing. "You do that, hon. He deserves it. Just remember one thing through all of this. You made the right decision for you. Don't let anyone tell you different."

No shit. She wouldn't have done it if she hadn't thought it over. Now if she could get everyone else in her life to look at it like Janet, her life would be so much easier. But Tranquility as a whole wasn't the most progressive town. They labeled any woman who didn't marry and have three kids by the time she turned twenty-five *eccentric*. *Not* in a good, Hollywood type of way, either. More in the she-desperately-needs-to-be-committed sort of way.

"This sucks," Lily said, shaking her head.

"Not so much. It's not like you took out a billboard advertising the pictures or anything. I'm sure hardly anybody even knew about you posing for *Seduced*."

"Well, they do now after this article."

"Who actually reads the crap that Toby spews in his editorials? By now everyone in town knows not to take him seriously." A look of pity crossed Janet's face. "Honey, this is Tranquility. What else do the men have to do with their time other than sit around looking at dirty pictures?"

"They're not dirty." Lily narrowed her eyes at Janet before spinning around and stalking into the kitchen. She needed another cup — or ten — of coffee if she planned to make it through this day. After Toby's little *column*, she had a feeling today would turn out to be…interesting, to put it lightly.

Janet followed her into the kitchen and helped herself to a cup of coffee from the small drip coffeemaker on the counter. "You know what I mean, Lily. We might not see the pictures as dirty, but the men around here probably do. They get off on that kind of thing."

Considering the physical state of most of the available men in Tranquility, she didn't care much for that visual. Evan across the street…the thought of him using the magazine for a little, um, *help* sent a little thrill through her. But Mel downtown at the butcher shop… *Eww*!

Janet shrugged and shook her head, her blonde hair whipping around her shoulders. Lily had always wanted hair like Janet's instead of her natural shade of dishwater brown. She'd even gone as far as trying one of those at-home hair color kits once. Big mistake. Nothing like bright orange hair to scare the men away.

"Hey, you look puffy." Janet fingered the skin under Lily's eyes. "Bad night last night?"

"No. Jake woke me up at six a.m. yelling about the pictures."

"How did Jake find out?" Janet brought the mug to her lips and gulped the coffee down in a few sips.

Lily laughed. "I think opening the magazine when he got it out of his post office box was his first clue."

Janet's eyes widened and she blinked in surprise. "No way. Jake? You're kidding."

"Nope. I'm totally serious."

"Wow. I never would have figured. Jake is so…"

"Boring?"

"Yeah, that about sums it up." Janet set her mug in the sink, quickly scooping it up to rinse it out when Lily glared at her.

"I've got to get to work before I'm late." She glanced at the clock on the wall. "Oops. Well, I should go before I'm *too* late. Do you want a ride downtown?"

Lily shook her head. "No, thanks. I've got a few things to do before I head over to the wellness center."

"Suit yourself. Though why you want to *exercise* for a living is beyond me. Talk to you later, hon." Janet walked down the hall with a shudder. Moments later, Lily heard the front door open and close with a clack.

Lily shook her head, still fuming over Toby. Toby the Traitor. A couple of months ago he'd wanted to marry her. A couple of weeks ago he'd asked if they could still be friends. A couple of days ago he called to ask her to take him back. And he thought dragging her name through the mud in print would convince her? *Jerk.*

* * * * *

Several hours later, in need of fresh air, Lily grabbed her duffel bag and headed out the door, hoping the ten-minute walk downtown to work would help relieve her of some of her murderous intentions. She laughed. Oh, yeah, getting arrested would do *wonders* for her reputation. She could see the headline now: *Town Tramp Arrested for Murdering Son of Local Newspaper Owner.* Yet another thing to make her family proud.

By the time she hit the sidewalk at the end of her short driveway, sweat beaded along her hairline. She had no idea how Evan could run in this heat. For the past week, they'd been stuck in a heat wave, the soaring temperature and humidity levels not even backing off at night. She swiped the back of her hand over her forehead. Even the trees that lined her quiet street seemed to feel it. They looked less full, less green, as if wilting under the scorching rays of the early August sun.

Mrs. Keever's yappy little puffball of a dog barked at her as she passed the fence that held the thing contained in the yard. Lily scowled. It looked like the heat didn't phase the little rat...er, dog next door. "Shut up, Contessa." The dog wagged its cotton-swab tail and yapped louder. The dog might be cute...in her own way, if she ever kept her jaw closed.

As she passed Mrs. Keever's house, she felt someone watching her. She glanced over her shoulder, expecting the paranoia Toby's editorial had caused to be at work. With all the publicity the article would bring her, she expected to get a lot of leers. Her breath caught in her throat when she saw Evan leaning against his classic sports car, his arms crossed over his chest, his hard, intense gaze following her down the street. Dressed now in khaki pants and a royal blue dress shirt that did wonderful things for his skin tone, he looked as good now as he had earlier in just running shorts. Maybe even better. *Wow.* Potent stuff. Her heartbeat skittered out of control just looking at him, and her panties dampened in a way that had nothing to do with the current temperature.

She added a sexy—she hoped—swing to her step. And tripped over a huge rock lying in the middle of the sidewalk. Catching her balance before she toppled to the ground in a heap of bruised embarrassment, her face flamed as she raced down the sidewalk toward town. *Please tell me he didn't just see that. Please. I'll give anything to have him not have seen that.* Maybe by the hyper-bright sun had temporarily blinded him.

She glanced over her shoulder, mindful of foreign objects in her path, hoping Mr. Fine Ass had disappeared. No such luck. He still leaned against his car, looking right at her. As she watched him, a full-blown smile formed on his sexy lips. A smile laced with a heavy dose of humor. Shit. *Now* she finally coaxed a smile out of the guy? What was he, some kind of a sadist? She'd almost smacked her face off the sidewalk, for crying out loud! Men.

"Grrr." She whipped her head around and kept walking, proud of herself when she only looked back in his direction once. Twice. Okay, five times. He had that kind of effect on a girl. No matter how much his attitude aggravated her and increased her embarrassment to criminal levels, she still couldn't turn her head away. She felt the heat of his stare on her back until she turned the corner and walked out of his sight.

By the time she got to work, her intense embarrassment had almost abated. If she didn't think about the near fall and Mr. Fine Ass's subsequent sexy-yet-utterly-annoying smile, she'd make it through the day just fine. She pulled open the heavy glass door of the Tranquility Center for Wellness and Personal Growth and walked inside. The blast of frigid air from the air conditioning system hit her, bringing back her goose bumps and pebbling her nipples. Or maybe the pebbled nipples were a delayed reaction to the way Evan had looked at her. She shrugged at the toss-up as she walked through the large, white-painted lobby. Her mother, Anne, sat in a gray swivel chair behind the white front counter, her black-framed glasses perched on her nose and the sides of her hair held back with a rubber band as her fingers pounded on the computer keyboard in front of her.

"Morning, Mom."

She glanced up from the computer screen and smiled. Her glasses slid down her nose and she pushed them up again. "Morning, Lily."

Anne had opened the wellness center ten years ago, a few months after her divorce from Lily's father. Lily had been in high school at the time, and had worked the reception desk after school and on weekends. Once out of high school she'd gotten her yoga instructor certification and had started working full-time at the wellness center. With the popularity of alternative health, business was very good. The wellness center had started out small, offering things like massage services and herbal facials, but it had grown into a health spa of sorts over the years, bringing in business to Tranquility from all over the area. That fact, unfortunately, didn't stop Lily's father from prodding her to get a real job.

"Real job, my ass," she muttered. "At least I don't sit around counting other people's money all day."

"What was that, dear?"

"How is everything today?" Lily asked. With this kind of heat, class size tended to diminish.

"Well, it's been an interesting morning." Anne tugged on a strand of gray-streaked brown hair, her fingers shaking a little as she smiled at Lily. "You know. With the full moon coming, everyone is a little...strange."

Strange? For Anne Baxter to say something like that, Lily expected to walk into the room and find everyone dancing around like monkeys. "What do you mean by strange?"

Anne stepped out from behind the desk, her multi-colored, ankle-length skirt billowing around her legs as she did. After the divorce, her former social-club-president mother had gone through some pretty drastic changes. She'd told Lily that her father, the president of the town's only bank, had repressed her natural tendencies. Lily laughed at the thought. Tendencies to what? Walk around looking like something out of a three-ring circus? Anne Baxter had always been a little flighty, but now...Lily couldn't even come close to understanding the changes in her mother. But she seemed happy. That had to count for something—although her father kept blaming Lily's impulsiveness on her mother's behavior. That was *so* not true. Frank Baxter should know that better than anyone. Lily had been born with an impulsive streak. Growing up, her nickname had been Lily Don't. She had sudden visions of the nickname, along with the string of sermons and reprimands, coming back to haunt her now.

Anne threw her arms around Lily and squeezed her tight. "No matter what happens, I love you."

Ooo-kay. Was there a firing squad waiting inside the yoga studio? "Mom, is something wrong?"

Anne pulled away and blinked, her gaze a little too innocent to be believed. "Well, no, dear. I just wanted you to know that before you go into your class."

The hair on the back of Lily's neck pricked. "What's wrong with my class? Did no one show up or something?"

"Oh, no. You most definitely have a full class today."

Lily shook her head as she set her bag behind the desk before going into the studio. If she had a full class, what could the problem be? It didn't make any sense. Were the women she taught ready to stage a protest against her because of Toby's article?

Her jaw dropped when she walked into the small, beige studio. The problem obviously had nothing to do with the women in her class staging a mass protest. None of them had shown up. But Anne had been right—the class was full.

Of men.

Chapter Two

"That's all for today. Thanks everyone." Lily grabbed her bottle of water from the floor and brought it to her lips as she watched the class file out of the room. She shook her head. Talk about embarrassing. It was a little hard to concentrate on yoga poses with twenty-five men trying to catch a glimpse down her shirt every time she bent over.

She drained the small amount of water left in the bottle and dropped it to the floor, trying to hold back a laugh until the room was empty. Seeing the men, most of who were horribly out of shape, try to maneuver their bodies into poses resembling pretzels had to be the funniest thing she'd ever seen. They'd be sore for days. Served them right, too, for thinking they could hit on her while she worked.

"Sticking around for the next class?" she asked the few stragglers. She didn't bother to hold back the laugh when they shook their heads, mumbling, and hurried out of the room. Never has there been a scarier sight than old, chubby men wearing spandex.

When the room finally cleared, she picked up her mat off the floor and rolled it up, sticking it back in the closet where she stored it between classes. She wandered out into the lobby, still struck by the surreal experience of the morning. Her mother sat at the reception counter, her feet propped up on the chair next to her, smiling as she waved goodbye to the class participants as they filed out the front door.

"Don't wave to them," Lily said. "That might encourage them to come back."

Anne waved off Lily's comment with a flick of her wrist. "Don't be so negative. How'd it go?"

Since when did not having a class full of sweaty, red-faced old men become a negative thing? Lily shrugged. "As well as could be expected with a bunch of novices incapable of touching their toes. You should have warned me."

Anne laughed. "I thought you had enough to deal with for one day."

So it would be better to throw her to the wolves? Yeah, *that* made a lot of sense. She shook her head. Obviously, someone had forgotten to warn her that it was Torture Lily Day. "Gee, thanks. Your maternal instincts never cease to astound me."

"Lily. Don't be that way. I just thought after the conversation with your father you had this morning—"

Lily held a hand in the air to stop her mother. "Hold on. I didn't talk to Dad this morning."

"Oh, dear." Anne wrung her hands together, mumbling. The incessant thump of her foot tapping on the short carpeting made Lily cringe. "He said he would call you. He must be madder than I thought. Well, I'm sure that when he's had some time to calm down he'll see what an ass he's making of himself."

"*You* spoke to Dad?"

"Well, yes. He called this morning to blame me for your decision to pose for that magazine."

"You've got to be kidding me." Lily tugged her hair out of the ponytail, stuffing the elastic in her pocket. She ran her fingers through the still-damp strands to get the tangles out. "What is everyone's problem? Dad calls you to yell at you, and Jake shows up at my door. How many men in this town subscribe to *Seduced*, anyway?"

Not that it mattered. Not after Toby the Traitor's little piece of crap article that told the entire town about it. She stormed through the lobby to the employee room in back and grabbed a yogurt out of the fridge. She peeled off the top, crumbling it on her fist, and tossed it into the trash bin in the corner. Grabbing a spoon out of the plastic cup on the counter next to the fridge, she slumped into a chair and banged her forehead on the worn wooden surface of the table.

"Your father means well, Lily," Anne told her as she followed her into the room. "Don't let anyone put you down. You're a beautiful girl, and there's nothing to be ashamed of with the naked female form."

"My thoughts exactly," Lily spoke, her voice muffled by the table. She lifted her head and rolled her eyes. "Maybe I should go over to the bank and talk to Dad."

Anne's eyes widened, a horrified expression coming across her face. "Well, maybe you should give him a little more time. You know how conservative your father is."

Talk about the understatement of the year. If Frank Baxter was wound any tighter, he'd implode. Unfortunately, Jake had followed in his footsteps and was currently vying for the title of Tranquility's Biggest Domineering Jerk. Growing up in that house had been *so* much fun. *A real picnic.*

"I hope you don't get too full from that yogurt. I ordered lunch," Anne told her.

Full? Lily glanced down at the tiny six-ounce container in her hand. "I think I'll still have a little room. What did you order?"

"I got a couple of dishes from that new place across the street."

"Marty's House of Tofu?" Lily's stomach churned. Suddenly she did feel full. Bloated even. "I don't think I could eat another bite."

Anne rolled her eyes. "Nonsense. You'll love it. I'll run across the street and grab it. You just sit tight. Oh, and if Marnie shows up before I get back, tell her there's plenty to go around."

Lily sat back in the chair and groaned. They were all nuts. Every single one of them.

Yes, there would be plenty left over, because Lily had no intention of eating a single bite. She didn't have anything against the stuff, she just preferred to avoid it whenever possible. Why hadn't she taken the leftover pasta from home like she'd planned? Oh, yeah. Jake and his early morning interruption—not to mention The Traitor's editorial—had thrown her schedule out of whack. It would serve her right to go hungry.

The door swung open not even five minutes later and Lily grimaced, waiting for the smell of special spices to send a wave of nausea rippling through her. When the room remained thankfully garlic-orange-rosemary free, she snapped her gaze to the door. Marnie Price, the wellness center's massage therapist and Lily's friend since second grade, stood in the open doorway, stifling a yawn. Her white-blonde hair brushed her chin in unkempt waves, her blue eyes looked glassy, and the dark circles under her eyes made her slim face look even thinner.

"Tough night last night?" Lily asked.

Marnie wandered into the room, dropped her purse on the counter, and dropped her butt into the chair next to Lily. She covered her mouth and yawned again. "Yes. Joe's been such a pain lately. He thinks we need time apart. Again."

Lily shook her head. "Didn't I tell you men suck? After five years, don't you ever wonder if it's time to give up?" At nearly six feet tall and probably no more than a hundred and twenty pounds, Marnie could have her pick of men. Why did she stick it out with Joe for so long? The guy couldn't make a commitment beyond buying the same brand of toothpaste for two months in a row.

"But what if it isn't?" Marnie sighed and took a big gulp from the blue plastic travel mug in her hand—probably some kind of herbal tea. "What if this is it? What if I never meet anyone else who wants me?"

Lily snorted and raised an eyebrow. Did she not have any mirrors in her house? Marnie was so laid-back that she appeared flighty, but she was the sweetest, kindest person Lily knew. Why she hung out with Lily and Janet was anyone's guess. "Trust me. You will have no problem finding someone else." True, Joe looked like a Sex God—and he probably was—but he acted like a jerk half the time and wasn't worth Marnie's trouble.

"Speaking of jerks," Marnie said. She cleared her throat and ran a hand through her knotted hair. "Why didn't I brush this today? Anyway, I saw Toby's editorial. Do me a favor. If you decide to kill him, make sure you don't get caught. I couldn't stand you going to jail for doing society a favor."

Anne saved Lily from replying when she bustled back into the room, set a big yellow and black plastic bag covered with smiley faces on the table. *Please*. Could it get any more corny than that?

"Isn't plastic bad for the environment?"

Anne shook her head. "Not if you recycle."

Anne said the word like it was some kind of religion. Most of the younger residents of Tranquility had gotten into the whole recycling thing, but the older, stuck-in-their-ways residents still refused to listen to reason. The most recycling done within that crowd was when Mrs. Ferguson made wind chimes out of her husband's empty beer bottles and sold them at a roadside stand to unsuspecting tourists. "Yeah. I'm sure everyone who orders there plans to recycle the bags." All two of their customers. Anne, and Marnie—a *serious* health fanatic. She made Anne look like a junk food junkie of the highest order. She'd probably love the meal Anne had ordered.

"Ooh, Marty's House of Tofu." Marnie eyed the bag covetously, licking her lips.

Lily rolled her eyes. Sometimes she thought Anne and Marnie, and the rest of their strange, taste-bud-deprived kind, came from another galaxy. One where moon rocks were a delicacy.

"There's plenty of food, Marnie dear. Help yourself," Anne told her as she unpacked four foam takeout containers from the bag and arranged them on the table.

"Wow. Thanks."

Oh, please. This was like a bad sitcom. "I think I'll go and get ready for my next class." If anyone bothered to show up this time, besides a room full of misguided perverts.

"Don't be silly. Sit. Enjoy with us," Anne urged. "I wanted to talk to you a little bit, anyway."

Uh-oh. "About what?"

"The pictures were lovely, Lily," Anne told her as she piled a paper plate high with mounds of weirdly-fragranced mush. It looked—and smelled—like someone had mixed a bag of potpourri with a container of ricotta cheese. "But they didn't look like you."

Duh. "Maybe they weren't. Maybe someone else posed for them and used my name." At least that would get the idiots off her back.

"Like I said, sweetheart. You have nothing to be ashamed of." Unease flickered in Anne's eyes when she said the words.

Then why do you keep repeating that line, Mom? Was that the new mantra of the week? Ohmm...Lily's a good girl...Ohmm...Lily's not a tramp. "Thanks. I think."

Anne stopped and stared at Lily, her hand holding a spoon full of something that came too close to resembling brain matter just over her plate. "I'm serious, dear. You're a young woman capable of making her own decisions. You made the one that's right for you, and I'm proud of you for it."

Liar. Why couldn't she just come out and say the pictures made her uncomfortable? No one else had that problem. "Thanks, Mom, really. I know all of that. I'm not ashamed of the pictures, and I'm not going to apologize for them."

Anne blinked at Lily. Her hand tipped the spoon and the gelatinous tofu mass hit the plate with a splat. "I never expected you to." She smiled that bright, somewhat vacant smile that indicated the subject was closed. "Why don't we eat before this gets cold?"

"Yeah. That would be terrible. If it got cold, it might taste bad."

"Lily, have some faith in me. I am capable of picking out decent food from a restaurant menu."

If her ordering skills were as bad as her cooking skills, Lily feared she might end up in the emergency room. She was lucky she'd made it through her childhood with only one bout of food poisoning.

"This really looks delicious," Marnie chimed in. Lily made a mental note to get the woman an eye doctor appointment.

She picked up one of the plastic forks Anne put on the table and dug in, holding her nose as she brought the first bite of tofu-something-puree-in-garlic to her mouth. Okay, so it wasn't hideous. It could have been worse. At least tofu could technically be classified as food, unlike some things Anne had served during her struggle as a stay-at-home-mother.

"It's not so bad, is it?" Anne asked, beaming.

"It's fine, if you like this sort of thing." Lily shook her head. She preferred to eat something a little less like hyper-spiced baby food. "What do you think, Marnie?"

Marnie rolled her eyes heavenward and sighed. "It's amazing," she said in between slurps.

"I'm so glad you enjoy it." Anne beamed even more. Marnie was like the daughter Anne had never had. Lily—well, she couldn't say she'd been a disappointment to her mother, just a surprise. She liked to cook, a lot, and she loved to eat. She didn't bother with salads or five servings of vegetables every day. And— *shudder*—she cooked with *butter*. Teaching yoga five days a week was the only reason she still managed to fit into a size eight.

"You know what? I think I really am full. I have another class to teach in a little while." She crossed her fingers and hoped the regular women—most of them younger and a little less...stuffy than the ones from the first class, showed up. If she ended up with another class full of men, she was going to need a margarita—or a whole pitcher—to teach it.

* * * * *

By the time Evan pulled his car into the driveway and cut the engine, he was just about dead on his feet. He got out of the car and wandered up the front steps, loosening his tie to ward off the shock of the evening humidity. At just after seven p.m., the street was quiet and calm, with only the occasional bird chirping to break the silence. The sun hadn't yet set, but he saw lights on in most of his neighbors' windows. All the houses, except the woman across the street. Lily Baxter.

If he'd been looking for a steady relationship—which he wasn't, not after the divorce from hell episode—she would be the type of woman he'd want. The type he had thought Jessica was, until he'd found out about her little side fling with his best friend. He shook his head. The whole sordid incident still left a bitter taste in his mouth. Especially since he'd gotten word from his sister that Jessica and Scott were now engaged—only two months after the divorce became final.

Jessica had moved on, and so had he. He'd moved past the stage in his life where he thought he could have it all—great job, nice house, perfect family. Hey, he had the house and the job, and two out of three was nothing to sneeze at. He didn't *want* the family. Not anymore. That was why he'd never done anything about his attraction to Lily, an attraction he knew she reciprocated. He knew she watched him after his morning runs. The idea gave him a little thrill, but also warned him to stay away. She wouldn't want the same thing he did.

Lily's friend, the blonde who liked to wear skimpy clothes and wiggle her ass as she pretended not to watch him, was the type of woman he went for now. The kind without any strings attached. The kind looking for the same thing he was—just a single night. Maybe two or three if it was really good, but after that he preferred to go his own way.

Lily...she was cute. He couldn't describe her any other way. She wore workout clothes all the time—little zip-front sweatshirts and tank tops and stretchy, loose pants. From what he could tell, she didn't bother with makeup. She'd had her light brown hair pulled back in a ponytail every time he'd seen her, so he didn't know how long it was. He liked women with very long hair. There was nothing sexier than tangling his fingers in hair like that in the middle of a bout of fast, hot sex. But Lily didn't inspire visions of sweaty sex. She inspired visions of home-cooked meals, a bunch of kids running in the yard, and slow evenings making love in front of the fireplace. He had nothing against slow and easy—for other people. For himself, he just wanted the thrill.

He unlocked the front door and swung it open, grabbing the pile of mail from the brass mailbox hanging next to the door as he went inside. He slammed the door shut with his foot, threw the deadbolt, and made his way into the kitchen. With any luck, he'd find something to appease his growling stomach.

He dropped the mail on the counter and sorted through it. A couple of bills, the weekly sale flyers, the usual junk...and a copy of *Seduced* magazine—a New Bachelor gift from his father when the divorce had gone through. He wouldn't say he didn't enjoy it, but it wouldn't have been his first choice. He preferred the real thing, and had never had a problem getting it when he wanted it. Lately, though, he'd been too busy—and too sick of women's games—to even want it.

He moved to the fridge and dug through it for something that passed as semi-edible. The only things he found were an almost-empty carton of milk and leftover pizza from last week. Looked like it'd be takeout tonight. Again. He made a mental note to take a run to the store the next night after work for a couple dozen frozen dinners. Life—or at least takeout—had been much simpler in Chicago. Who needed to cook when any kind of food could be delivered to one's front door, cooked to perfection and piping hot? Tranquility, being a relatively small town, had a limited selection. If he wanted good Chinese, he had to go about a half hour out of town. Thai food—forget it. The closest place was probably a good forty-five minutes away. So most nights it was either settle for pizza, or starve.

He picked up the magazine and flipped it open to the first page. He scanned the contents half-heartedly, not putting too much focus on any one face. Until he came to one that looked familiar, in the form of the magazine centerfold. The woman was stretched out on a bed, lying on rumpled, black satin sheets, masses of chestnut-brown hair fanning the pillow under her head. The bedroom in the picture had a dark, almost gothic feel. The pose was tasteful, as far as those kinds of things went, reminding him of the pictures of sirens he'd seen in art books. Her eyes focused on the camera, her full lips pursed, a sexy come-hither look on her face.

His cock hardened against the zipper of his dress pants and a sheen of sweat formed on his brow. Why did that one woman, out of the many he'd seen in his lifetime, affect him so strongly?

Because you know her, dummy.

Was that possible? Had he met the woman in the picture? She looked familiar, but where would he have seen her before? Maybe…the answer hit him so hard he nearly stumbled into the wall behind him. He knew exactly where he'd seen that woman before.

Across the street.

What the hell was sweet little Lily doing in the centerfold of a trashy magazine?

He reached into the fridge and pulled out a can of cola, popping the top and taking a big gulp. No wonder those shockingly bright Caribbean blue eyes looked so familiar. He glanced down at the picture again, seeing Lily in a whole new light as he took in the sight of her dusky nipples against her fair skin, and the neatly trimmed thatch of cocoa-colored hair resting on top of her mound. He licked his lips. What was the reason he didn't want to pursue her obvious interest in him?

He shook his head and resisted banging it off the cabinet doors. He felt like his world had been turned upside down. Why was that sweet little small town girl in the centerfold of *Seduced* magazine?

Shit. His cock was rock-solid now, and he had no hope of getting rid of the almost painful erection. All those times he'd passed her by, thinking she was too innocent for him. All those times he'd wanted to take her out to dinner, and back to his bed afterward…he hadn't even had an inkling of the wild woman beneath the innocent exterior. The girl he'd overlooked for months had suddenly become a hell of a lot more interesting. Would she be up for a little fun, no commitments, no strings? There was only one way to find out. He debated for a split second the sanity of his plan before he grabbed the magazine and a pen and headed out the front door.

* * * * *

Lily turned the pork cutlets on the broiler pan, careful not to dislodge the delicate breading, and stuck them back in the oven. Five more minutes should just about do it. She stirred sesame oil and honey into the peanut sauce, her mouth watering already—which probably had something to do with the fact that she'd skipped breakfast and had a yogurt for lunch. She moved the saucepan off the burner just as she heard a knock on the door. She went to answer it and dropped into utter shock when she saw Evan standing there.

"Hi," he said softly in that deep, honey-smooth voice of his.

She swiped a hand over her suddenly sweat-ridden brow and tried to smile. It fell flat as her nerves jumped and her heart skittered to a stop. Lord, the man did terrible, wonderful things to her insides. His intense gaze locked with hers and she had to clear her throat twice to get sound to come out of her mouth. "Is there something I can do for you?"

A sexy smile formed on his lips, taking away her ability to breathe. Did he know CPR? She felt a sudden need for mouth-to-mouth resuscitation.

And then, like the typical man he was, he had to go and ruin it all by opening his big, stupid mouth.

"Maybe. Do you do autographs?" He thrust something at her—a magazine. No, not just a magazine. *The* magazine.

Aggravation clenched her gut and she fisted her hands at her sides. The guy was lucky she was a pacifist—for the most part. If she'd been a violent person, she would have knocked him out cold.

Chapter Three

"Are you out of your mind?" Lily put her hand on the door, starting to try to slam it shut, but Evan stuck his foot inside before she could complete the movement. The door bounced off his foot and smacked her in the chest.

"This is you, isn't it?" he asked, a smug smile on his face she would have found attractive if he hadn't turned out to be such a moron.

At least he'd answered her question. Not just men in Tranquility had been born with the idiot gene. They *all* had.

She spread her arms out and glared at him, her face reddening as her temper rose. "I don't know. What do *you* think?"

Okay, that was a bad question to ask. Very bad. She shook her head. It had sounded more like an invitation, and he obviously took it as such. His gaze traveled over her, up and down, with an excruciating slowness that sent shivers down her spine and made her want to scream. Her mouth went dry when his gaze lingered on her breasts, his lips parting, before he dragged his gaze back up to her face. "Looks like you. Kind of. It's hard to tell without all the makeup."

She snorted. "Maybe I should take off my clothes so you can judge." *What's the matter with you? Did you leave your brain back at the wellness studio?*

"Well, I don't think it's necessary. But it would be a big help." The look on his face told her exactly how *necessary* he thought it was. She narrowed her eyes.

"That's it. This conversation is over. I don't need some jerk ogling me—"

"Like you ogle me every morning after my run?"

She froze, her jaw dropping to the floor. *Busted.*

She let out a harsh breath, shaking her head and hoping he didn't catch what promised to be a mortified look in her eyes. "You saw me?"

"Every single morning." He touched her chin with the tip of his index finger, brought her gaze back to his. "Almost every damned morning for two months. Do you have any idea what that kind of rapt attention does to a guy?"

She blinked, taken aback by the husky tone of his voice. "Um, no. And I don't think I want to find out."

His deep, rich laugh rumbled through her senses and made her feel all tingly inside. She shook the thought off. Tingly was unacceptable. Hard, angry, ready to beat the crap out of him — *that's* what she should feel. Tingling with desire had no place in the equation. The guy was an asshole. He didn't deserve her lust. He deserved to be castrated. Still…

"You're joking about the whole clothes thing, right?" she asked, raising an eyebrow as she crossed her arms over her chest. She wanted to give him the benefit of the doubt. She'd been watching the guy for weeks. Months. And despite the brazen and oh-so-chauvinistic attitude, the man was a complete hunk.

"Yeah." He laughed, and she felt better until she heard his next words. "When I want a woman naked, I don't usually have to ask."

Oh, boy. Her pussy clenched at just his tone of voice. "Awfully full of yourself, aren't you?" As much as she hated to admit it, that one sentence made her angry and dampened her panties at the same time. *Get a grip, Lily. He's just another jerk. Don't let the melted-dark-chocolate eyes fool you.*

He lifted one shoulder in a casual shrug. His gaze locked with hers as he leaned a hip on the doorframe, *the* magazine still dangling from his fingers. "Maybe I have a reason to be."

"And maybe I have a reason for slamming the door in your

face."

"You haven't yet."

She blinked at him. "Well…I tried once. You wouldn't let me. Now I'm just being polite."

"I think you should stop being so polite."

"Excuse me?" He *wanted* her to slam the door in his face?

"I smell something burning. You might want to go check that out."

Her eyes widened and a cold chill ran through her. Dinner. Damn it. "You know what? Slam the door in your own face for me, will you? I've got to go turn the pork before it burns."

She hurried back down the short hallway, making it in time to save the macadamia- encrusted pork from demise. The three-cheese garlic bread, unfortunately, hadn't been as lucky. She said a silent prayer for the ruined food as she dumped the whole tray into the trash can. What a waste of a good loaf of Italian bread. With a frustrated sigh—and a muttered curse to the man who'd kept her away from her meal—she took the finished pork out of the oven and gave the peanut sauce a final stir.

"You didn't ruin it, did you?"

The voice behind her caused her to jump what felt like a mile in the air. She smacked her knee on the oven handle and cursed. She turned around to find *him* standing, of all places, right in the middle of the kitchen. Was he nuts? Was he some kind of crazed serial killer?

Why hadn't she shut and locked the door?

Because she'd grown up in a small town, where everyone knew everyone else. She'd never thought an outsider would come in and do something like this. Perhaps she needed to reevaluate her apparently too-trusting ways.

She grabbed the first weapon-like object she could find and spun on him. Unfortunately, he didn't seem to be intimidated by the cheese grater.

He laughed, holding his hands in front of him in a gesture

of mock surrender. "Relax. I'm not going to hurt you. I promise."

"Then why are you still here?"

"I figure you owe me for watching me stretch every morning. Since you're not receptive to the autograph idea, how about dinner instead?"

This guy must have a set of brass balls, to be trying to worm a dinner invitation out of her. "Do you think I'm stupid?"

"No, but I think from the smell of the food you're an excellent cook, and from the amount in that pan, you're either expecting a dinner party to come rushing in here any second or you have a hell of a lot of extra."

"As a matter of fact, I'm expecting guests. A couple of big, brawny guys I've been seeing. Two of them. And they're the jealous type. They should be here, oh…" She made a show of checking her watch. "Five minutes ago. You'd better leave before they get here."

He laughed again and pointed to her shirt. "Good thing you're not trying to impress anyone."

She glanced down at her T-shirt. Red with little white puppies all over it, the fabric so thin in places her skin showed through. Damn. "It's a fashion statement."

"Yeah, and it's screaming 'zero fashion sense' loud and clear."

She set the cheese grater on the counter and put her hands on her hips. "Really good way to earn brownie points, Mr. Fine—Acardi." Whew. *Close one.*

He propped a hip against the back of a chair and crossed his arms over his chest. "Look, I'll be honest with you. I have no food in my house and I'm sick of pizza. I can barely heat a frozen dinner without overcooking it and turning it hard as a rock. I don't think I've had a decent meal since I moved here. Your dinner looks really good. What is it?"

"Macadamia encrusted pork with a warm peanut sauce," she mumbled.

A frown marred his more-perfect-than-a-Greek-god features. "Excuse me? Are you a chef or something?"

"No. I just like to cook."

"I guess so."

He started to step closer to her, but a wave of panic seized her and she waved him off. "Stay right where you are." *If you come any closer, I'm liable to need to change my panties.* Her pussy quivered at the thought and she bit back a moan just in time.

"So, are you going to let me stay, or do I need to go slam that door in my face now?"

She shook her head. "Why would you even want to stay? You don't even know my name."

"But you know mine? I don't remember us being formally introduced." He laughed. "And, for your information, I do know your name. Lily Baxter. There. Happy now?"

She glared at him suspiciously. "How did you know *my* name?"

"I'm pretty observant." He winked one of those sexy brown eyes at her. "Your name is on your mailbox."

Oh, yeah. She shot him another glare. He had her so flustered she couldn't think straight.

"What do you do for a living, Evan?" She felt herself softening to his unique brand of humor and forwardness, and she did everything she could to ward herself against it.

"I'm an architect. I work in Concord at Mills and Downey. I can provide you with references, if it would help."

Either he was too cute for words, or a total nutcase and she needed to call the loony bin right now to come and pick him up.

"I'm not sure if references are necessary," she told him, eyeing him with a new wariness.

"I'm just trying to promote neighborly relations." That sexy smile held firmly in place as he took one step toward her, then another. This time her whole body quivered.

"Oh, really?" She shook her head. *Give it up, Lil. It's a lost cause. You both know you're going to invite him for dinner, so get on with it before the food gets cold.* "Fine. Sit down. I'll make a plate up for you. But after you eat, you leave. Right away. And no autograph. Got it?"

"Is that negotiable?"

She gave him a sugar-coated-cyanide smile. "Depends. Are any of your masculine parts?"

She'd never seen a guy drop into a chair and put his hands in his lap so fast. "Okay. No autograph."

She walked to the stove and piled pork and green beans on a plate. She lifted the ladle and drizzled peanut sauce over the macadamia-breaded cutlets—and almost dropped the entire plate when she felt breath on the back of her neck.

"Relax. It's just me," Evan said, his fingers the lightest touch against her waist. Lord, if that didn't make her skin break out in goose bumps she'd have to dump the food down his shirt. "That looks amazing. Where did you learn how to cook?"

"I took some classes a few years ago." She sucked in a deep breath, drawing the clean, freshly masculine scent of him into her lungs. She could live on that alone. *Get over it, Lil.* Why hadn't he stayed in his seat? "My mother gets me a few cookbooks for Christmas every year. It's a hobby. That's really all."

She set his plate down on the counter and sliced off a sliver of pork, turning to him with the fork raised in front of her. Her expression faltered when she saw the heated look in his eyes—directed in the vicinity of her lips. She opened her mouth to speak, hoping she didn't stutter.

"Do you want a taste?" *Great going, genius!* "Dinner, I mean?"

Evan's smile came slowly, sensually, and made her tingle all over. She gulped down the basketball-sized lump in her throat. "It's really good. I promise. I make this all the time."

"Sure. I'll try some."

She started to hand him the fork with the cooling piece of

pork on it, but he shook his head. He smiled, obviously noting her confused expression, and opened his mouth. She blinked. He wanted her to feed him? *Oh, boy.* She whimpered.

She shoved the fork toward his mouth, praying she didn't puncture a lip or crack a tooth. She watched, held rapt by the sensual way he closed his full lips around the fork. She slid it out of his mouth slowly. When she heard his murmur of appreciation, she glanced into his eyes before dropping her gaze back to his mouth. She just couldn't seem to draw her eyes away for long.

It amazed her that even the way he chewed could be orgasm-inducing to a woman. He had this way about him, this…sensuality that seemed to come from within. The way he spoke, the way he moved his long, lean muscles brought to mind satin sheets and multiple orgasms. The man was pure, undiluted, liquid sex. She shivered down to her flip-flops when he ran his tongue over his lips. "What kind of pork is that, again?"

"Macadamia encrusted." She ran a hand across her suddenly sweaty forehead. "With a warm peanut sauce." She rolled her eyes at her own stupidity. *You sound like a teenager on a first date, Lil. Knock it off.*

"How is it that you can eat like *that* and look like…?" He gestured to her body, his hands moving up and down in front of her, way too close to touching for her own sanity. If she moved just a step closer— *no.*

"Like what?" she asked, trying to lighten the mood before she ripped his clothes off and did him right there on the cold tile floor. The fact that he'd probably file assault charges dampened her lust. A little. "I'm nothing special." Unlike you, Mr. Fine Ass, with a body like sin personified and a voice like sex, she added silently. "Should we sit down to eat before this gets cold?"

She picked up the plate she'd dished up for him and thrust it at him. He grabbed it before it fell to the floor and followed her to the table. She had to give him credit. She'd been ogling him all night long like a serial dieter in the Godiva chocolate shop, and he hadn't once asked her to stop. Either he didn't mind, or he filed the information away to tell the police when he filled out a potential stalker report. They didn't really have those, did they? If so, she was in huge trouble.

* * * * *

Evan watched Lily move around the kitchen with more grace than he'd ever seen someone have while cooking a meal. Never mind that the fare sounded like something out of a gourmet restaurant—and tasted just as good. He'd just have to find a way to work around her attitude. She was prickly, but he could handle prickly. She just needed the right man to relax her. He could have her purring like a kitten in no time.

And he would pursue her. He'd seen just about every inch of her body in that magazine, and he'd be willing to bet that the real thing was even better. She looked a little softer, less dramatically wanton sitting across from him at her small, round table. He kept his gaze on her for most of the meal, devouring every inch of Lily as he devoured the entire plateful of food.

When he finished, he put his fork on his plate and pushed the plate a few inches across the table, prepared to get up and rinse if off in the sink. Probably nervous that he was coming after her, Lily stood and grabbed the plate before he had a chance. "Sit, Evan. I'll get you seconds."

He raised an eyebrow at her back. What was with the sudden compliance? Her hands shook as she brought the plate back to the table and set it down in front of him with a clatter.

"Here. The poison is supposed to be slow-acting, so you shouldn't drop dead until you're out the door."

"Gee. Thanks. I could have dished up my own, though. You didn't have to do it for me."

"You wouldn't have gotten the sauce-to-pork ratio right. If I do it, it leaves a lot less margin for error."

Snappy and intelligent. He liked that in a woman. He liked a woman who could stand on her own, and not let him get away with too much. Half the fun was in the arguing. The other half was in the making up. "This is an incredible meal, by the way. Do you cook like this every night?"

She started to nod, but then apparently thought better of it. "No. Of course not. Most nights I just make tuna casserole."

He laughed. "I love tuna casserole."

"With mangoes and hot peppers mixed in."

"Liar."

"Just like you *love* tuna casserole, right?"

She had him there. He shook his head and ate a couple more bites of the food—food that reminded him of a few of his favorite restaurants back in Chicago. "Are you sure you don't do this professionally?"

Her eyes shot fire. "The pictures?"

"No. The food."

"Oh, that." She laughed nervously. "No. In real life, I'm a yoga instructor. I told you the food is just a hobby…"

The rest of her words drained away, his mind still stuck on her occupation. She still spoke to him, but he couldn't grasp any of what she said. Yoga instructor? Weren't they *really* flexible? His cock, semi-hard since he'd seen the pictures, tightened against his khakis. He'd really hit the neighbor jackpot with this move.

"Yoga instructor, huh?"

"Pig." He felt her toes connect with his shin under the table. "Why did I know you were going to zero in on that one thing?"

"Because I'm a man?"

He felt the swat of her foot again and wondered if she was flirting. No, probably not. Having talked to her for a while, he figured she was trying to beat him up. But no one said flirting wasn't allowed. "Men do those kinds of things, honey."

"Honey?" Her voice rose as she spoke, his words having the desired effect. He felt her foot brush his shin again, but this time he was ready for her. He snagged her foot between his calves, squeezing tight enough that she couldn't pull away. She gasped and squirmed, but he didn't let go.

"Stop it." She brought the other leg to his and kicked him a little harder. He let her go, laughing as she turned red and huffed. "What's wrong with you? Are you always this…this…?"

"Annoying?" he offered. She shook her head.

"No, that's not quite the word I'm looking for. It's a noun, begins with an 'a'," She brightened, holding her index finger in the air. "I've got it. Asshole. Are you always this much of an asshole?"

He laughed. "Sorry. You must bring out the worst in me."

"Nice try, buddy. Don't you go blaming your problems on me."

"I wouldn't dream of it." He went back to eating, but Lily hadn't finished her tirade.

"Just because you have an incredible body doesn't mean I'm going to fall to my knees and kiss your feet."

He'd prefer she stopped closer to his hips and kissed his cock—which jerked painfully in response to the thought—but if he told her that he'd probably loose a nut. "You think I have an incredible body?"

"Duh. Like you've never been told that before. You wouldn't wear those skimpy shorts if they didn't make you look good. Eat your dinner. It's getting late and I want to get to bed."

"Is that an offer?" He cursed himself for his forward behavior with a woman he barely knew—one not quite receptive to his *charms*—but he couldn't seem to stop the words from pouring out of his mouth.

"Don't push your luck, buddy." She shook her head and smiled as she spoke, and he took that cute, sexy smile to be a good sign.

"Sorry." He smiled back. He liked how she reacted when he smiled at her. She flushed. He wouldn't say he'd never had that reaction before, but he'd never gotten it from a *Seduced* magazine

Elisa Adams

centerfold, either. He'd never gotten *anything* from a *Seduced* magazine centerfold. No time like the present to start.

And Lily...he wanted her with a hunger he couldn't explain. He barely knew her, wouldn't have picked her out as a potential bedmate if he'd run into her on the street, but she'd had his gut clenched from the second she'd opened the door, and his cock hard from the time he'd flipped open the magazine. He blew out a breath to help gain control of his reaction to her. He knew how strongly she affected him—he didn't need to let her see it.

"So about those guys you have coming to dinner."

She shrugged. "No guys. I lied."

Honesty—another quality he found admirable in a woman. "Why?"

"Because I didn't know you. I still don't. I don't know if you're safe."

Well, he wouldn't hurt her. But safe? Nah. He wasn't boring. "Ask me anything. I'm an open book."

She stopped eating and blinked at him, her eyebrows drawing into a frown. "You're clinically insane."

"I'm serious." He set his fork down and looked across the table at her. "Ask me anything. I promise I'll answer." As long as it wasn't too personal. He shouldn't be worried. In his experience, a woman asked a few personal questions, usually about jobs and living situations, before moving on to a subject she found much more fascinating. Herself.

"Okay. What the hell are you doing in my kitchen?"

He laughed. She was going to be a tough one. But he knew she was attracted to him. He saw it in her eyes even as she just about told him to buzz off. "I told you."

"Yeah, yeah, yeah. Neighborly relations and all that crap. Whatever. You're lying, but I can live with that. For now. How about this...are you married?"

"Why would you want to know something like that if

you're not interested in me?"

"Duh. So I can tattle to your wife since you're over here hitting on me."

"I'm not hitting on you." He tried to look casual, but feared he failed miserably.

"Yes, you are. That's okay, though. You're a guy who thinks I'm a slut because I posed for a couple of naked pictures, so I can forgive you for hitting on me, too. Just a quick warning, though, Casanova. I'm not interested in what you have to offer, so you might as well give up while you're ahead. Now answer the question."

He gaped at her, wondering where all that had come from. The woman had to be hyperactive. "No. I'm not married. I was, but now I'm not. Next question."

"What happened to your marriage?"

Okay. Bad idea. Amazing how she'd zeroed in immediately on the most uncomfortable subject he could think of. What happened to checking his financial status? "My best friend happened. Rather, my former best friend. Can we change the subject to a less personal one?"

"Suit yourself. This whole 'ask me anything' crap was your idea, though." She shrugged, and he was relieved that she didn't mention another thing about the breakup of his marriage. She smiled instead. "Why did you move to Monotony—I mean, Tranquility?"

"Monotony? I don't think it's that bad. It's quiet, which is a nice change of pace. And it's cheap. The cost of housing here floored me. I moved here because I got a new job in Concord, and this area suited my needs—close enough to work, and a lot less expensive than living in the city."

"True. So why the new job?"

Did she never let up? "I heard about this job from a friend of my family, and the timing was perfect. One, because my old job had gotten stale. And two, because I wanted to get away from Chicago and my ex-wife and former friend."

"I'm sorry."

"Don't be. I'm not." He recognized the words for lies as soon as they were out of his mouth. He *was* sorry. Sorry he'd ever married Jessica, and sorry he'd trusted Scott. Now...now it was time to move on with his life. He smiled to himself. Maybe if Lily felt badly enough, she might offer to console him. That sounded like a nice thought. He started making a lost-puppy-dog face at her, but then remembered how she'd tried to attack him with a cheese grater. His gaze fell to the steak knife lying next to her plate and he closed his eyes. She didn't really strike him as the consoling type.

"How about you?" he asked her. "Are you married?"

"God, no." Well, okay. *Why don't you tell me how you really feel, Lily?*

"Ever been?"

"No. I was engaged a couple of months ago, but it ended. Now I'm glad I didn't marry the guy. He turned out to be a real jerk."

"What did he do?"

"Publicly accused me of contributing to the moral decline of modern society."

Huh? "Oh, yeah. What a complete scumbag."

She pursed her lips and nodded. "My thoughts exactly."

"Any plans for marriage in the future?"

"Maybe. I'm still young. I have plenty of time to make up my mind." She shrugged. "I just want to live a little first."

And Tranquility was the perfect hotbed of nighttime activity for that? "How old are you?"

"Twenty-seven."

He nodded. Not too young. Good thing. She looked it, though. Without all the makeup, she could easily pass for eighteen or nineteen.

"How old are you?"

"I'll be thirty-six in a couple of months."

Her eyes widened and she dropped her fork to her plate. "You're kidding. I never would have guessed."

"Does it bother you to have an old man hitting on you?"

"You're *not* hitting on me. Remember?"

"Oh, yeah." Why was that again?

Evan took the last bite of pork and pushed his chair away from the table. He stood and carried his plate to the sink and started to rinse it, but Lily had other plans. She jumped up from the table and pulled the plate out of his hand. "I'll get this."

"I'm just trying to help."

"Yes, but I want to make sure it's done right. Rinse, stack, put in the dishwasher."

He shook his head. "Huh?"

"My method of organization. I like to do things my way."

Control freak. "They make medication for that you know."

"Very funny."

They stood close together, a little too close, since his cock was ready to reach out and touch her. She was an interesting woman, one he found himself more and more attracted to as he got to know her better. He'd never met anyone like her. She puzzled him. She gave him hell, and drove him mad with arousal at the same time. He smiled. He'd always enjoyed a good mind fuck. He was going to love this…thing—whatever to call it they'd started over dinner tonight.

And they'd definitely started something. She could deny it all she wanted, but they'd started something that promised to be very good. And they'd finish it, too. With a bang.

Just not tonight.

"Well, thanks for dinner." He started to walk across the kitchen, turning around when she didn't follow. "Hey, aren't you going to walk me to the door?"

"Why?"

"Because that's the polite thing to do with guests."

"Barging in and inviting yourself to dinner doesn't make you a guest," she mumbled, but she followed after him as he walked back down the hall to the front door.

He came to such an abrupt stop in front of the door that Lily ran into him. With a soft "Oof" she pushed herself away from his back. "Nice of you to give me a little warning, there, buddy."

He turned back to her, his head cocked to the side, studying her eyes. Then he smiled. And ran his tongue over his lips. She watched him, her expression softening into a nice glaze of arousal. Her lips parted. Her cheeks pinkened. It would be so easy to lean in and kiss her. She wanted him to kiss her. He saw it in her eyes.

He wanted it, too. So badly he could taste it. Every nerve he had yelled for him to do it, and his cock enthusiastically agreed as it throbbed against the zipper of his pants. But he wouldn't. Not tonight. It would be more fun to keep her off-balance—and would lead to a much more gratifying experience the next time they met.

"Thanks again," he told her quietly, leaning close enough for his breath to brush over her lips. A shock ran through him at being so close to her and he had to fight an almost insatiable urge to close the inch between them. "We'll have to do it again sometime."

He heard her growl of frustration—the one that matched the howl inside him—as he turned his back on her and walked down her front steps.

* * * * *

"We'll have to do it again sometime," Lily mimicked, pacing her kitchen floor as she cleaned up after the meal. "Do *what* again? Annoy the hell out of each other over an otherwise perfectly good meal? I think not. It's not worth ruining an excellent recipe."

If he wasn't so damned sexy with all that dark skin and even darker eyes and perfect white teeth, she would have kicked him out a lot sooner. As it was, by the time he'd left, she'd been ready to throttle him. He was arrogant, selfish, presumptuous...of course, none of her current level of aggravation had *anything* to do with the fact that he'd had a perfect opportunity to kiss her—and he hadn't. He might as well have laughed in her face. What was all that flirting during dinner about? What was with the footsie? Did he just want to embarrass her at the end of the evening because she wouldn't give him a stupid autograph? Men. They all sucked. It didn't matter what Janet or Marnie said. Men sucked, plain and simple. Every last one of them. Including Mr. Fine Ass—who had just become Mr. Arrogant *Ass*.

She finished the dishes, loaded the dishwasher, and poured in the orange-scented detergent. Once she'd started the machine, she gave the counters a final swipe with the dishcloth. She'd had enough of masculine jerks to last a lifetime. But Mr. Arrogant— *Evan* was *so* sexy. He didn't have to do anything beyond breathing to be sexy. She couldn't help but be affected by that. Any sane woman would feel the same way—and that was even more reason to avoid the guy. Too much time around him and she'd end up having to check herself into the mental ward.

Thanks to Evan and his intense brown eyes, she wouldn't get a wink of sleep tonight. She settled onto the couch with the remote. Why even bother going to bed, when all she'd do was think about him and the kiss that never happened? She huffed a sigh and sank deeper into the plush cushions. She was *so* done with men and all their stupid games.

Chapter Four

The blaring country music, clanging glasses and raucous laughter of people well on their way to advanced stages of inebriation pounded through Lily's head. The dimly-lit, dark wood paneled bar room smelled of smoke, beer, and sweaty bodies. Dampness hung in the air, the air conditioning system unable to accommodate the extreme temperatures, and the throng of people with nothing better to do than get drunk and yell at each other. She pinched the bridge of her nose and sucked in a deep breath through her mouth, hoping she had a bottle of aspirin in her purse.

"Are you okay?" Janet nudged her in between sips of her margarita. "You don't look very good tonight."

"Yeah. Tired." And in no mood to be partying with half the town. Why had she agreed to come out tonight, anyway? Did she have some kind of untapped masochistic streak?

Janet clicked her tongue and shook her head. "See, you're working too hard. I told you that you need to find a less strenuous job."

"This isn't about work. I haven't been sleeping well for the past couple of days." And that fact had absolutely nothing to do with the upstairs light on across the street until all hours of the night. *Nothing.* Evan had probably just been reading.

She sighed. She didn't really want to think about his choice of reading material — and her starring role in it.

A tall, burly man wearing a gray T-shirt and a pair of long denim shorts walked by the section of the bar where she, Janet, and Marnie sat. His leering gaze fell on Lily. She squinted. Did she know him? Probably. He looked familiar, and she knew most everyone in town, but it was kind of hard to tell with the lighting so low, it looked like the room was lit with nothing but birthday candles. She rolled her eyes, resisting the urge to give him the finger. Thanks to Toby and his article, she couldn't get a moment's peace. The editors at *Seduced* should send the guy a thank you for increasing their sales by such a high margin.

"This is a joke," she said to Janet. "I can't go anywhere without someone staring at me, thanks to Toby. I should just go home and hide under the covers until it all blows over."

"Do you plan on dragging a man under the covers with you?" Marnie asked.

"No." Even if she could find a suitable man, she didn't think she wanted him around. He'd probably just want her because of the pictures.

Marnie laughed. "Then you're not going anywhere. Did you ever stop to think that Toby isn't entirely to blame for all the attention you're getting?"

Lily quirked a brow. "What do you mean?"

"Well, *Toby* didn't pose nude."

Of all the nerve… "So you think this is my fault?"

Janet shook her head, her lips pursed. "No, Lily. I think what Marnie's trying to say is you're placing some of the blame on a convenient source. I know Toby is responsible for a lot of the attention you're getting, but not all of it. You don't know how many men in town subscribe to the magazine."

Lily opened her mouth to argue in her defense, but she snapped it shut when she realized she had no argument to make. As much as she hated to admit it, Janet and Marnie were right. She wrinkled her nose and blew out a breath.

Janet patted her shoulder. "Relax, hon. You should be happy with all the male attention. Sit down and enjoy all the drinks you're getting us. For *free*."

Not interested in any of the men who had been sending her drinks all evening, Lily passed the drinks to her friends. She had just finished her first diet cola with lime, while Janet and Marnie had consumed at least a pitcher of margaritas.

"Thank you, by the way." Marnie giggled like a seventh-grader, a sure sign she was well on her way to getting stinking drunk. Lily laughed. It wouldn't be pleasant for Marnie, but it would be a lot of fun to watch. It might be just what she needed to lighten her stormy mood.

"Excuse me. Again." The bartender set a glassful of dark liquid in front of her, an amused grin on his suntanned face. "Here's another one. From the guy over there." He gestured with his chin to the other end of the bar. Lily followed his gaze.

Damn it. What was *he* doing here?

Evan sat on the last stool at the other end of the bar, glancing her way and tossing her another of those sexy half-smiles. He winked and shook his head when she started to push the drink away. She frowned as she picked it up and sniffed it. Tasted it. Cola? Finally, someone around here got something right. She took a big, grateful sip to wet her parched throat and mouthed "Thanks" to Evan. Janet, who must have been watching the whole exchange, poked Lily in the ribs with the tip of one long fingernail. "You're been holding out on us, hon."

"Not me."

"Yes, you have. I saw that. Mr. Fine Ass just winked at you." She fanned herself with a cocktail napkin.

Lily sighed. "His name is Evan Acardi."

"Evan Acardi? Ooh, sexy." Janet fanned herself harder, and Marnie joined in.

Soon they were reduced to fits of giggles, leaning against the bar for support. Marnie's face had turned red and Janet had tears coming out of her eyes. Marnie hiccupped. Shit. Lily had nightmarish visions of the two of them wrapping their cars around trees on the way home. Not much of a drinker, Lily would have made the perfect designated driver. If she knew how to drive. So she settled for the next best thing. "Girls, I'm going to need you to hand me your keys," she told them, trying to keep a straight face.

Janet frowned at her and Marnie gave her a pleasantly

blank stare. "What for?" Janet asked. "I'm fine."

"When you've had enough tequila to put down a bull, there's a problem." Lily held out her hand and waited until each of them placed their keys in her open palm. "Thank you." She shoved the two sets of keys into her little black purse and picked up her drink.

Janet stuck out her tongue at her and Marnie burst into another fit of giggles. Marnie had never been much of a drinker, either, and it amazed Lily that she managed to stay perched on the little stool without slamming her face into the bar.

As if on cue, Marnie teetered. Lily shook her head. "There's an open booth. Why don't we grab it before someone else does?"

Janet made a beeline for the table and Lily and Marnie followed. When Lily sat down, she realized their new location put the end of the bar where Evan sat in her direct line of vision. And he was staring right at her. He gave her a smile and her own grin faltered.

"So, you're doing Mr. Fine Ass now?" Janet asked.

Lily nearly choked on her cola. She sputtered, setting the glass down hard enough to splash half of it over the tabletop. "Doing him? I barely know the guy."

"Well, let's get to know him." Janet yelled to him, making come-here gestures that involved her whole arm. "Hey, Evan Acardi! Get your sexy ass over here."

A hush fell over the bar for a few seconds as all eyes turned toward Janet and her wildly gesturing arm. Evan shook his head. He pushed away from the bar and walked over to the table, standing over them and filling Lily's personal space with his big, sexy, annoying presence. Annoying mainly because his attention currently focused on Janet. "Interesting summons. Thank you for the compliment."

Janet beamed. "I only speak the truth."

"Is there something I can do for you, or did you just call me over to tell me that?" he asked, an eyebrow raised, an amused grin on his face.

Marnie got up from next to Lily and scooted into the bench next to Janet. She patted the portion of the table in front of the empty space she'd created. "Sit, Evan. Tell us about yourself."

Evan turned his amused gaze to Lily and stage whispered, "Is it safe?"

Lily shrugged. "Probably, but I wouldn't let your guard down. You never can tell with these two."

He nodded as he scooted onto the bench, his knee brushing Lily's. And not moving away. A chill ran down her entire leg, all the way to her toes. "Good to see you again."

She snorted. He said it like he hadn't been at her house three days ago asking her to autograph a picture of her naked breasts. "Hi."

"You don't sound very happy to see me."

"Nonsense," Janet chimed in, patting Evan's hand and making a curl of jealousy rise in Lily's stomach. "She's very happy to see you. You'll get used to her attitude. So...tell us everything about yourself. We like to get to know the men Lily is interested in. We look out for each other that way."

Lily shook her head. No way were they going to pull this crap. The poor guy didn't need their third-degree. He'd already gotten it from her. "He's thirty-five, divorced, an architect, came from Chicago, works in Concord."

Evan shook his head and laughed softly. "Nice summary. Concise. A little more information than I would have given, but you're good at this. Have you considered writing biographies for a living?"

"Thanks." Lily wrinkled her nose at his sarcasm, but Marnie frowned.

"That's nothing. We want to know more about any man who has his sights set on Lily. You've got to tell us a little more. You have an interesting last name. It sounds like Bacardi." She giggled. "Are you Italian?"

Evan shook his head. "Nope. My family originally comes from Argentina. I still have relatives there."

So she'd been right about his Hispanic ancestry. Damn, the guy was hot. Every second she sat next to him, breathing in his clean scent, he just got hotter. Maybe she should have something stronger than soda.

Janet eyed the almost-empty glass in front of Evan. "Do you want another drink? My treat. I have plenty of cash. Haven't paid for a single thing all night."

Evan swirled the amber-colored liquid in the glass before he downed it in one sip. He shook his head at Janet. "No, thanks. I'm all set."

Janet shrugged. "Suit yourself." Apparently, seeing she wasn't going to get any further information from Lily, she turned her attention to Marnie. "How's everything going with Joe?"

Marnie shrugged. "It's going. But he's not as sexy as..."

She snapped her mouth shut and waggled her fingers at Evan.

He leaned close to Lily's ear, sending a shiver up her spine as he whispered, "She's not always like this, is she?" He pulled back and sat up.

She closed her eyes and savored the lingering chills. When she let her eyelids flutter open, her face flamed when she saw Evan watching her, intense interest on his handsome face.

She brought her mouth to his ear to whisper back, resisting the urge to nibble on his earlobe. He smelled so good, clean and spicy and warm. His skin would probably be warm and soft under her touch. "No. She's a health nut. One drink hits her like a whole bottle of vodka. She's had at least four margaritas."

He turned his head toward her, putting his mouth only a few inches from hers. "The other one's in pretty much the same state."

"Janet? Yeah, I suppose she is."

"They're not driving, I hope."

"Nope. I've got their keys."

He patted her leg, his hand so high on her thigh that it made her panties go damp. She squirmed. Could she get drunk from the alcohol fumes in the bar? Because she was starting to feel a little buzzed. She snapped her head away from him and sucked in a deep, calming breath.

His hand didn't leave her leg, but instead rested there. He gave her thigh a light squeeze and leaned in to whisper again. At least she thought he would whisper, but instead he brushed his lips against the skin of her neck, just below her ear. She let out a little whimper and Marnie and Janet swung their heads in Lily's direction.

"Oh, get a room," Janet said on a giggle. She shook her head and turned back to Marnie, who was starting to get that not-so-good look about her. That might turn out to be a problem in a little while.

"Stop," Lily told Evan, lifting her hands to his chest to push him away. But once she settled her palms against his well-defined pecs, she didn't feel so much like pushing anymore.

"Why should I stop?" he asked, his tone laced with humor. He winked. He knew he was getting to her, and was loving every second of it. She ought to punch him—and she would, if she could get her hands to move away from his chest.

"Because I said so." Oh, yeah, Lily. You sound oh-so-convincing.

"Give me a valid reason to stop and I will." He sucked her earlobe into his mouth and bit down gently. She shuddered. If he went any lower with that clever tongue, she'd embarrass herself by screaming out his name in front of the whole bar. This could get out of control very quickly from here, and he had to be stopped. Though it felt so good…

"Bad spot. We're in a public place. Don't touch me there." She shook her head when he released her earlobe but didn't move away. His breath feathered across the ultra-sensitive skin of her neck, making her squirm in her seat. Why couldn't he see how badly he was affecting her? Her face had to be flushed, and her eyes had probably taken on that pre-orgasmic glaze. She frowned. He probably *did* see, and chose to push her further. *Jerk.*

"Nice skirt."

"Thanks." She groaned when her voice came out as a semi-breathless whisper.

"You should always wear skirts," he told her. "Much sexier than those athletic pants you wear all the time."

She made a mental note to go out and buy ten more pairs of yoga pants. Dull, boring, gray ones a couple sizes too big. "Whatever."

His deep laugh hit her hard, right where it counted, and she sighed. Why couldn't she be attracted to a guy she didn't want to throttle?

His fingers worked their way down her leg to the hem of her skirt. Before she could stop him, he'd pushed the stretchy black fabric up a good three inches and worked his fingers up the inside of her thigh.

"Stop it." *Keep going. Just a little higher. Oh, yeah. That's really nice.* "We're in a public place."

He shrugged and moved his fingers up another fraction of an inch.

"Evan," she warned loud enough to get Janet's attention. Janet turned her head toward them, took in their faces, and burst out laughing. Some friend she was.

"Evan, what?" Janet asked, giving Evan an exaggerated frown. "You *are* behaving yourself, right, mister?"

Evan blinked his eyes at Janet, the picture of innocence. "Always. I'm a perfect gentleman." As he spoke, he nudged his fingers higher until he brushed them across the triangle of lace covering her pussy. The *soaked* triangle of lace. He turned his heated gaze to Lily and smiled.

Lily snorted to cover her extreme discomfort. "Perfect gentleman, my ass."

Evan leaned in and chuckled against the side of her neck. "I'm sure your ass is as lovely as your front." He punctuated his words with little taps against her clit. She squirmed against his hand, about two seconds away from coming. She couldn't let that happen, not with Janet and Marnie staring right at her.

Her face must have turned a thousand shades of red. She tapped her nails on the table to get his attention. "You have no idea what my front really looks like. Have you ever heard of airbrushing techniques?"

"Sure."

"How do you think they made those pictures look so flawless?"

He shook his head, a look of mock disappointment on his face. "I've been disillusioned. And here I thought you had to be the prettiest little thing I'd ever seen."

"Bullshit." She turned her attention back to her drink, though it was difficult to concentrate on anything other than his fingers and what they were doing to her.

"No, really." He slipped one finger under the fabric of her thong and stroked the tip of it over her clit. She tried her best not to arch into his touch.

"Don't lie to me, Evan. If you hadn't seen those pictures, you wouldn't have even given me a second glance. Look at how long it took you to come up and talk to me."

"I didn't talk to you sooner for other reasons."

Like, he hadn't been able to find his voice? Or the pictures made him think she was Head Slut in town? She yanked his hand out of her panties and pushed it away. "What other reasons?"

Evan shook his head. With his gaze locked on hers, he brought his finger to his mouth and licked the tip. He closed his eyes and gave a groan of appreciation that sent a quiver through her cunt. When he finally spoke, he leaned back to her ear and kept his voice low. "Look, Lily, I'm not looking for marriage."

She nearly choked on her drink. "Well, good, considering

we've only really known each other for three days."

He continued, ignoring her quip. "I'm very attracted to you."

The way he said it made her toes curl up in her sandals. She opened her mouth to speak, but no sound came out. Thankfully, Janet had turned her attention back to Marnie. The two of them appeared to be scoping out the bar, probably looking for eligible men.

"As strange as this sounds," Evan started, "I could see us becoming friends."

"And it seems strange, why? Because being my friend is so weird?" She glanced at Janet and Marnie and nodded. "Okay, I see your point."

"I don't think you do." He kissed her cheek in a gesture that seemed a little too intimate, given the fact that they'd had a total of one and a half real conversations past a simple greeting when they ran into each other outside. "I haven't been here very long, and I haven't had the chance to make many friends. I do want to be your friend. The problem is, I want more than that, too. I don't know if I can separate the two."

She started to ask what he was talking about—as if she didn't know, she just liked to torture the guy—when Marnie stood up from the bench. And toppled to the floor in a heap. Janet snorted a laugh. "I think she's had a little too much to drink."

"No shit." Lily poked Evan in the stomach. "Move over, will you? I've got to lift her up off the floor before somebody steps on her."

Evan stilled her with his hand as he slid off the bench. "I'll get her." He bent down and scooped Marnie up like she weighed no more than ten pounds. Knowing Miss Salad Queen, that assumption might not be too far off. Evan stood her on her feet, catching her when she started to topple again. "You've got her car keys, right?"

Lily nodded.

"Can you drive her home?"

She'd probably drive her *through* her home. "Um, no."

"Well, why the hell not?"

Janet wrapped an arm over Lily's shoulder and smiled at her. "She can't drive."

"Do you have bad night vision or something?"

"No, dummy. I really can't drive. At all. I don't know how."

"Lovely." Evan rolled his eyes. He glanced down at Marnie, who was now drooling on his shoulder. "Fine. We're leaving. I'm driving everyone home. Let's go."

"I think I'll just walk," Lily said, backing away a step when Evan shot her an intense glare.

"No, you won't. These are *your* friends. You're not leaving me alone with them in this state."

Lily started to protest, but then she thought about Janet sitting in the front seat of Evan's car, her hand touching his knee, his thigh, maybe higher. Jealousy clenched tight around her throat and she nodded. "You're right. I can't leave you alone with them."

Evan half-walked, half-carried Marnie through the crowd in the bar. He let out a sigh of what could only be described as relief when they finally made it out the door into the warm dampness of the night. Lily helped Janet and Evan pile Marnie into the back seat of Evan's car, saying a silent prayer that she didn't throw up. Marnie would be embarrassed about it in the morning, and probably a little—okay, a lot—hung over at work, but Lily couldn't help the chuckle. Marnie very rarely lost control, and when she did, she went all the way with it. At least Lily wasn't the only one tonight with control issues.

* * * * *

This was definitely *not* the way Evan had planned to spend the evening. He'd gone to the bar to relax after another grueling week at work. If he'd known Lily and her friends would be there, he would have stayed home and parked his ass in front of the TV instead. Lily, he didn't mind. Not in the least. Running into Lily had been a very nice—and very arousing—surprise. Her friends he could do without.

Blondie number one, the loud one who he always saw at Lily's house, couldn't seem to stop giggling. And blondie number two…well, there would be hell to pay if she puked in his car.

Lily sat in the passenger seat, quietly giving him directions to the ditz twins' houses and, he suspected, fuming. Her grip was so tight on the door handle he worried she'd snap it off. If she harmed any part of his car…even the woman who'd become his current obsession wouldn't be safe. He'd spent all his spare time in the past three years restoring the classic car to mint condition, and no one who harmed his baby would be safe from his wrath.

How had this happened? What had started out as a not-so-innocent flirtation with Lily had turned into a road trip with a couple of drunk blondes—one who couldn't stand on her own two feet. He'd just wanted to tease Lily enough to tempt her into coming home with him, and somehow he'd ended up the designated driver.

"Stop here," Lily told him, an annoyed edge to her voice.

"Whose house is this?" He pulled the car to a stop in front of a tiny cottage smaller than the little ranch Lily lived in. "Ditz one or ditz two?"

"Huh?"

"The one who can walk, or the one who might fall over and smack her face off the concrete?"

"The second one."

"Wonderful." He got out and helped Lily ease the woman from the car. There was a tense moment when she coughed and started to gag, but she made it out of the car without losing her dinner all over the leather seats. *Lucky woman.* What was her name again? It began with an 'm'. Marly? Marcie?

Marnie. The health food nut who worked with Lily.

And the other one was Janet. He remembered *her* name— and her blatant way of trying to get him to notice her on a near daily basis. He helped the women walk Marnie up the front walk. Lily used Marnie's keys to open the door and instructed Evan to lay her on the couch.

"Think she'll be okay?" Lily asked Janet, who slid down into a beige recliner and toed off her shoes.

"I'll stay the night to make sure she doesn't do anything stupid." Janet laughed. "We can keep each other company in the morning."

"Are you sure?" Lily asked. Evan grabbed her arm and tried to drag her from the house before she changed Janet's mind. Lily swatted him in the arm and shot him a dirty look.

"Yes, I'm sure. Go home. Have fun with your man." Janet giggled as she leaned back and closed her eyes. "Don't let this pretty boy go too soon."

Evan frowned. Pretty boy? *What the hell?* Lily must have noticed the change in his expression, because she dragged him outside. She shook her head at him as she got into his car and shut the passenger side door. He glanced back at the house before he turned and followed.

"I'm not a pretty boy," he told Lily as he backed the car out of Marnie's driveway.

"Actually, you kind of are."

He slammed his foot on the brake and glared at her. "What's that supposed to mean?"

She sighed and shook her head, looking at him like he was an insecure child. Her hand came to rest on his knee and she squeezed gently, sending a jolt of heat straight to his cock. "It means that you're beautiful. Chiseled. Polished. *Perfect.*"

Huh. When she put it that way, it didn't sound like such a terrible thing.

* * * * *

He'd barely pulled his car into the garage when Lily opened the passenger door and jumped out. She was out of the garage and halfway down the driveway before he caught up with her. What was her hurry? She spun when she heard him approach, her eyes glittering with unease in the light of the streetlights overhead.

"Well, thanks for the ride home. It's not that far from the bar to my house, though. I could have walked."

"I already explained my reasoning. No way was I getting stuck with your buddies by myself." He reached his hand out and wrapped a finger in a lock of her silky hair. She'd worn it down tonight. It hung long and straight and glossy to the middle of her back, a warm color he couldn't quite call brown, but not light enough to be blonde.

She drew her lower lip into her mouth, holding it lightly between her teeth, and his cock tightened. He wanted to do that to her — as well as many other things.

"Well, thanks. I mean it. I'll see you later." She stepped away and her hair slid from his finger. "Have a good night."

No. He wasn't ready to let her go so soon. "I'll walk you home."

She glanced at the distance between the end of his driveway and her front steps. And laughed. "Why? There's no need. It's not like I'm going to be kidnapped or mugged as I cross the street. If it makes you feel better, stand here and watch me walk home."

As much as he'd love to watch that delicate swing of her ass as she walked — provided she didn't trip on another rock and almost take a header into the sidewalk — he couldn't let her go home alone. "What kind of gentleman would I be if I didn't see you to your front door?"

"A *normal* one." She turned to glare at him, her hands on her hips, her mouth pursed as if fighting laughter. "You're something else, Evan. You know that? Number one, we aren't on a date so I don't need you to go all chivalrous on me. Number two, I happen to know that you aren't a gentleman so it negates what you're saying now."

She had him there. Still, he didn't want to let her go yet. After the way she let him touch her in the bar, he had to find out how much further she'd let him go. He needed *something* from her, he just didn't know what yet.

"Too bad," he told her with a shrug.

"Too bad, what?"

"Too bad you don't get your way this time. I'm walking you home. If you don't like it, get over it."

She rolled her eyes. "We'll see how much *you* don't like it when I grind my heel into the top of your foot."

"Go ahead." He smiled and shoved his hands into the pockets of his pants to keep from grabbing her.

Lily blinked her big Caribbean blue-green eyes, a shocked expression settling firmly in their depths. She sucked her full lower lip into her mouth again and let it slide back out slowly, making him pant with need, before she spoke. "Excuse me?"

"I said go ahead. You want to crush my foot, I'm not going to stop you." He laughed. "Hell, maybe I even *like* pain." He didn't usually, but with Lily he had a feeling he'd be open to a lot of new things.

"You're impossible." She started walking away and he followed, grabbing her hand to keep her from running away. She slowed, but slid him a glare out of the corner of her eye. "What do you want now?"

What *did* he want? Everything. And he'd get it, too. Just not tonight. He saved his answer until they reached her front steps and he walked her up to her door. When she opened the door and started inside, he spun her around and tugged her back to him. "What do I want? A kiss. For starters."

Lily gave him a smug smile. "Sorry. I don't kiss on the first date."

And she thought she was so smart. He returned the smile

with one of his own. *You're mine now, Lily. At least for the next ten minutes or so.* "It's a damned good thing we're not on a date, then." He registered the shock in her eyes seconds before he cupped her chin in his palm and crushed his lips to hers.

At first he didn't push her for more, just contented himself with the fact that she hadn't shoved him away — or tried to break any of his bones. She seemed to move closer, to press her soft little body against him, but that might have been the product of his hopeful imagination. He realized she was, in fact, enjoying the gentle kiss when she wrapped her arms around his neck and she licked his lower lip. His cock hardened even more, passing the point of painful, fighting against his zipper. His mind started to shut down. He threaded his fingers in her silky hair, holding her head in place as he repeated her action, running his tongue along the plumpness of her lower lip. Her lips parted on a gasp and he slipped his tongue into her mouth.

She tasted sweet and hot and, somehow, exactly like he thought she would. Her light floral fragrance wrapped around him, combined with a scent that he could only describe as "Lily", and he had trouble breathing. Everything in his mind screamed that this was right, take it slow, while every cell in his body screamed to get closer — *much* closer. The conflicting signals only served to spur him on. His mind could wait. He'd been *thinking* all day. Time for his body to take over and give his poor brain a rest.

He pushed her back until her hips bumped the porch railing. Her breathing hitched and she caught his tongue with her teeth, tugging gently. A shiver skittered down his spine as her short nails ran down the back of his neck. A new and far more pressing urge took over, the urge to expose a little more of her soft, pale skin. He lowered his hands to her thighs and shoved her skirt up a few inches, giving him better access to the skin he wanted to feel against his, hot and sweat-slicked, between his sheets. He nudged her thighs apart and fit himself against her, his mouth leaving hers to trail kisses along her jaw and down the side of her neck. When he pushed the neckline of her shirt out of the way to brush his lips over the top swell of her breast, she gave his hair a sharp tug. Blinking in lust and confusion, he lifted his head. "Huh?"

"Damn it, Evan. What are you doing?" The words had bite behind them, but her eyes held the same desire and confusion he felt inside. He'd gotten a little carried away with the kiss—okay, a *lot* carried away—but he couldn't help it. She brought out the worst in him, the animalistic tendencies he tried to keep caged when he hadn't even taken the woman out to dinner yet.

"I don't know," he answered, his tone breathless as he struggled to draw air into his lungs. The sharp breath he sucked in didn't help. It was filled with her. A car passed on the usually quiet dead-end street, its headlights illuminating Lily's features for a brief moment, giving him a glimpse of her face. Gone was the set jaw, the argumentative expression. He saw the woman in the magazine—the woman she swore she was nothing like. He knew the truth, even if she didn't see it yet. Shaking his head at the hopelessness of the situation, he leaned in and claimed her lips again.

He struggled with the tiny buttons of her blouse, finally losing his patience and thrusting a hand under the short hem of the shirt to cup her breast. The lace cup of her bra abraded his palm as he kneaded the fabric-covered mound. She moaned into his mouth when he flicked his thumb over her nipple, arching against his touch.

And suddenly it wasn't enough, yet it was too much at the same time. He'd caught a glimpse of the passion in her eyes, and he wanted to bring it out. It didn't matter that, before he'd invited himself to dinner, they'd only known each other in passing. It didn't matter that she fought him at every turn, challenged everything he said. Maybe that was why he felt so strongly for her so quickly. She didn't make things easy. She didn't give in to what he wanted just to make him happy. She made him *feel*, in a way Jessica had never been able to do. He wanted *everything*.

He abandoned her breast, his fingers trailing a teasing path down her stomach, past the skirt bunched at her hips, until he came to a triangle of fabric that covered her mound. He pushed it aside and ran his fingers along her slit. He dragged his lips from her skin and looked down into her eyes. "I swear you're trying to kill me with these underwear."

"I didn't even know I'd see you tonight," she whispered. Her teeth caught her lower lip and dragged it into her mouth.

"Are you sorry you did?"

"No." Her chest was heaving, her eyes wide. She gave him a small, uncertain smile and it nearly undid him. When she sucked that lip back in between her teeth again something snapped inside him. How could one woman be so many contradicting things? He barely knew her, but he wanted to protect her from the world—though he knew she'd never allow it. His heart clenched with the knowledge, but he pushed it to the back of his mind. Sex and emotion were two things he'd learned not to mix. Especially when the woman had managed to bury herself under his skin within a few short days.

"Good." He leaned in and bit her shoulder through the thin fabric of her shirt. She moaned softly and let her head drop back, giving him the perfect opportunity to put his mouth to the smooth skin of her neck. Her fingers tunneled in his hair, tightening to the point of pain. If they kept this up much longer, he might embarrass himself and come in his pants. He was harder than he could ever remember being, and he'd barely touched her. What would happen when he finally got her clothes off? He shook his head. He'd be liable to explode on contact.

"Evan," she moaned, her voice soft and throaty.

"I'm right here." He slipped his fingers past the folds of her pussy, finding her drenched, hot and throbbing. Her pussy muscles quivered as he stroked the slick skin. His cock wanted inside her. *Now.* He let out a frustrated sigh. Since that wouldn't happen tonight, he'd have to settle for his fingers. He kissed her hard and fast before pulling back, wanting to look into her eyes as she came.

He lifted one of her legs up, setting her foot to rest on a wooden planter on the porch floor. Surprise registered on her face seconds before he thrust two fingers into her dripping cunt. His groan rumbled through his chest as he fought to hold back his powerful response. She was so impossibly tight, so wet, so...*perfect*. He found her clit with his thumb and pressed down as he stroked his fingers inside her, curling them up slightly to increase her pleasure. Lily's whimper let him know she liked what he did to her as much as he liked doing it. He could spend hours exploring her body, making her come over and over again.

Her eyes started to drift closed, but he snagged her gaze and shook his head. "Keep your eyes open," he whispered. He leaned in and ran his tongue along the ultra-sensitive spot under her ear he'd found earlier in the bar. She shuddered, a soft sigh escaping her lips. He loved how responsive she was to his touch, how much she enjoyed him. She let it show. She didn't try to hide it like most of the women he'd been with. Lily, in everything, was open and honest—a change he found utterly refreshing and intoxicating.

He nipped her earlobe, tugging on it lightly. She cried out and her inner muscles clenched around him. *Damn*. He'd never felt anything like it before—a woman so willing, so responsive, so on the edge after only a few minutes. Maybe the play in the bar had turned her on as much as it had him. Or maybe she was always like this, always ready, always hot and passionate. Either way, he didn't care. He wanted to feel her clench around him as her orgasm shattered her.

He released her earlobe and kissed her mouth again—hard, claiming, possessive. "Come for me, Lily," he spoke, barely above a whisper, as he played his thumb over her clit.

"I can't just..." Her voice trailed off on a moan as he deepened his strokes within her.

"Yes, you can." He drew his tongue down the side of her neck from just under her ear to where her neck met her shoulder. One final flick of his thumb over her clit brought her orgasm crashing down on her, her cunt muscles sucking hard on his fingers as shudders racked her body. Her body pitched forward and he pulled her close to steady her. She let her head drop to his shoulder and her hands dropped to his arms, her fingers digging into his muscles. He withdrew his fingers from her still-spasming cunt and kissed the top of her head. "Amazing, Lily. Absolutely amazing."

" *Yeah*," she breathed. She pulled away and leaned against the railing, looking for all the world like a wanton sex goddess who'd just been thoroughly fucked. Her cheeks were red, her lips swollen and parted, the tip of her tongue resting on the top one. Her eyes had the glazed-over look of a very satisfied woman, and her hair hung in ragged waves around her face and shoulders.

He smiled at her as he brought his fingers to his lips and sucked them into his mouth, drawing them back out with excruciating slowness. Her gaze followed his every movement. "Next time, sweetheart, I want it to be my mouth that makes you come."

She shivered and closed her eyes for a brief second. When she opened them again, he watched the emotions flash across them at lightning speed — lust, satisfaction, annoyance, and fear. *Damn it.* She wasn't going to accept what had just happened between them easily. She was going to fight him on yet another thing. This woman and her mile-long stubborn streak would be the death of him.

She pushed away from the railing and made a show of straightening her skirt, her lips pursed and eyes narrowed. "Who says there's going to be a next time?"

He did. They both knew it. Why did she even bother to deny it? He shook his head. It wouldn't be worth the argument. Walking away now would be his best course of action — his apparent indifference would get her thinking. "Whatever you say, Lily. You'd better get inside before one of the neighbors sees you out here."

Her eyes widened and her face flushed as his words hit

home. She glanced down at her clothes and then around the neighborhood, her eyes searching the empty streets. "Oh, my God. I can't believe I...we...you... What the hell is wrong with you?" She slapped him upside the head. "Don't you ever do that again!"

She turned to rush into her house and a wave of panic hit him. What if indifference didn't work? What if she decided she didn't want to see him again? He couldn't let that happen, not when he was so close to getting her right where he needed her. "Don't what? Make you come so hard you see stars?"

She froze for a second before turning slowly back to him, a frown marring her pretty features. "No. You can do *that* again. Maybe. Just not outside under the porch lamp, okay?"

He had her. It couldn't have been easy for Lily to admit she wanted him. He gave her a slow smile designed to make her relive what he'd done to her—and let her know that he planned to do it again. *Soon.* "Whatever you want, sweetheart. Anything."

Lily shifted her gaze to the floor, scuffing the toe of her sandal on the porch's wooden surface. Evan felt the change in her more than saw it, as the uneasiness took over. If he didn't leave now, he ran the risk of Lily losing her nerve—and Evan losing his chance to get more from her than a hot kiss on her front porch. He cupped her chin in his hand and drew her gaze back to his. "I'm going to go home and get some sleep now. Go ahead inside. I'll talk to you soon, okay?"

"Okay." She pulled away, glancing back over her shoulder as she stepped through the open front door. "Goodnight."

"Goodnight." He waited until she shut the door before he turned and headed to his house. By the time he got inside, the warm glow had started to wane. His smile faded fast as his cock made a desperate bid for attention. *Shit.* The next time he had Lily alone, half-naked and willing, he planned to get a little satisfaction himself. But now—well, he couldn't very well go across the street and demand Lily give him a hand with the issue, no matter how much his cock begged. He'd have to deal with the problem himself.

But not for much longer.

Next time he had Lily alone, he promised himself not to be such a gentleman. Hadn't she told him she didn't expect that from him, anyway?

Five minutes later, he stood under the hot spray of the shower in his upstairs bathroom. He leaned his arm against the beige tile wall and let the steaming water sluice over his bare back. As much as he hated to admit it, he did some of his best thinking in this shower—the one he'd had built to his specifications when he'd bought the house four months ago and done some remodeling before he'd moved in. He'd modeled the bathroom, and the shower in particular, after the one he'd loved in his Chicago condo.

Jessica's condo now, he reminded himself. She hadn't cared for the huge expanse and open space of the shower, but he loved it. When they bought the condo he had envisioned mornings of hot, steamy sex in a shower big enough to hold them both—and accommodate a variety of positions comfortably—with plenty of room to spare. Having multiple showerheads meant that neither of them would be accused by the other of being a water hog. He laughed bitterly at the memories. Too bad Jessica hadn't enjoyed sex in the shower—or water at all, for that matter. She'd never wanted to ruin her hair or makeup.

The shower itself took up more than half the bathroom—a six by six, uncurtained space tucked into the corner of the room. Cream-colored Italian tile covered the entire surface of the shower, including the bench that ran along the entire length of the back wall. His favorite feature, though, had to be the four separate shower heads, one in each corner, all pointing toward the middle of the tiled floor. It had cost a small fortune, but it had been worth every penny.

Lily would probably love the shower. He smiled at the thought of her being in there with him, on her knees in front of him. He imagined her running her hands up his thighs, cupping his balls in her warm palm just before she closed those full lips over his aching cock. He closed his eyes and groaned, the thought leaving him weak and wanting. She'd probably tease the head of his cock with her tongue, treat the rest of his cock to long, lapping strokes...

He opened his eyes and glanced down at his cock, now jutting straight out in front of him, the head an angry red. A cold shower wouldn't have any effect on him except aggravate him more. He closed his fist around his cock, knowing release would be the only way he'd be able to settle down enough to sleep. It took a total of three strokes before he came on a groan, his mind still stuck on Lily's incredible lips and what she'd be able to do with them.

said a word to her in the half hour since she'd arrived, and the stepcow...step*mother* hadn't even bothered to meet her eyes. Of course, Hannah was a little, okay a *lot* wrapped around Frank Baxter's finger. And not in a good way. The woman hadn't had an original thought since they married six years ago.

"Speak of the devil..." Tony made the sign of the cross as Hannah waddled into the room, her hugely pregnant stomach protruding out into the atmosphere around her. All women gained weight when pregnant, but Hannah, it seemed, had gained enough for *all women.* She had to have put on at least a hundred and twenty pounds. She'd been thin before when Frank had married her, and Lily didn't know how her father was handling this. She wasn't due for three more months, and she looked like she was carrying septuplets. The bright purple and orange tent-style dress she wore only exaggerated her swollen figure.

"Dinner's ready," Hannah told Tony, strategically ignoring Lily. Lily wondered at the turn-around. Only six years older than Lily, Hannah had spent the early years of her marriage to Frank trying to be Lily's best friend. Probably on Frank's orders. Now things had certainly changed — and she bet her father had a hand in this as well.

Tony pushed himself up from the couch and started to follow the three boys out of the living room. He turned to Lily when he got to the door. "Are you coming in to dinner?"

"You mean I have a choice?"

Tony laughed. "No. Jake skipped out on us this week. We've got to stick together or we might not make it out alive."

She fought against the laughter bubbling in her chest but in the end lost the battle. "Oh, yeah. It's us against the world." She followed Tony out the door.

They made their way down the hallway to the dining room in the back corner of the house. Frank sat at the head of the table, his beefy arms crossed over his chest, a solemn expression on his round face. Lily stifled a groan when he directed his reproving gaze at her. Having a daughter appear in *Seduced* magazine must be hard to take for a man so bent on controlling the world around him to suit his needs. Normally she didn't mind visiting for dinner every Saturday, but when he refused to speak even a word to her, it brought back bad memories of growing up, when it seemed like nothing she did pleased him.

"Your brother and his wife have decided to stay at home today," he said to Tony as they settled into their chairs around the oval mahogany table. He shot Lily another disapproving glare that told her he blamed her for Jake and Mary's absence.

Was it her fault her brother was an unprogressive, chauvinistic pig?

Hannah set the plates and bowls in front of Frank before taking her seat next to him. Lily wanted to scream at him. *Don't you realize your wife is, like, twenty months pregnant, you arrogant jerk?* But when Hannah smiled at him, she understood why he didn't bother to help her. Because he didn't have to. Their whole relationship was a little too 1950's for Lily to stomach.

Frank heaped mounds of food onto his plate—obviously living with Anne for so many years had dulled his taste buds—and passed the plates along to Hannah. Her much smaller portions were probably due to the fact that her uterus was so big, she no longer had room for her stomach.

Lily took as little food as she could without offending the hormonal pregnant woman, cutting tiny pieces off her chicken and pushing the food around her plate, only taking a bite whenever Hannah wasn't looking.

"How is work, Lily?" Hannah asked her plate.

Lily had to bite back a snort of laughter at the last second, when Frank glared at her again. Was Hannah so cowed that she wasn't even allowed to meet Lily's eyes? Or was she as ashamed as Frank and Jake were—and as Anne pretended not to be? "It's great."

Hannah smiled at her mashed potatoes. "That's terrific. I'm thinking about taking some yoga classes after the baby is born."

Frank cleared his throat.

"Or not," Hannah added, for the first time daring to look Lily in the eye — and sending her a warning glance.

Lily fought the urge to roll her eyes in response. She'd lived with the man her whole childhood. She knew how stubborn and pig-headed he could be. But she knew better than to purposely bait him at the dinner table. When this whole mess blew over, he'd still be her father.

Eddie, Hannah's thirteen-year-old son, sat to Lily's left and spent most of the meal gawking at her, his pimply jaw practically in his lap. She tried to ignore it, but it got a little difficult when she felt him breathing on her neck. Obviously, he'd seen firsthand what Frank was so upset about. Where had a thirteen-year-old gotten a copy of the magazine? And didn't he realize they were *family*? Sick.

She forced herself to eat half a plate of leather chicken and lumpy mashed potatoes, gulping water in between every bite to wash down the charred taste of everything Hannah cooked. How did her father put up with this? Did he have no taste buds? His wife couldn't manage peas. *From a can!* And Eddie, poor kid, was as skinny as a broomstick. She didn't blame the kid for not eating. She'd cook something for the little geek, but she wouldn't be able to deal with all the openmouthed staring.

"Anthony, would you ask your sister to pass the rolls?" Frank asked Tony. Tony snorted a laugh.

"Hear that, sis?"

Didn't this kind of thing only happen on TV shows? She closed her eyes and drew a deep breath, hoping when she opened them the surreal feeling that had settled in her stomach would be gone. No such luck. When she opened her eyes she found everyone staring at her, waiting for her reaction. She'd been sucked into a soap opera. "Here, *Dad*." She resisted the urge to throw the basket full of half-cooked dough lumps Hannah passed off as rolls. "It's okay to ask me directly, you know. This isn't middle school."

"Watch your mouth, young lady," he said, glaring and pointing a finger at her. "You cannot come into my house and talk to me like that."

Okay, that's it. I've tried to be adult about this whole thing, but since no one else is, why should I bother? "Like what? Like you're being a jerk and you need to lighten up? Excuse me for speaking the truth."

"It's about time somebody did," Tony murmured.

Frank slammed his fists down on the table, shaking plates and bowls and making Hannah and the little ones jump. "Do you see what you have your brother doing, Lily? He's following your example. You need to learn to be a better role model."

Hello? "Dad, Tony is twenty-five." And he didn't need any help misbehaving. Tony got into trouble just fine all on his own.

"And what about Eddie?" Hannah added, her voice pitched so high dogs in the next state must have heard her. "He's at such an impressionable age."

Yeah, it showed. Eddie was no innocent, either. She dropped her fork to her plate and sat forward. "Why don't you both just say what the problem is and get on with it, so I can get on with my life."

"You want to know what the problem is, young lady? Fine. What were you thinking, posing for those *dirty* pictures?" Frank roared, standing up from the table. Hannah widened her eyes and threw her hands over her youngest, Bradley's, ears.

A little late for that, isn't it? "I was thinking that I'm old enough to make my own decisions. And there was nothing dirty about those pictures. We're all born naked, aren't we?"

"I didn't raise a hussy," Frank continued, going into full preacher mode. Shit. She didn't need this today—she wouldn't let it ruin her mood, not after her amazing night with Mr. Fine Ass.

"No, you didn't." She stood up and shoved her chair in. "You raised a free-thinker, able to take care of herself and make her own decisions. If you don't like them, too bad. This isn't your life. I don't like every decision you've ever made, either." She glared at Hannah, and then down at the food. "I don't think these *family dinners* are really a good idea anymore. I think I'm going to go out and find a new family."

She stormed away from the table, her hands clenched into fists. Like none of them had ever made a decision their families didn't like. She rushed out the front door into the hot, breezy air, amazed that she could breathe better in ninety-percent humidity than she could in her father's air-conditioned dining room.

She was halfway down the walk when she heard the front door shut and footsteps behind her. She turned to see Tony coming after her. "Hold on. I'm not going to let you walk home in this condition. You'll probably beat some old man up if he looks at you the wrong way. I'll give you a ride."

She started to protest, but Tony held up his hand. "Just let me take you home, okay? I want to talk to you about something."

Great. Another one who wanted to chastise her for what he saw as a bad decision. And she'd thought Tony, of all the people she knew, would support her. Moving to California and changing her name sounded like a better and better idea every day. She glanced around the quiet street of large houses and well-manicured lawns. Several of her father's neighbors were outside, and a couple even waved to her. Frank would never forgive her if she made a scene, so she climbed into Tony's black SUV and buckled her seatbelt, leaning back against the burgundy leather and closing her eyes. If she didn't look at him, maybe he wouldn't push her.

She should have known better. The second he got behind the wheel, he cleared his throat. "Are you okay?"

She cracked one eye open and glanced at him. "Just fine for a woman who's apparently been labeled Town Slut."

Tony's laughter filled the truck as he pulled out of the driveway and onto the street. "No, that's not you. Janet, maybe, but not you."

"Hey! Janet's my friend."

"And do you deny she has a little problem in the commitment department?"

"Well, no."

"There you go. I just wanted to say I'm sorry for what happened in there." He stopped for a stop sign and glanced her way. "Dad had no right to talk to you like that."

Lily laughed, despite her anger. "Must be nice to have him yelling at me for a change, instead of you."

Tony shook his head, a smile on his face. "Yeah, it's nice to have someone else be the family disappointment for once. But seriously, you didn't do anything you should be ashamed of. I admire you for following your heart. Maybe you are taking after me, after all."

"Funny. Really funny." Despite Tony's joking tone, his words made her feel better. He knew exactly what to say to get rid of her doubt. She *had* done the right thing by following her heart. If everyone else took issue with it, it wasn't her problem. Eventually this would pass and life would be back to some reasonable facsimile of normal. Until then, she'd just have to deal with it. Though hiding under the covers for a couple of months still sounded like a pretty good idea—especially when she thought about bringing Evan under there with her.

From the way he'd acted last night, first in the bar and then on her front steps, she had a feeling he'd be more than willing. That sent a giddy feeling shooting through her stomach. The man she'd been…well, ogling for the past few months had suddenly noticed her. Granted, it had taken him seeing nude pictures of her to jumpstart his interest, but at this point she had to take what she could get. And what exactly would she get from Evan? She couldn't wait to find out.

Tony pulled into her driveway a few minutes later. He put the truck in park and turned to her, a rare serious expression on his face. "Do me a favor, Lily."

"Anything, kiddo."

"Next time you decide to pose like that, let me know ahead of time. It was quite a surprise to open the magazine and see you on the pages."

Her eyes widened and she felt her face flame. Why hadn't she thought to let her family know? "Sorry."

"Don't be. This month's issue will make great kindling for my fireplace come winter. Talk to you later."

She slid out of the truck and with a wave, Tony pulled out of the driveway. She watched him drive down the street before she walked up the walkway, grabbing the mail out of the mailbox on the stair rail before letting herself inside the house.

She dropped the mail on the kitchen table and tried to settle in to read the fitness magazine she subscribed to, but she couldn't get her nerves to settle down. Instead of throwing her expensive glass plates against the wall — which would have been very satisfying since Hannah have given them to her for her last birthday — she put on some shorts and a tank top and went for a run.

A half-hour later she turned back onto her street, sweat pouring down her face and coating her body, her lungs protesting the thick air she'd been inhaling. A fine coating of dust from the dirt-packed, back roads she'd jogged covered her skin, mixing with the sweat and dripping down her arms and legs in rivulets. *Gross.* A shower would be wonderful right about now. More than wonderful. A shower was *necessary.*

Her thoughts of getting clean were sidetracked when Evan walked through the gate in the fence surrounding his back yard, a hammer in his hand, wearing nothing but a snug pair of denim shorts. Her throat went dry and her heart hammered harder against her ribcage. Even his bare feet turned her on. She tried to turn away before he saw her in her present disgusting state, but her feet seemed glued to the sidewalk. To make matters worse, her hand lifted — all on its own, of course — and waved at him.

"Hey, sexy," he called, stopping in the middle of his yard and propping his hand on his hip. The move outlined his toned shoulder and arm muscles and served to make *her* muscles fail. Her legs felt like melting. Must have been the heat.

"You have great timing," he continued. She frowned, her eyes narrowing in suspicion.

"Great timing for what?"

He walked up to her and tugged a strand of limp, sweaty hair that had escaped her ponytail. He gave her a smile so potent that she nearly grabbed him and ripped his jeans off. His voice broke through the heat-induced fog in her mind. "Can I borrow you for two minutes?"

Men. Always wanting favors. Always thinking of themselves. Did any of them actually say "please"? She shook her head. "Two minutes? That's all? What a disappointment. I would have figured a young, healthy guy like you could go for at least ten."

"Smartass." He ruffled her hair, using a strand to tug her a step closer. "I need a little help with something in the back yard." He waved the hammer in the air.

"Does it involve getting naked?" *Please?*

He leaned in close—obviously the man was in possession of defective olfactory senses if her running-in-ninety-degree-heat fragrance didn't bother him—and sent a series of little jolts up her spine as he breathed on her neck. "I think we proved last night that naked is optional."

Oh boy.

Chapter Six

Evan glanced back a few times at Lily as she followed him through the gate into the back yard. She'd probably sock him for saying it, but she looked cute all sweaty and breathless from her run. *He* wanted to make her sweaty and breathless. He would, too. Soon.

She wanted him as much as he wanted her. He saw it in those ocean-colored eyes that hid none of her feelings. But he wanted her to want him more before he got her into his bed. He wanted her to be so wild for him that she wouldn't be able to help herself. He wanted her completely out of control. He'd give anything to see calm, no-nonsense Lily lose herself in the moment—especially if the moment involved him and a bed.

When they got to the kitchen window that overlooked his in-ground pool, he stopped and picked up the black shutter off the ground. When he stood and handed it to her, he watched the confusion cloud her expression. He smiled. "What I need you to do is hold this." He took her hands and guided them to the window, using her hands to place the shutter next to the window, right where he wanted it. The position stretched her arms over her head, lifting the hem of her shirt to expose the soft line of her abdomen. His heart rate picked up, sending his pulse pounding. "Right about here. Don't move while I nail this in place, okay?"

The corners of her full lips tipped into a frown. "Um, okay."

He grabbed a couple of nails out of the plastic bucket on the ground and placed one against the shutter. To get the angle right he had to stand behind her and press his front against her back. The second his bare chest touched her, he felt her muscles stiffen. He resisted the urge to kiss the side of her neck. He could do that later, when she wasn't holding something that could do serious damage to his face.

"Can you hurry up? My arms are getting tired. Do you generally start home improvement projects you can't finish by yourself?" she asked. "What would you have done if I hadn't been around?"

Silly girl. He had no problem hanging the shutter himself, but when he'd seen her coming around the corner in those skimpy clothes — and he knew just what she had under those clothes — he'd seen it as a perfect opportunity. "Hold it steady for just a second more so I can nail it to the window."

He really wanted to nail *her*. And he would. Soon. But he had to be careful. She'd bolt at the first sign of losing control, so he wanted to make her think she had it until he'd already pulled its tenuous strings from her slender fingers. And then he'd have her right where he wanted her. In his bed. Or hers. The location didn't matter. The only thing that did was that his cock got a little satisfaction out of the deal. He loved pleasing a woman, but he didn't particularly care for being left hard and aching.

Lily let out a sigh and started to slouch. "Sure. Whatever."

Even though the windows at the back of the house were low, he had to stretch to put the nails through the top half of the shutter. But stretching allowed him an unimpeded view down the front of Lily's tank top when he glanced down, so he didn't mind the effort. When he finished, he dropped the hammer into the grass by his feet and put a hand on her damp shoulder. "Thanks. I appreciate the help."

She spun around and blinked at him a few times, the confusion in what she took as a dismissal obvious in her eyes. "Oh, okay. You...um, don't need me for anything else?"

Woman, you have no idea. "I'm done for the day with the home improvements, if that's what you mean."

He watched her try to school her reaction, but she couldn't quite do it. He'd be willing to bet she had no idea how much of her emotions showed on her face. It was one of the major things that made the woman so appealing. She frowned. "Of course that's what I meant. What else would I mean?"

He cupped her chin in his palm and smiled down at her. "I don't know. Can I make you an early dinner, seeing as you fed me the other night and helped me with this today?"

She laughed, somewhat nervously, and shifted under his touch. "I think I owe *you* after last night." Her eyes widened. "Wait. I didn't mean it that way."

"You might be on to something there." He smiled when she smacked his arm. "Or not. How about this instead. I'll take you out for dinner. Do you want to take a shower and get cleaned up? I have the best shower. You'd love it."

She raised her eyebrows. "Does it have built-in hands that give massages while you shower?"

No, but he could do that for her. All she had to do was say the word. "No, but it's almost the size of the bathroom and it has four shower heads."

She looked like she might be contemplating it, but then shook her head. "No, I'd better get home. You don't want to deal with me all hot and sweaty like this."

She really had no idea how appealing that sounded. "Why not? It's best when it's hot and sweaty, sweetheart." He leaned in and brushed his lips over hers, not forceful, not possessive, but playful and teasing to keep the mood light. "This humidity today is a killer. Can you swim?"

She nodded. "Yes, but I'm not getting into your pool all gross and dirty like this."

"Wanna bet?" He lifted her into his arms and brought her kicking and screaming with laughter to the edge of the deep end of the pool, dangling her over the water.

She pounded on his back with her fists, trying to speak through the laughter. "You wouldn't dare! I still have my shoes on."

"They'll dry." He let her go, but she snagged his wrist as she dropped, pulling him into the water with her. The splash of the water over his face was at first a shock, but the warm depths felt good after spending the afternoon outside in the heat. He came up first, standing in the chest-deep water, when she came up behind him and jumped on his back.

"Think you're so funny? My turn." She tried her hardest to dunk him under the water, but he was too tall and too strong. He eventually went down anyway, bringing her with him, both of them laughing as they floated back to the surface.

He raked a hand through his soaked hair, slicked it back from his face. It had been so long since he'd had fun with a woman—not the kind of fun sex involved, but actual *fun* that didn't involve getting naked. He'd closed himself off since the divorce, even long before the divorce if he had to be honest about it, and it felt good to let that part of him out again. With Lily, he didn't feel the need to try to impress her with his maturity—because she didn't care. He could be who he was without worrying about her judging him. If she liked him, she'd stick around. If she didn't, she wouldn't hesitate to let him know. She didn't play games, and she didn't try to be someone she wasn't, so he didn't have to either. It took away a lot of the stress he usually associated with relationships and flings, and left him free to pursue what he knew would make them both happy.

Lily waded to the edge of the pool and lifted her leg up on the side, her fingers working to untie her shoes. His stomach clenched with a sudden rush of need as he took in the flexibility she had to be able to lift her leg that high. If he tried, he'd pull some important muscles and possibly cause permanent injury. She seemed to do it without any effort at all.

"Need some help?" he asked when she struggled to get the tangled laces untied.

He expected her to say no—or tell him where to shove his chauvinistic behavior—but she surprised him. "Actually, yes. Since you started this, I think you should take them off for me."

He put one of her legs on his knee, pulled off the waterlogged shoe, and tossed it out of the pool. It hit the grass behind him with a wet splat. When he'd stripped off the other shoe and both her socks, he gave her a smile. "Better?"

She wiggled her toes against his leg. "Much. Thank you."

"Anytime."

She sucked her lower lip into her mouth—did she know how crazy she drove him every time she did that?—and put her hand on his chest. He thought she might push him away, but she surprised him yet again when her hand went around the back of his neck. "You were pretty sweaty yourself."

"Yeah. I spent most of the morning working on the house." He tried to smile, but failed when her tongue traced her top lip. She reached up and took out the clip holding her hair. The soaked strands fell over her shoulders. He couldn't resist moving closer, pressing her into the side of the pool and tangling his fingers in all that hair.

"Good for you," she told him, her smile taking a decidedly sensual turn. What did she have planned? He felt the control that he'd hoped to gain slowly slipping away from him, falling right into Lily's hands. He didn't care. Just the way she looked at him, with that hot-yet-innocent expression, was almost enough to make him come. He could see the outline of her nipples perfectly through her soaked white shirt. His mouth watered at the sight and he leaned in to her, his lips brushing her jaw.

"What are you doing?" she asked, her fingers playing with the short hair at the nape of his neck.

"Kissing you."

"Just checking. I thought maybe you were trying to convince me to mow your lawn or something."

He looked up at her and laughed. "Or something."

"Shut up and kiss me already, will you?" She pulled him down and crushed her lips to his. She tasted like salt and chlorine and hot summer sunshine. She felt amazing against him, even through the layer of her wet shirt. His cock ached, needing more of her touch, and he pressed his hips against hers. "Do you feel what you do to me?" he asked between kisses.

She nodded as a soft moan escaped her lips. "Yeah, you have a pretty strong effect on me, too."

"Maybe we should do something about that."

"What do you have in mind?"

He smiled at her devilishly. Just the opening he'd been hoping for. "I think we should get naked."

"In your back yard? Are you nuts?"

"No, I'm hot for you. So hot I can barely breathe." He ground his cock against her to prove his point.

"It's the summer heat. I assure you it has nothing to do with me," she told him, her eyes sparkling with humor.

He frowned. "It's not the heat. It's you. I can't stop thinking about you, how wet you were last night, how tightly you clenched my fingers when you came. Do you know what I did after I left you last night?"

Her lips parted, her expression growing serious. And more than a little aroused. "What?"

He took her hand and brought it between them, resting her open palm on his cock. He arched his hips against her, unable to help it once he felt her warmth envelop him. "I came home this hard. Harder even, since I'd had my fingers inside your sweet cunt. My cock wanted to be there instead."

She whimpered, her fingers curling around his arousal. "Very nice," she whispered with an almost reverent tone that only served to make him harder.

He shook his head. "Very aroused. Care to do something about that?"

"Now that you mention it…" Before he knew what she had planned, she unzipped his shorts and freed his cock from the confines of his briefs. He hissed as her warm, wet hand circled his throbbing shaft.

"You're so hard."

"Well, yeah. With you stroking it like that, did you expect any different?"

She smiled at him, her fingers running up his length, brushing over the head with a caress too soft, too light to be anything but a tease. A maddening promise of things to come — things he didn't want to wait for. She let him go long enough to push his shorts down past his hips, giving her better access. One warm hand cupped his balls, rolling them gently, while her other hand folded around him again, playing slowly and determinedly with every inch of his cock until he felt the need to scream. She seemed to be learning him, memorizing every little bit, playing the tips of her fingers over every centimeter with excruciating slowness. He couldn't take much more of this. "Harder," he ground out. "You're killing me."

"What?" She paused in her stroking, blinking up at him, her expression guileless.

Oh, damn it. Could it be possible that she didn't know? "You're not a virgin, are you?"

He expected her expression to chill, for her to focus an icy blue-green gaze on him, but she didn't. She laughed. "No. I'm not a virgin. I'm twenty-seven, not eighteen." She smiled, her chin shaky and her gaze a tinge apprehensive.

Okay. So she wasn't a virgin. But she didn't have a lot of experience, either. That surprised him. After he'd seen the pictures, he'd expected something completely different. He chastised himself for stereotyping her, this woman who was a bundle of intriguing contradictions.

He opened his mouth to ask for more clarification, but she tightened her hand around his cock and chased all thoughts of conversation from his mind. "Harder, huh?" she asked, sucking that damned lip into her mouth again. Next time, he planned to suck it into his.

"Yeah, like that," he breathed. He looked down into the water, seeing as her small hand encircled the red, throbbing length of his cock. Her touch was almost perfect. Just a little more...

"Show me," she told him, her words dragging his gaze back

to her face. "Show me how you want me to do it. Teach me, Evan. I want to know how to please you."

Her words nearly undid him. He let his eyes drift closed long enough to regain a tiny bit of his composure. When he opened them, she met his gaze, a resolute and very sexy smile on her face. She might not have much experience in this department, but what she lacked she made up for in eagerness and determination. It made him even harder, if that was possible.

He brought his hand between them, wrapped it around hers, tightening her grip a little more. He guided her hand into the rhythm he knew would drive him crazy in a matter of minutes. Seconds even. "Just like this." He brought her hand up the full length of his shaft before guiding her down again. He wanted her mouth on him, his hands in her hair as he taught her how he wanted her to move over him.

Fuck. He leaned in and kissed her, hard and quick. "Perfect. Use your thumb over the head. Oh yeah, like *that*." He moaned when the pad of her thumb circled over the head of his cock on the upstroke. He only needed ten more seconds, maybe twenty, before he exploded in her hands.

"You should stop now."

She paused and raised an eyebrow. "Don't tell me you don't like it."

He barked a laugh. "Hell yes, I like it. Way, way too much. If you don't stop, I'm not going to be able to."

"And what's wrong with that?"

He leaned forward and rested his head on her shoulder, burying his face in her wet hair. He pushed the strands aside and nuzzled his lips against her neck, flicking his tongue over her earlobe. She shivered, her grip tightening even more. He reached between them and stilled her hand, pulling her away from his cock before he lost control. He wouldn't come in her hand, in his pool. He would come in Lily's hot little cunt, or he wouldn't come at all. "Nothing's wrong with it. There are a few other things I'd rather be doing."

He pressed her into the smooth tile side of the pool and wrapped her legs around his hips, grinding his rock-solid cock against her mound. The only thing separating them were her too-thin shorts, and it was the most amazing thing he'd ever felt in his life. He rocked against her, nuzzling into her neck and pressing kisses along her jaw. He felt her fingers dig into the bare flesh of his back, his biceps, his shoulders, the sharp sting of her nails adding to his arousal.

With one final, hard thrust against her cotton shorts, he held her in place against the wall of the pool, his breathing heavy on her neck. She arched against him and he pushed back, willing her not to move. If she moved, even one inch, he'd explode. He didn't even dare let her down for fear that the motion of the water would send him over the edge.

When he felt controlled enough to speak again, he raised his lust-hazed gaze to her face. "Ever been skinny-dipping?"

She shook her head, confusion settling into her Caribbean eyes. "No. Why?"

"Because you're going to now."

Her frustrated sigh reverberated through his strung-too-tight body as he set her back on her feet. She frowned at him, her expression annoyed. "I don't want to swim, Evan, I want to...oh."

Her sentence stopped when he brought his hands to her breasts, his thumbs flicking over her beaded nipples. She sighed and arched into his hands. "I have things other than swimming in mind." He smiled down at her as he lifted the hem of her shirt and pulled the wet material over her head. The tank top was the athletic kind with a built-in bra, and freeing her of the shirt bared her breasts to his heated gaze. He tossed the shirt, not bothering to look where it landed, and brought his lips down to those incredible breasts.

They weren't quite as full as they'd looked in the magazine photos, but he'd never seen anything more perfect. He closed his mouth over one pebbled, dusky pink nipple, and sucked in the musky sweet taste of Lily. Pure perfection. He took her nipple between his lips, rolling gently, squeezing until she gasped. Her fingers flew to his hair, tangling and tugging the strands. It only spurred him on. He wanted more. So much more.

Too much more.

He pushed any thoughts of affection out of his mind and threw all his concentration into appeasing the tremendous, white-hot need that surged between them. His whole body shook as he laved her nipple, suckling her with a fierceness he felt running through his entire body. When he finally got inside that hot cunt, he'd be blown to pieces with the force of the power between them. They both would.

He released her nipple with a soft, wet pop and turned his attention to her other breast, sucking the beaded nipple deep inside the recesses of his mouth. She squirmed against him, fighting to wrap her legs around his waist. He felt her stomach tighten against his, the soft moans and whimpers escaping her, driving him crazy.

"Evan," she whispered, her tone hoarse. "Evan, please."

"Please, what?" he mumbled around her stiffened flesh. He'd never get enough of her taste, her smell...her responsiveness. He'd never met a woman like Lily, a woman who could be this close to coming just from his mouth on her breasts.

"Please touch me." She dug her nails into his scalp and he hissed out a breath. He wanted to make her wait, to drive her crazy a little longer, but at this rate she'd kill him before he got where he wanted to be. Not willing to risk his health since she was probably a second or two away from scalping him, he reached between them and pressed his index finger to her cloth-covered clit. At the same time, he sucked hard on her nipple, swirling his tongue over the tight bud. Lily came with a sharp cry, her hands pulling so hard on his hair he feared she might tear it out in clumps.

He moved his hand away from her clit and grasped her wrists to loosen her hold, at the same time leaving her breasts to bring his lips to her mouth. He slid his tongue into her mouth, his kiss claiming, possessive. Hard. Fierce, like the feeling welling in his lower abdomen and tightening his cock. Her arms came around his neck and she rode out the spasms, her body finally settling against his, shaking, as she came back down. She jerked her mouth away from his, her gaze searching, her breaths coming in short, ragged pants.

Her tongue traced the line of his collarbone before moving down to flick over the flat disk of his nipple. And suddenly the pent-up need inside him blossomed into something more—a raging, burning compulsion he had no hope of controlling. He pushed her shorts down her hips, taking her panties along with them, fighting the water that made undressing her near impossible. She helped him rid her of the only obstacles keeping him from where he needed to be, kicking her shorts and panties off as he brought them down her legs. He shoved his own shorts and briefs down his hips and struggled out of them, leaving them both naked in the warm, soothing water.

He snagged her gaze, his eyes searching her face for some kind of rejection, a denial of what he knew they both wanted. Finding none, he lifted her legs around his waist, settling her back against the tile as he pulled her wet, slippery cunt over his throbbing cock. She whimpered, her cunt sucking him in, clenching around him, and he didn't stop until he'd seated himself fully inside her. The whole time their gazes held, personalizing the intensity of the moment.

"Oh my," she whispered, her tongue darting out to moisten already-wet lips. "I didn't expect this."

"Neither did I." He held her hips steady, not willing to move yet, not when he hadn't memorized the feel of her tight cunt enveloping his cock, nothing between them. A cold chill ran through him. "Lily, I...shit. We have to stop."

He started to pull out, but she dug her heels into his ass and barred any further retreat. "It's fine. I'm on the Pill. I'm clean."

A flash flood of relief filled him. He'd never been so out of control with a woman that he'd forgotten to protect her. And he'd never had sex without a rubber with any woman besides the one he'd married. "I'm clean, too." The feel of her tightness around him, almost as tight as a fist and twice as hot, made him realize what he'd missed. Without the thin barrier of a condom, he felt every nuance of movement within her muscles, every ridge and curve in her inner walls.

"Good." She threw her head back and moaned when he captured her earlobe between his teeth. "But don't you think you should move?"

Her laugher vibrated through his cock, her muscles squeezing him even tighter. *Fuck.* So much for savoring the moment. He was going to come—soon—whether he moved or not. He pulled back until he'd almost withdrawn before slamming back into her, over and over again, not giving her any break in between forceful thrusts. He'd lost control, was acting like a rutting animal, but he didn't care. Lily didn't seem to, either—in fact, from the glazed-over look on her face and the way those nails found their way to his shoulder blades again, he'd say she was enjoying the fast, hard fuck as much as he was. Next time, he'd take it slow. Next time he'd lay her out on the bed and eat that sweet pussy until she begged for mercy. Next time—when he wasn't two seconds away from exploding inside the hottest cunt he'd ever fucked.

Lily's soft gasps turned into whimpers, which turned into moans as he slammed even harder into her. He angled her hips up just a little higher, wanting to pleasure her as much as she pleasured him. Almost immediately, he felt her tense around him, her body stilling just before she screamed his name and shattered around him. Her body bucked hard, her cunt clenching him so tight he could barely move. The spasms that ran through her inner muscles sucked him deeper, pulling him in, sending him over the edge into the most powerful climax he'd ever felt. He spurted his hot cum inside her in seemingly endless streams, his balls drawn up tight as they emptied, his teeth locking on the tender skin between her neck and shoulder. One word ran through his mind as his body convulsed and her spasming cunt milked him dry.

Mine.

It should have shaken him, made him want to run for cover, but it didn't. He was too lost in the sensations to make any sense of the word and what it might mean. He only knew one thing. Lily's cunt had been made for his cock. She fit him like no other—and this would not be the last time he had her. He'd make sure of it.

He pulled out and let her down slowly, every inch of her curvy body sliding down his front. He shuddered at the loss of contact as he set her on her feet, needing more. He leaned in and kissed her, gently this time, stroking his tongue into her mouth in a slow rhythm until she swayed against him. When he finally broke the kiss, he could barely breathe. He didn't want to feel this way about a woman he barely knew—a woman who wanted no more from him than a few mindless encounters. He ran a hand down his face. He didn't want mindless. He didn't want only a few encounters. He wanted more. He didn't know how much more, or why the thought scared him as much as it did, but he couldn't shake it.

Lily looked up at him and smoothed her finger down his jaw, her brows drawn together in a frown. "Why so serious? Was it that bad?"

He barked a laugh. "Bad? No, honey. It was that amazing. I'm practically speechless."

He watched the play of emotions in her expression, her gaze torn between fear, lust, and some nameless emotion that echoed deep inside him in a place he'd ignored for so long. His gaze held hers, strong and steady, and he fought the urge to confess to her the feeling she stirred inside him, this amazing woman he had no hope of figuring out. She blinked, the fear in her eyes taking over for a brief second before she settled a mask of humor firmly in place. She stood on her tiptoes and kissed him softly before ducking out of his grasp and lifting herself out of the pool.

"Thank you, Evan," she said, her back to him. "That was the most amazing—and unexpected—sex I've ever had."

"Yeah, me too."

Her ass swayed in a very enticing way as she padded the few steps to where her shirt had landed when he'd tossed it. He licked his lips, wondering if she knew how much he wanted her still. When she bent down to pick the shirt up from the ground, she gave him a perfect view of her pussy, glistening with his seed. A trickle of cum ran down the inside of her thigh and lust surged inside him again.

He snorted a laugh as she tried to pull the soaked shirt over her head. "What are the odds of getting you to have dinner with me?" Of course she'd say yes. After what they'd just shared, why wouldn't she?

He felt something in the vicinity of his heart clench painfully when she shook her head. "Not tonight. Sorry. I have other plans."

"Other plans," he echoed, a hollow feeling filling his stomach. "With that guy I saw you with earlier? The one with the black SUV?" She wouldn't do that to him, would she? She wouldn't be so warm and willing with him, only to leave him and go to some asshole that didn't deserve her. He clenched his hands into fists as he watched her gather her shoes and socks. "Lily?" he asked, his tone more jealous and demanding than he'd meant—but he couldn't help it. Thinking of her with another man brought out some pretty murderous instincts.

She turned to him, wearing nothing but the tank top she had bunched at her waist, her hands on her hips. And then she laughed. "That *guy* with the black SUV is my brother Tony. And, no, I don't have plans with him."

"Oh." His anger and jealousy receded in a burst like the air escaping from a balloon, leaving him with only humiliation. "Your brother, huh?"

"Yeah. My brother. Now would you mind getting my

shorts?" Her laugh sounded husky, and it hit him low in his gut. He fought against his burgeoning erection as he dove under the water and retrieved their discarded clothing. When he broke the surface of the water, Lily had moved to the patio and flopped down in a chair, her skin tinged red with what he assumed to be embarrassment. He waded to the shallow end of the pool and climbed out, walking across the grass to where she stood. He dropped her clothes onto the glass top of the table with a splat. "Here you go, honey."

"Thanks." Her eyes widened as her gaze settled on his flaccid cock. "Wow. You're big even now."

He bit back a laugh at the innocent look in her eyes. "Not really. I'm pretty average."

She shrugged, her face flaming even as she kept her expression casual. "Not in my experience."

Shit. Did she have any idea what she did to him when she perused him so openly? "Keep staring like that, sweetheart, and it's going to get a lot bigger."

Her eyes widened and she turned away, grabbing her shorts off the table and struggling to get into them. In the end she yanked them up as best as she could, grabbed her panties, socks and shoes, and smiled. "I suppose I should go now, before I end up not leaving at all."

Now that sounded like a plan. He took a step toward her, but she held her hand up to stop his advance. "Whoa there, Naked Guy. As appealing as you are in your natural state, I really do have somewhere to be and I don't want to be late. I want to stay, more than anything in the world, but I have to go."

Her confession helped a little, but he still felt far too much loss at the thought of her leaving right after that incredible sex. Any loss he felt was his own fault, though, since she'd been clear with him on the fact that she didn't want a relationship. She wanted his body. Only. That should have bolstered his ego, but it just made him feel empty inside.

He shook his head, water from his hair spraying across the

yard in front of him. What was his problem? He wanted the same thing she did. Sex. *Only* sex. Not a lasting commitment, not anything beyond a summer fling. Yes, she melted under his touch. Yes, she affected him in a way no other woman had. But none of that had anything to do with emotions. It was all about sexual chemistry — and they owed it to each other to ride this thing out to the end and see how far it would carry them. But he didn't have feelings for her — at least not beyond warm feelings he could see turning into friendship.

He genuinely liked Lily, but he'd be better off not confusing that with the emotional infatuation that would turn into love. Because he couldn't love her. Ever. He didn't love anymore, not in the romantic sense. No matter how tempting falling into that infatuation might be.

He let out a strangled groan. Maybe it would be better if she did leave. *Now.*

"Will I see you later?" he asked her, guiding her toward the gate. He needed to get rid of her before her scent, her presence scrambled his mind even more.

"Yep. Definitely. Oh, you might not want to walk me out this time."

She waved her hand in front of his body, calling his attention to his state of undress. *Shit.* And he'd planned to walk her back across the street like this? He had to be losing his mind.

Lily gave him a quick kiss and started out of the yard, turning back to look at him when she reached the gate. "Oh, by the way. I think we're even now."

"Not a chance," he mumbled as he watched her amazing ass sway in those clingy, damp shorts as she walked out of sight. They wouldn't be *even* in the pleasure department. Ever. He'd see to it personally, and make sure she kept coming back for more.

Chapter Seven

Lily sat between Janet and Marnie on Janet's overstuffed blue couch, a huge bowl of popcorn balanced on her lap and her eyes glued to the TV screen in front of them. She reached blindly for a handful of popcorn, not caring if she dropped half of it on the floor as she brought it to her mouth and munched. The movie Janet had rented for their girls' night in — Marnie's suggestion after her little mishap with the margaritas during their last girls' night *out* — should have sucked her attention in from the very beginning. The latest psychological thriller had promised to be haunting and captivating. Her favorite type of movie. And it would have been, had her mind not been stuck on Evan and the way he'd taken her with such force in his pool. She creamed her panties just thinking about it.

She snapped out of her daze as the credits started rolling. When had the movie ended? When had it *begun*? She frowned, mentally cursing Evan for destroying her concentration.

"You're distant tonight," Janet observed, snagging a handful of popcorn as Marnie stood up to remove the DVD from the player. "What's on your mind? And don't tell me you were just interested in the movie. Your eyes were so glazed over I don't think you could even see the screen."

How could she explain this delicately, without giving away too much of what had happened? They might be her friends, but they didn't need to know every tiny detail of her life. She pursed her lips, determined not to tell them anything they didn't need to know.

"Come on, Lily. Fess up," Marnie goaded, a wide smile on her face.

Lily opened her mouth to deny everything. They needed to

learn to mind their own business. "I had sex with Evan."

Her jaw dropped after she listened to the words pour from her mouth. *Way to go, Lily. Good thing you're so excellent at keeping secrets.* She looked from Janet to Marnie, hoping they'd been rendered temporarily deaf and hadn't heard her. When she saw the look on Janet's face, she changed her wish. It would be so much better if they'd been rendered temporarily mute. She was about to get an earful.

Marnie froze, pivoted, and slumped to the floor. "No way."

"You had sex with Mr. Fine Ass? For *real*?" Janet dropped her empty can of diet soda onto the hardwood floor, her gaze never leaving Lily's. "I don't believe it."

Lily glared at Janet. Was it so hard to believe that she could interest a guy like Evan? Well, maybe not to the world who only knew her as a naked chick in a magazine, but to the friends who knew her best...well, she saw Janet's point. But only a small percentage of all the people in the world knew Lily wasn't the wanton sex queen on the magazine pages. The staff at *Seduced* had obviously thought she had something special, or they wouldn't have invited her to pose.

"No, I'm lying. I'm making the whole thing up." She rolled her eyes. "Yes, I really had sex with him. This afternoon."

Janet's eyes widened, sparkling with interest. "How was it? We want details."

"Oh, yeah," Marnie agreed, nodding her head vigorously. " *All* the details."

Like hell. Lily snorted. Like she'd really tell them everything. She shook her head. Well, a few details wouldn't hurt anyone. She started her story. "Okay. I can tell you a little. I came home from a run and saw him in his yard, wearing practically nothing, as usual."

Janet and Marnie sat in rapt attention while Lily relayed the details of the encounter. "We were fooling around in his pool, but I didn't expect anything else to happen. Before I knew it, we were both naked and he was inside me," she ended, swiping away the sweat that had formed on her brow just from speaking about the incident. Janet fanned her face and Marnie let out a dramatic sigh.

"Did you want it to happen?" Janet asked.

Well, *duh*. Who wouldn't? "You've seen Evan. Of course I did. I just didn't expect it when it actually happened. I probably should have, but after that first orgasm I think my mind took a nap."

Marnie blinked, apparently having trouble digesting the sentence. She finally shook her head and shoved a handful of popcorn into her mouth. "You had more than one orgasm?" she asked as she chewed.

"Uh-huh."

"How many did you have?" Janet asked, her gaze intent as she leaned forward, apparently waiting on bated breath for the answer.

"Just two," Lily said slowly. Why did she suddenly feel like she was a guest on some late night talk show? "Is that okay? Is it not an acceptable number?" *Is there a wrong answer?*

"Okay? Are you nuts? It's two more than I usually get," Marnie grumbled in between shoveling handfuls of popcorn into her mouth.

"You know there's extra butter on that, right?" Lily asked, not knowing whether to laugh or feel dismayed. Joe wasn't a slouch in the looks department. Though he could be a little intimidating at times.

Marnie glanced at the popcorn, frowned, and shoveled in another handful. She chewed for a moment, a thoughtful look on her face, before she spoke again. "How was it? Was it completely amazing?"

"Oh, yeah. There's something about water and sex—"

Janet held up a hand to stop her from speaking, her eyes narrowing. "Wait a second. You said you were fooling around in the pool. You mean, when you had sex with Mr. Fine Ass, you actually had sex *in* the pool?"

"Yeah, that's what I said before. Why don't you try listening?" Lily nodded, feeling her face flame. *What happened to not revealing all the details, Lil?* She set the bowl on Marnie's worn oak coffee table with a thunk, scattering a few kernels across the surface, and pushed up from the couch to pace the room. "Am I supposed to feel guilty for having good sex?"

Janet heaved a sigh and leaned back against the couch cushions, her hair draping over her face. "Of course not. But I can't help being a little jealous. It's so hard to find a good man around here."

Probably because she'd already been with all the eligible ones. "Not if you pose nude for a magazine," Lily muttered.

Marnie burst out laughing. Lily snapped her gaze to her friend, her eyes narrowed. "What's so funny?"

"If I had the body to pose for one of those magazines, I might think about it. But I'm not lucky to be curvy like you are."

Lucky? She'd dieted for two months and lost fifteen pounds before she'd posed. Even then, she wasn't thin like Marnie. With her curves and medium bone structure, she'd never be. As long as she kept up with the yoga and the occasional runs, she'd stay fit and toned, but once she gave that up, she'd probably blow up like a blimp. In all honesty, gaining a few pounds really wouldn't bother her. But it wouldn't help her social life either, as far as dating and men were concerned. She was just glad she didn't do the modeling thing full time. She'd really be in trouble if she had to live off salad and carrot sticks for the rest of her life.

"Are you kidding me? You have the type of body men love."

Marnie snorted. "No, I have the type of body clothing designers love. Men, well let's just say I've heard different."

Lily shook her head. "Okay. Whatever." True she'd never heard any complaints about her body from the men who'd seen it before the infamous centerfold and photo spread—all two of them. And out of all the men who'd seen her nude body, a whopping total of three had seen all of her flesh...well, in the flesh. It wasn't that she didn't believe in casual sex, she was picky when it came to the men she slept with. And most of the time she was able to satisfy herself better than any man ever could—and now Evan had come along and shattered that illusion.

Janet flopped onto her stomach and bent her knees up, kicking her bare feet into the air. She propped herself up on her elbows and frowned at Lily. "So I suppose you're going to get all possessive now and stop letting me watch him after his morning run."

As if she'd be able to stop Janet, even if she wanted to. "I don't care if you watch him. And I have no right to be possessive. Evan and I are not involved."

Marnie cleared her throat. "Sex in a pool doesn't constitute involvement?"

"Not that kind of involved. We're just..." She stopped and rolled her eyes toward the ceiling. How did she put this without making herself sound like a tramp? Unable to think of a delicate way to tell them she only wanted Evan for his body, she shrugged. "You know."

" *I* know," Janet told her, nodding. "But I didn't think *you* did."

Maybe she hadn't before, when her only experience had been that fumbling guy in high school followed by Stumpy...er, Toby—who didn't know how to please anyone but himself. But now she knew, and she saw what she'd been missing for so long.

"This is so unlike you," Janet continued. "I thought you didn't have sex with anyone until you practically had a ring on your finger."

"Seeing as the ring has been rather elusive these past years, what's the point of saving myself for something I'm not ever going to get?" She grinned as she thought about all she'd gotten from Evan, and how much more she wanted. "Besides, after the fiasco with Toby, I'm done looking for a relationship. I've told you that a hundred times."

Janet smiled. "Yeah, I know. I just thought you'd run away to a convent instead of seducing the guy across the street."

Lily lifted a pink chenille afghan off the chair next to her and tossed it at Janet. "Funny. Really funny." It hit Janet's ankle before sliding to the floor. "I didn't seduce him."

At least she didn't think she had. Evan had come to her that first night with his flirty ways and the magazine in his hand. Had the magazine caused the whole chain of events that led to Evan's sudden interest? If so, she'd have to do it again in a few years and see what kind of fun she could shake loose.

Janet and Marnie collapsed into laugher, and this time Lily joined them. So what if she was acting out of character? So far, she was having the time of her life.

* * * * *

So much for the time of my life. It's just sex, Lily. Get over it already. Her fling with Evan seemed to be turning into an obsession. She groaned in frustration, flipping onto her stomach. Obsessions were not welcome in her life, not even if they involved a very sexy Latino hunk who lived across the street and supposedly had the best shower in all of creation.

Speaking of that shower…

Stop it, Lily. This is ridiculous.

She flipped onto her back and pulled the pillow over her head. "Quit acting like some teenager with a crush."

She huffed out a breath. This was getting her nowhere. Obviously she wasn't going to get to sleep, not without some kind of distraction from thinking about Evan's hands, and the way he kissed, and…*oh, brother.*

After a few hours of tossing and turning, Lily finally flipped on the light over her bed and picked up the paperback she'd been reading. She tucked the sheet up around her to ward off the chill from the air conditioner in the window, curled her knees up, and propped the book on her thighs. Most nights, all she had to do was open a book in bed and she'd be asleep. It figured that tonight, a night she wanted to sleep and not rush to finish just one more chapter, her eyes wouldn't close and her mind wouldn't fall into the sleep she needed to make it through her classes tomorrow without dosing off during a few of the less-than-rigorous poses.

And no matter what her mother said, that had only happened once.

She didn't care to see it happening again. Anne shaking her awake in front of the whole class, complaining about the snoring, had been enough to convince her to never fall asleep in class again, no matter how relaxing some of the beginner sessions were.

She rolled her head from side to side and took a few deep belly breaths. The fact that she couldn't unwind was all Evan's fault—him and his stupid pool and that amazing sex she couldn't get off her mind.

The phone rang, snapping her out of her lack-of-sleep pity party. She shot her gaze to the clock. One a.m.? Who would be calling her *now*? She lifted the phone off the cradle and brought it to her ear, expecting to hear Janet or Marnie's voice. "It's kind of late for a social call, isn't it?"

"Personally, I'd prefer to think of it as early since it's past midnight."

Her heart lurched into her throat when she heard Evan's voice on the other end of the line. So much for trying to sleep. Now she'd probably be up all night. "Forgive my directness, but it's one o'clock in the morning. What the hell are you doing calling me?"

"I saw your light on. Can't sleep?"

She felt as much as heard his deep chuckle. It hit her low in her belly and tied her all up in knots. She squeezed her thighs together in an attempt to tamp down her arousal, but it only put pressure on her clit and made her ache more.

"No, I can't sleep," she grumbled, slamming her bookmark into her book and dropping the book onto the floor. "Thanks to you."

"What did I do?"

She heard the humor in his voice and she wrinkled her nose. "You know damned well what you did. You and your amazing hands, and mouth, and…other parts. I can't stop thinking about earlier, and it's keeping me awake."

She heard him exhale a slow breath.

He didn't speak for a never-ending second. When he finally bothered to respond, his voice had taken on a deeper, husky tone. "Oh, I get it. You're horny."

Bingo! "Excuse me? That's a little presumptuous of you, isn't it?"

"No, I don't think so." He paused again, the charged silence dragging a little longer between them this time. "I've been thinking about you, too."

"You have?" Her voice sounded small and weak. *Unacceptable.* She cleared her throat. "I mean, of course you have. Why wouldn't you? I mean, I'm probably the best you've ever had, right?"

As soon as the words left her mouth, she wanted to bite them back. *Geez. Next time why don't you brag a little more?* Why did he have to bring out her feisty side at one in the morning, when she'd been awake for a lot longer than she should and she couldn't find the wit to defend herself?

"It was pretty amazing," he answered, his tone sincere enough to shock her. "I'm still shaking. It's been a long time since I've had a lay that good."

She should have been offended by his comment, but coming from him, it only ratcheted her arousal up another couple of notches. She knew what he was doing—he was trying to get a rise out of her. She smiled at the thought, wondering if she was getting a *rise* out of him.

"Did you have a good time tonight?" he asked in that deep voice that had her dripping wet in seconds. She pressed her thighs harder together, but it still didn't help her any.

"Yes."

"What did you do?"

"Watched a movie with Marnie and Janet."

"That's nice."

How could he hold a normal conversation with her now, while she lay on her bed ready to explode? "Yeah." She let out a breath on a long sigh. Just listening to him speak sent chills through her and made her blood run hot and cold. She needed so much more than just a phone conversation. "Do you want to come over?"

"Not tonight. It's late."

She snorted. "No shit. Either that or it's early."

"Cute. Keep giving me attitude and I'm not going to help you with your little problem."

"You just said you wouldn't come over."

"Not everything has to be face-to-face."

His words stopped the teasing reply she'd planned. She snapped her mouth shut as an icy-hot shiver ran through her entire body. Her nipples beaded under the thin fabric of her over-washed T-shirt.

"No comment, sweetheart?"

Nope. No comment. Nothing at all. She wouldn't let him bait her. Not in this lifetime. "What do you have in mind?"

So much for not letting him bait you, Lil. Maybe she should look into having her mouth stitched shut. She rolled her eyes and smacked herself in the forehead. Evan wasn't like most of the men she knew.

He actually had a brain.

One he used, even. He knew just how to get her going, in more ways than one, knew how to get her to respond — both to his barbs and his body. In his perfect world, she'd have to worship at his feet.

"I want to help you sleep."

My ass. "And how do you plan on doing that? Are you going to read *War and Peace* to me until you hear me snoring?"

"No, silly. I have something much better in mind than that."

"Oh, really?" Though now that she thought about it, *War and Peace* might do the trick. Did she still have a copy of it laying around here somewhere?

"Are you wearing pajamas?" Evan asked, putting an end to her mental search for the hardback her father had given her one year for Christmas.

What was he thinking? Was he going to get her all worked up and hang up, leaving her aroused and miserable all night? Not in this lifetime. "Yes. But before you get any ideas, I don't sleep in sexy little nighties. I'm wearing a faded gray T-shirt with holes in it and a pair of white granny panties."

Okay, so she'd lied about the granny panties, but she really did have on one of her most worn-out T-shirts. They were the most comfortable to wear to bed.

"I don't care *what* you're wearing. That isn't what I asked. I wanted to know *if* you were wearing something." He paused, the silence between them electrical. She could almost imagine him at the foot of her bed. "Take them off."

"Excuse me?" What did he think she was? Some kind of loose woman? Well, yeah. After the encounter in the pool he probably did. She shook her head. "Okay. I'm undressed."

"No you aren't. If you lie to me, I'm not going to help you. I'll hang up."

The hair rose on the back of her neck. How would he know she hadn't undressed unless he had a view into her room? "Can you see me?"

"No. I can only see the light in your window. But I know you didn't take your pajamas off. You're too relaxed. Do it for me now, Lily. Take everything off and lay back on your bed."

She weighed the pros and cons of listening to him. If she did what he wanted her to, she'd be giving in to his demands.

Demands that, provided he gave her a little relief from her problem, weren't so unreasonable. She could go to sleep happy and satisfied and not be a living zombie in the morning. Why was that a bad idea again?

"Hold on." She set the phone down on the satin comforter and stripped everything off, letting it pile in a heap at the foot of the bed. She lay back against the sheets, the cool, smooth fabric like a caress against her back. Goose bumps covered her skin, more from nerves and arousal than the cool air in the room. Her nipples hardened even more, and the ache between her thighs intensified to a fevered pitch as she thought about Evan and what he might say to her. Or what he might tell her to do.

Breathing heavier than normal, she picked the phone up and brought it to her ear. "Okay. I'm undressed."

"Now I believe you." He chuckled and she wished she could reach through the phone lines and strangle his sexy neck. She didn't find anything funny about her current state.

"Gee, thanks. So...I'm undressed. What now?"

"Spread your legs."

The comforter whooshed softly as she slid her legs apart, exposing her drenched pussy to the cool air. She arched her hips off the mattress and bit back a moan at the sudden rush of desire that filled her. "Okay," she whispered.

"Do you have a vibrator?" Evan asked, sending another shiver through her. This time she didn't try to hold back her moan — one of disappointment. She'd never felt the need for a toy more than she did at that moment.

"No."

"You don't?" He sounded surprised. "Why not?"

"I have a detachable shower head. It's always suited my purpose before."

He sighed. "Okay. I suppose you'll have to use your fingers for tonight."

"My fingers?" A gush of cream drenched her cunt. She wet

her lips with her tongue and tightened her grip on the phone. Her body had turned into a huge bundle of nerves, and even the slightest touch might cause a major explosion.

"Oh, yeah. Your fingers, sweetheart." He let out a soft sigh. "Are you wet for me, Lily?"

Huge understatement. If she got any wetter, she'd flood the bed. "Yes."

"Good. I want you to touch yourself. Touch your pussy. Spread that wetness all over. Slowly, Lily. But first, touch the rest of your body. Start at your collarbone and work your way down to that sweet cunt."

She let out a soft sigh as she placed her fingers above her breasts, dragging them down her skin until she reached the tuft of hair above her mound. She whimpered when she slid her fingers lower, dipping them into her folds and drenching them with her own moisture. She did as Evan asked, spreading that moisture over her entire pussy with excruciating slowness. When her fingers brushed her clit, she cried out at the jolt that ran through her.

"That's right," Evan urged, his voice sounding strained. "Stroke that hard clit. Circle your finger over it. Bring yourself right to the edge."

She closed her eyes, soft moans escaping her lips as she did as he told her. She spread her legs wider, pressed a little harder with her strokes, until Evan had her gasping for breath and right on the edge.

"You're close, aren't you?" he asked. From his ragged breathing, she wondered how close *he* was.

"Yes...*oh*..." A wave of heat washed over her. She bit the inside of her lip to keep from screaming. He probably wouldn't look too kindly on being deafened.

"Does that feel good?" he asked.

"Yes." The end of the word came out on a hiss. "Are you touching yourself, too?"

He was silent long enough that she knew his answer before

he spoke. "Yeah. Pump your fingers in and out of your cunt. Pretend it's my cock hammering into you."

She hesitated for a split second before she leaned over and put the phone on speaker mode, freeing her other hand. She brought the fingers of her free hand to her cunt, sliding two inside her wet heat. It wasn't a replacement for Evan, but it felt damned good to bring herself to climax while he talked her through it. She stroked slowly at first, increasing her rhythm as the tension built, centered on the tight bud of her clit. She moaned. The scent of her arousal filled the room, pushing her even closer to the climax that waited just past her reach.

"Fuck," Evan muttered. "This is good. I can't wait until I can get inside you again."

Neither could she. She wanted to talk to him, tell him to do things to himself like he was doing for her, but she couldn't form the words. From the sounds coming through the phone line, though, she had an idea he was doing okay all by himself.

She arched her hips against her hand, pumping them in time with her thrusting fingers, yelling out as her orgasm took her by surprise—a ball of fire that spread from her pussy out to her limbs, reaching all the way to her fingertips and the top of her head.

She closed her eyes and floated, her sated body limp and unmoving, her mind protesting even the smallest thing. She might have even stopped breathing for a few moments. She didn't know. Evan's harsh groan brought her back to reality. She smiled to herself, wondering if he felt as boneless as she did.

"Feel better?" he asked, his voice husky.

She sighed in answer. Oh, yeah. She felt *much* better. "Do you?"

"Yeah," his answer was long and drawn out. "So much. It's supposed to rain on Monday. Call me if you need a ride to work."

As if. Even if it did rain—which she hadn't heard anything about—she wouldn't melt. "Sure."

"Goodnight, Lily." She heard the click of the phone and knew he'd hung up. She reached over and hit the end button, the room thrown into silence with the absence of the dial tone. She might have protested the abrupt dismissal if she hadn't fallen right to sleep.

* * * * *

Lily glanced out the window when she first got out of bed on Monday morning. The sky had opened up sometime during the night. Rain pelted the ground outside, gray clouds covering the sky, tree branches swayed in what promised to be a cool, strong wind. Lovely. Why did he have to be right about this? Contrary to what she'd thought when Evan had told her to call, she did *not* enjoy walking to work in the rain. Toby used to pick her up on the bad days and give her a ride—but she couldn't very well call him. She had a strict policy against accepting rides from scumbag losers. But she didn't want to call Evan, either. She didn't want to start relying on him for little things, because someday, when the fling had ended, he wouldn't be around. She refused to depend on anyone but herself. But every muscle in her body cramped at the thought of walking to work in the rain.

She heaved a sigh as she went into the kitchen for breakfast. "Well, Lily, you'll just have to think of something else."

Something else ended up being an extra set of clothes wrapped in a green trash bag and stuffed into her duffel bag. *How innovative.* After assuring herself she'd make it to work alive despite the nasty turn the weather had taken, she slipped on a pair of ratty sandals, grabbed her umbrella, and headed out the door.

Her morning soured even more when she opened the umbrella. *Tried* to open it would be a better description. The mechanism seemed stuck, and the more she forced it, the more stuck it became. She banged it against the porch steps and finally freed the trapped metal—only to find the nylon had four gaping holes the size of softballs in it. Wonderful. So much for the hope that she might make it to work at least partially dry. She tossed the umbrella into the trashcan sitting next to the garage on her way down the driveway and slicked her now-soaked bangs back from her face. Could this day get any worse?

She found out the answer to her question when the strap on her bag broke and the whole thing tumbled off her shoulder. Into a puddle the size of Lake Michigan. Maybe she should just call in sick. At this rate, she'd end up in the emergency room with a broken ankle by lunchtime.

A chill skittered down her spine and she looked toward the sky. "I didn't mean that." *Please, please let this day improve. Even just a little.*

She bent to pick up her sopping bag, taking it as a good sign that lightning didn't strike her butt. She heard the rumble of a powerful motor behind her when she stood. Damn it. *Not him. Not now that I'm in the process of making a complete fool of myself.* She spun slowly, hoping it would be someone else pulling up alongside her. His car wasn't the only one with the big engine in town.

She wasn't that lucky. Evan's vintage sports car sat idling at the curb. He rolled the window down, his gaze annoyed. "What happened to calling me for a ride?"

Did he not notice her dripping hair and soggy clothes? Did he know what they would do to his butter-soft leather seats? "I'm not going to get into your car like this. I'll ruin it."

Panic flashed across his eyes before he let out a breath and smiled. "Yeah, I know. So go home and change. I'm not in any hurry."

She glanced at her watch. She might be a few minutes late, but if she had to walk to work, dry off and change, she'd be late for class anyway. She nodded. "Okay. Thanks. Give me five minutes."

She dashed down the street and into her house, probably setting the record for fastest change and repack in history. After she tugged her hair back into a messy bun and grabbed her newly-packed backpack, she ran out the door and jumped into the passenger seat of Evan's car, which he'd pulled into her driveway. She checked her watch. She'd done it all in just over four minutes. "Thanks for waiting."

"What are you, some kind of speed dresser?" he asked, laughing.

"I didn't want to keep you waiting."

"Thoughtful of you." He backed the car out onto the road and started the short drive toward downtown Tranquility. "You still should have called."

She bit back a snappish reply, not wanting to sound ungrateful. She leaned back in the seat, inhaling a deep, relieved breath to be out of the rain. She slid a sidelong glance to the man next to her. Her day had already started to improve.

Evan looked damn good dressed for work in his burgundy shirt and navy patterned tie. He smelled good, too. Better than good. He smelled...orgasmic. Some sort of spicy, sensual cologne that had her panties damp just from inhaling it. She leaned a little closer and drew a deep breath. *Mmm.* She leaned back against the seat and closed her eyes.

"Mmm, what?"

She froze. Did she say that out loud? "Excuse me?"

"You said 'mmm'. What are you referring to?"

She thought about lying, but one glance into those deep brown eyes and she couldn't do it. He was so sexy, so persuasive—so hers, at least for a little while. "You smell great," she told him, hoping she didn't blush. That would ruin her delivery for sure.

He smiled. "Thanks. So do you."

This time she couldn't help it. She blushed. "You know where the wellness center is, right?"

He nodded, his gaze glued to the road but that smile that drove her crazy firmly in place on his lips. "Right downtown, across from that godawful tofu place."

She laughed. Finally, someone with a little taste. "Yes, that's right. You can just drop me off out front."

"No problem." He reached across the console and rested his hand on her knee. She didn't think he meant it to be a sexual gesture, but her body responded as if he'd just asked her to bed. Her nipples beaded, a line of sweat formed on her forehead, and she'd have to change her underwear when she got to work. She sank further into the seat, hoping he didn't notice how strongly he affected her.

"Tell me, Lily, why is it that you don't have your own car?" His words should have snapped her from her lust-induced daze, but the sound of his voice was enough to keep her locked in her wanton state of mind. How did he expect her to make conversation when she could barely breathe?

It took her three tries to get her reply out of her mouth. "I live so close to town, I don't see the point. I work fifteen minutes away from home."

"Don't you ever get out of town?" His fingers tightened on her thigh, his thumb tracing patterns on her leg. She gulped.

"Well, yeah. With Janet or Marnie or my mother."

"You don't ever borrow a car?"

She snorted. Oh, yeah, like anyone would be dumb enough to lend her a car. They'd all seen her driving. "No, Evan, I don't. I don't have a license. I don't know how to drive, remember?"

He trailed his hand a little higher up her thigh—too high. If he came any closer to her pussy he'd know how wet he'd already made her. She'd be lucky if the seat didn't have a big wet spot when she stood. "Why not?" he asked.

Why not what? Oh, yeah. The license fiasco. "Because I failed the test."

"So take it again."

"I did. Two more times."

"And you still couldn't pass?"

He looked ready to laugh. She rolled her eyes. "No, obviously I couldn't. I made stupid mistakes. I just couldn't get it right. After the third time, I gave up. I think my father was very relieved."

"How long ago was this?"

"When I was in high school."

"So, what? Like ten years ago?"

"About that."

Evan slowed his car to a stop in front of the wellness center. He put it in park and turned to face her, cupping her chin in his warm palm. "Did anyone ever take the time to teach you how to drive?"

She shook her head. "My mom has no patience for that sort of thing, and my dad…well, if you knew him, you'd understand why I didn't want to get behind the wheel with him in the passenger seat."

"That's really too bad." Evan moved closer, and she backed toward the door. If he kissed her here, in front of her mother's business, she'd have to maim him.

It was one thing for them to carry on in private— *or semi-private*, she amended when she thought about what had happened in his back yard—but a whole new entity to fool around in downtown Tranquility, where everyone already thought she was some kind of slut. She tried to jump out of the car, but he caught her face again and brought his lips to hers. She sighed. He was so soft, so warm, and he tasted like sex personified. Well, maybe one little kiss wouldn't hurt. She relaxed and let him hold her, let him sweep his tongue into her waiting mouth. And then he pulled away, leaving her breathless and aroused and confused. It must have shown on her face, because he laughed.

"Have a good day, Lily." His voice sounded impossibly husky and irresistible and she almost told him to take her back home and take her to bed for the day. But then she came to her senses.

"You can't kiss me in public!"

He sat back in the seat and smiled. "Why not?"

"Because it doesn't look good."

"Sweetheart, you bared your entire body in a national magazine. What difference will one kiss make?"

He had a point—but so did she. What was it again? "I don't need any more gossip surrounding my name, if you don't mind. I have no problem with this little...fling in private, but I absolutely want no part in making it public knowledge. Okay?"

"You have such a sexy mouth. *Somebody* should be kissing it."

She sucked her lower lip between her teeth and stared at him, his words sending a shiver down her spine. She didn't want just *somebody* kissing her. She wanted it to be Evan. "Well, then. I guess if it has to be somebody, it should be you." She moved to get out of the car, but he cupped her chin in his hand and kissed her one more time—short and sweet this time, but with a domineering edge that should have bothered her.

"Behave at work today, okay? I'll talk to you soon."

She got out of the car and shut the door, half in a daze over his possessive attitude. If she hadn't liked it so much, she might have had to yell at him for it. She wandered inside the center and found Marnie sitting at the front desk. "So that's Evan, huh?"

"Don't you remember him from the bar the other night?"

She blinked, embarrassment flashing across her delicate features. "Um, not so much. Janet is right. He's cute."

Lily turned back toward the front door just as Evan's car pulled away from the curb and drove out of sight. "How can you tell from way over there?"

Marnie rolled her eyes. "I had my face pressed to the glass about two seconds ago. *Duh.* So, he's the new guy in your life, huh? The one in the pool."

"I told you we're not really involved. He's just a friend." Self-conscious about her non-relationship, Lily shrugged and brushed her drying bangs out of her eyes. "It's just a thing, you know?"

Elisa Adams

Marnie laughed. "Lily, if I had *friends* like that, I'd never need another loser boyfriend again."

Lily chuckled at Marnie's joking comment, but a chill passed through her at the same time. She understood what Marnie was saying—and unfortunately, agreed. Now that she'd spent time with Evan, she didn't think any other man would ever do.

I am not falling in love with him!

She shook her head as she set her bag down behind the counter and slipped off her shoes. She couldn't be falling in love with him. She didn't know him. She didn't plan to get to know him. She just wanted him for his body. She had no problem admitting how shallow she sounded, but it was the truth. *Right?* A little voice in her head started to answer, but she ignored it.

Please, please, please don't let me fall in love with him.

The sadistic little voice in her head whispered that it was too late. The fall had begun, and the only thing she could do was protect her heart and hope she had the strength to let him go, before she fell any further into the bottomless pit of unrequited affection.

"Are you okay?"

She snapped her gaze up to find Marnie watching her with a worried look on her face.

"Oh, yeah. Sure. I'm fine." She tried to smile, but couldn't get her muscles to work. *Just fine for a woman who just realized her life as she knows it is coming to a screeching halt.*

124

Chapter Eight

If the rest of his day had gone as well as his morning ride with Lily, Evan would have come home in a much better mood. But things had a way of going south just as they started to look up. After a generally crappy day of dealing with project after time consuming project and picky clients who wanted things not architecturally possible—at least not on this planet—he came home to an envelope with Jessica's return address printed in the upper left corner.

Well, *shit*.

He tore the top of the envelope open and pulled out a pink sheet of paper scented with Jessica's perfume—and nearly gagged on the memories. His anger at her infidelity returned full force. He didn't want her back, but he didn't want to see her happy, either. He shook his head as he read her words.

Evan,

I want you to know how sorry I am that our marriage didn't work out. I know it upset you when we ended it, but I think if you look back, you'll see it hadn't worked from the start. We confused passion with love, and really, never should have married at all. Scott and I...well, we fell in love almost at first sight. I tried to ignore what I felt for him, but I couldn't. He couldn't pretend he felt nothing for me, either. I hope you understand. We had passion, Evan, for a short time, but that fizzled out soon after we took our vows. Some people are not meant to be together. I never should have agreed to marry you when I knew it wouldn't be right. Scott has shown me that I can have passion back in my life again.

I also wanted to ask if you could try to forgive Scott. He misses you. We both do. As friends, of course. I wanted to let you know that Scott and I are getting married next month. We would both very much like for you to be there. You know how to reach us. Please call us and say you'll come.

I hope you've found the happiness you deserve in New Hampshire. I understand why you felt the need to get away, but your family and friends here are all hoping you'll be back. We miss you, Evan, and love you very much. Feel free to contact us at any time — even just to let us know how you're doing. Be safe, be well, and be happy. You're a wonderful man and you deserve to find a woman who completes you, like Scott completes me.

Love, Jessica

Love? *Love?* According to her letter, the woman had never felt love for him. What was this shit, anyway? Come to the wedding? Was she on crack? No way in hell would he subject himself to that, not when she'd practically accused him of being a lousy lover.

He crumpled the letter in a ball and tossed it across the room, clenching his hands into fists so tight his knuckles turned white. How dare she disturb his life like that? Anger spiked in him, numbing his extremities. Just when he'd thought the day couldn't get any worse, it had taken a nosedive and plummeted straight into the ground, exploding on impact.

He paced the room, raked a hand through his hair. Yes, she'd been right as she said they'd confused love and passion. But he *had* loved her. It hadn't been a lasting kind of love, but she could have talked to him about it. Maybe then it would have made the end easier to take. But she'd done what he considered the unforgivable. She'd screwed him over by sleeping with Scott, and lying about it for months. Sure. He'd go to the wedding.

When little green men came down from Jupiter and dragged him to Chicago.

And where did she get off telling him the passion fizzled out? It had waned, but only because she'd had excuse after excuse to keep them from making love. She was too tired. She'd had a long day at work. She had cramps. Ha! What she'd really had was an affair with a man he used to think he could trust with his life. He gritted his teeth, his face flaming from the anger over her words.

He was *not* a lousy lay.

He'd been with enough women before his marriage to know that he could please them. But he hadn't pleased Jessica. And there hadn't been another woman since the divorce. Until Lily. He'd pleased her. She wasn't shy about showing how much. Every reaction she'd felt had been clear in her heated gaze. But still… What if that was a fluke? What if he really didn't know as much about pleasing a woman as he thought?

Bullshit.

Since when had he gotten self-conscious? He knew what he was doing when it came to sex. He'd never once had any complaints—well, unless he counted the ones from Jessica. He didn't. She didn't deserve to be included on the list. Not after that damned letter. Talk about a serious blow to a man's ego.

He paced to the living room and glanced over at Lily's house. *She* wouldn't tell him he sucked in bed. No way. She'd writhe and whimper and moan and…*shit*. His cock tightened in his pants and some of the tension eased from his mind. Yeah. Lily wouldn't try to hurt him with obviously false statements. She'd welcome him with open arms—and hopefully open legs. He smiled.

He needed that. More than he could even explain.

He marched across the street to Lily's house and banged on the door.

She smiled as she swung the door open and saw him standing there. "Hey. What's up?"

Those lips. They haunted him every night in his dreams. "Can I talk to you for a second?" He wanted to do a lot more than talk, but if he told her what he had planned, she'd never let him in the door.

"Sure," she said, moving aside so he could enter the house. A touch of unease flickered across her gaze. "I just finished cooking dinner. Do you want to stay?"

He shut the door behind him and shook his head, crowding her against the wall. "Dinner can wait."

"What?" She gulped, blinking those huge, guileless eyes up at him in a way that clenched his heart. "Why? What's wrong?"

"I don't need food. I need you."

Her eyes widened as he pulled her closer and kissed her hard on the lips. She succumbed, not fighting at all, even when he lifted her into his arms and asked her where the bedroom was.

* * * * *

Lily gasped as Evan hurried down the hall to her bedroom. Shouldn't she protest this little show? Something about woman's rights and all that?

Nah.

She kind of liked when a guy took charge and told her he was taking her to bed. Especially a guy like Evan, one she hadn't been able to get out of her dreams for weeks. Months. One who didn't finish himself off in five minutes and leave her hanging.

He set her down on her feet as soon as they crossed the threshold into her tiny room. He pulled her into his arms and kissed her hard, long, and deep, until she felt the shiver right down to her toes. She wrapped her arms around his neck, not knowing what brought on this sudden lusty attack—and not caring. Only an insane woman would push Evan away at a time like this. He obviously needed her. Who was she to deny a man who needed her support…as well as other things?

He broke the kiss and looked down at her, the lust in his eyes making her nerves do the happy dance. Something there in his eyes, something darker hidden behind the lust, made her heart go out to him. Something had upset him. Maybe she should try to get him to talk it out.

He leaned in and nipped her earlobe before dragging his tongue down the side of her neck.

Talk? Who needed to talk? That could wait. She melted against him and leaned up for another kiss.

"You don't have the stove on or anything, do you?" he

asked, his gaze darkening as she ran her fingers through the hair at the nape of his neck.

She shook her head. "I turned it all off just before you tried to bash my door in with your fist."

"Good." He dipped in for another kiss. His tongue traced her lower lip before sucking it into his mouth, rolling it gently between his teeth. One of his hands rested on her lower back, keeping her close, while the other trailed lower to cup one of her ass cheeks in his palm. He gave her a squeeze that lifted her up on her toes. An impressive erection pressed against her stomach, and she couldn't wait to get that delicious cock inside her. She wanted him so badly she could taste it. Or maybe she was tasting him, since she had her tongue jammed down his throat. She licked the inside of his lips. A ragged groan rumbled through him.

He pulled back, his lips parted and his eyes glazed in a way that made her mouth water. "Do you know what you do to me?"

She laughed and gave his cock a squeeze. "I think I have some idea."

He shook his head. "There's so much more to it than that. You mess with my mind. You challenge me, get me thinking things I wouldn't have thought before. You don't take any crap, and you constantly give me attitude. I shouldn't like that, but I do. You're amazing."

Why did his compliments sound more like insults? She frowned. "Oh, yeah, that's me. The Amazing Bitch Woman."

"That's not what I mean. You're perfect the way you are. Don't change a thing."

She hadn't planned on it. But to hear him say it...it made her feel good about herself. There weren't many people in her life who tried to do that purposely. Most people wanted to change her to fit their ideal of a normal woman.

"That's really sweet. At least I think it is." She smiled up at him, using her hands around his neck to drag him closer. "Either that, or it's the most insulting thing I've ever heard."

Evan shook his head. "Definitely not an insult. I have a feeling an insult to you would be calling you conventional."

Hallelujah! A man had finally gotten her right. Why had it taken her almost thirty years to find the one who understood her?

"What's running through that incredible mind of yours, Lily?" Evan asked, backing her toward the bed.

"Not a thing past what will happen when we get naked."

He laughed. "It's going to be good. Better than last time. Way better." He leaned in and licked the shell of her ear. *"Way better."*

He thumbed her nipples through the loose fabric of her T-shirt and they hardened against his touch. The rasp of her cotton shirt over the sensitive peaks sent tingles down her stomach all the way to her pussy. She gasped when he gently pinched her nipples between his fingers and thumbs, rolling them back and forth.

"You like that?" he asked in a raspy voice.

She couldn't manage more than a mumble of assent. Evan's fingers stroked her waist as he lifted the hem of her cropped T-shirt and pulled it over her head. She'd gone braless after her post-work shower—a fact he didn't mind at all, if she could judge by the way his eyes flashed as he took in the sight of her naked breasts. He brought his hands up to cup them before lowering his mouth and sucking one of her nipples inside.

His teeth and tongue played across her nipple, sending little electric jolts straight through her. Her legs wobbled. She gripped his shoulders to keep from falling, sure his teeth would cause her nipple damage if it was yanked out of his mouth. She winced at the thought.

Evan snapped his gaze to hers, her nipple popping from his mouth. "Am I hurting you?"

"No, but I'm going to hurt you if you don't stop teasing me soon."

He blinked at her a few times before a sensual smile spread

over his lips. "All in good time, honey."

He started to bend to her breasts again, but she'd had enough. She wanted nothing to do with this kind of torture. Not tonight. She gripped his hair and pulled his gaze back to hers. "No, Evan. That's enough. I can't take much more. *Any* more."

His laugh reverberated through her as his lips closed on her neck. He licked the skin there before he pulled back. "Okay. Just don't be sorry you asked for it."

What was that supposed to mean? Her legs picked that moment to stop supporting her. She would have fallen if Evan hadn't dropped to his knees in front of her and put his big palms on her hips. "Easy now. We haven't even begun yet."

Speak for yourself, Stud Boy. She'd *begun* the second she'd opened the door and seen him standing there. Right about now, she was beyond ready to *end*.

Evan took his sweet time — too much time, in Lily's opinion, peeling away her cotton shorts and panties and helping her step out of them. He pressed his face to her mound and drew a deep breath that had her feeling as if she could melt into a puddle on the floor.

"I love the way you smell," he told her, his hot whisper brushing over her pussy. "Earthy and tangy and sweet. I could eat *you* for dinner."

She held back a laugh at the exaggerated leer on his face. It sounded like a great idea to her. "So why don't you?"

"I thought you'd never ask." He nudged her legs apart and delved his tongue into her pussy. The wet, soft heat of him pressing so hard against her made her knees let go. She moaned, so close to orgasm and knowing she'd topple over the edge at any second. She put her hands on the top of his head to steady herself, burying her fingers in the short curls too soft to belong to a man. It just wasn't fair that he would be blessed with such a head of hair when he kept it so short.

He tongue flicked over her clit, bringing a shock through her body. He always knew what to do — or what to say — to get an intense reaction out of her. He read her so well sometimes, she felt made for him. And then she came to her senses and remembered it was all about sex. Grand destiny didn't even come into play. And she didn't *want* it to.

Yeah, right.

She shook her head, wishing she was close enough to a wall to bang her head on it and knock some sense into herself. *Sex, Lily. It's about sex. Only.* She held back a snort. If it had been more, he would have sat down to dinner with her, asked her about her day instead of rushing her to the bedroom and stripping her naked in a matter of minutes. The thought should have reassured her, but it left her cold.

For all of ten seconds.

And then Evan thrust his tongue inside her, stroking in and out in a maddening rhythm and she lost her train of thought. Heat spiraled in her, crackling with electricity and ready to snap. She tugged on his hair. If he didn't get inside her soon, she might have to kill him. "Stop. I'd rather be in bed with you."

He didn't stop. He shook his head, which only served to make the steady ache inside her jump a few notches as his lips brushed back and forth against her clit. Her moan turned into a sound very much like a scream, her grip on his hair tightening. "I'm going to fall over."

He broke away from her long enough to say, "I've got you," before moving between her legs again. His insistent mouth and tongue continued to stroke and tease her until she rocketed into one of the most powerful orgasms ever to shake her body. She convulsed, moaning and panting as Evan let her go. She fell back to the bed. Her gaze settled on his face, his lips and chin glistening with her moisture, and a spasm ran through her cunt.

She lay back on the bed, her eyes closed and her hands clenching fistfuls of comforter. "That was incredible."

"I'm not done."

She snapped her eyes open, expecting to find him standing naked over her, but he was still kneeling close to her crotch, as far as she could tell completely dressed. Oh, no. Not another one. "My hearing must be going. I thought I heard you say you're not done."

He laughed even as he licked her moisture off his lips. "That's exactly what I said. Ready for round two?"

Round two? She'd never had a round two before the guy even got undressed. With Toby, she'd be lucky to get a round one once a month. *He* always got round one, but he'd never really cared if she did. Evan...what was he thinking? Had he lost his mind and forgotten to mention it to her? If he expected her to come again now, and then later when he got naked and joined her in bed... "How many rounds are there?"

"It's endless, babe."

Endless. *Oh man.* Maybe she should call the hospital now and tell them she'd be coming in a little later, suffering from heart failure.

He brought his mouth back to her pussy, laving her in long strokes, coaxing a few more shudders out of her. "Evan, really. I can't take another second of this. It's torture."

He nipped the tender skin of her inner thigh. "Isn't it, though?"

He was *so* dead later. She was going to *kill* him for putting her through this.

Tomorrow.

For now, she'd just enjoy it while she could get it. He wouldn't be around forever, and then it would be back to the detachable showerhead or men who only cared about their own release. He brought his mouth back to her pussy, latching onto her clit and sucking hard. She bucked against him, a strangled scream escaping her as another orgasm swept her away on a tide of light and electricity. It felt like her whole body left the mattress, her only anchor, Evan's mouth against her spasming flesh.

He didn't let up as she drifted through lust-filled bliss. He kept his lips and tongue right at the center of all her sensations, alternately laving and suckling, nibbling and tugging. She couldn't hold still, couldn't breathe, couldn't even think straight. She moaned, incoherent ramblings, tugged on his hair to get him to stop before she really did have a heart attack—but he didn't comply.

He brought her to climax yet another time before he finally lifted his head. Still fully clothed, he knelt between her knees and pressed his thumb against her overly-sensitized clit. She bucked against him, helpless to stop the tremors running through her. "No more, Evan. I can't take another second."

"You're going to take a lot more than a second, Lily." He thrust first two, then three fingers inside her, forcing her body into spiraling close to another orgasm. She teetered on the precipice, doing all she could to hold herself back, knowing one more time would mean certain death. Yes, it would be a very nice way to go, but she wasn't ready to die.

With his other hand, he fingered her clit. He stroked and soothed, light touches that eased some of the spring-tight tension inside her—until his next move. He pulled his drenched fingers out of her cunt and traced the tight ring of her anus with the tip of one of those fingers. She tried to sit up, shocked at the sudden turn of events, but couldn't seem to get her muscles to move. "What are you doing?"

He pushed just the tip of his finger inside her anus, sending a shock of pleasure-pain straight to her clit, and paused. "You don't like it?"

Like it? It was incredible. She couldn't describe it any other way. It burned a little, but the pleasure far outweighed the pain. Her muscles clenched around his finger at first, but as they relaxed, he pushed his finger deeper inside. He increased his pressure on her clit, picking up a fast rhythm that had her bucking her hips against him, the peculiar full feeling of his finger in her anus adding to the intensity. She moaned and squirmed, sure she couldn't take any more. When he started to rotate that finger slowly inside her, she screamed. "Oh God, Evan!"

"You are so amazing, Lily," he told her before he pressed a wet kiss to her clit. "So fucking unbelievable. I want to fuck your cunt. Hell, I want to fuck your ass."

A shudder coursed through her at his words. She wanted that, too, though she'd never known it before tonight. The scope of her feelings for Evan shocked her. Scared her. She didn't want to feel so strongly for him, but he'd worked his way into her heart. She cared about him, wanted to make him happy—wanted to pleasure him like he pleasured her tonight. A tear slid down her cheek, followed by another, the sensations and emotions becoming too much to bear.

"Come for me, sweetheart," Evan urged, stroking her clit with a heavy and demanding touch. She could do nothing except obey his request.

She exploded in the most powerful of her orgasms. Her whole being shattered, the pieces drifting through space as her heart beat against her chest and she struggled to draw a full breath. When the pieces of her soul came back together, they fit differently. Better.

Everything had changed because of Evan. She was the same woman, yet she wasn't. The colors of the world seemed brighter, the light in the room had changed, dulled at the edges in a way that emphasized the one thing at the center of her universe—Evan. She fought back a sob. Nothing would ever be the same. That thought both thrilled her and scared her to death at the same time. Her eyes drifted closed and she let herself go to the emotions taking over her body. Her heart and soul. He'd broken her and put her back together in a way that suited just him, and no one else would ever do.

He withdrew his finger as she lay there with her eyes closed. She felt the dip of the mattress as the springs let out a soft *screech*, letting her know he'd come up beside her on the bed. He pulled her close and she realized while she'd been drifting he'd stripped off his clothes. His cock pressed against her thigh, moistening her skin with the drop of precum that had gathered at the tip, and she licked her lips.

"Think you can handle a little more?" he asked, his tone caught somewhere between teasing and dead serious. She snapped her eyes open to find him looking down at her with uncertain eyes. Maybe one more climax wouldn't kill her. She caught the look in his eyes, all hot and dark and intense.

Then again, maybe it would.

She reached between them and grasped his cock in her hand. He was hard, more than ready, and a shiver ran through her. She groaned. Her muscles were so fluid she wasn't going to be able to walk for weeks.

"Of course I can take it." Her smile faltered at the shaky tone of her voice. What was *that* all about? After a couple of orgasms her brain turned to mush?

"Good." She nearly laughed at his relieved sigh. He bent down and kissed her, long and slow, before fitting the head of his cock against her entrance. "I'm sorry. I promise I'll take it slower next time."

He couldn't possibly go any slower without killing them both. "Trust me. You're fine." Better than fine. The man was a god.

He slammed into her so hard he moved her a few inches up the mattress. She had no doubt her head would have smacked the headboard had she been laying in that direction. As it was, if he pumped into her too much harder he'd probably shoot them both off the other side of the bed. His powerful thrusts might have hurt, if she hadn't been so sated and pleasantly numb.

He put one of his arms behind each of her knees and pushed her legs forward and out. The new position made the penetration deeper, and the angle created a furious, sweeping tension low in her belly. Evan's pace picked up a frantic rhythm just as another orgasm took her by surprise, pulling her along on a tide of sensation she had no hope of controlling, and didn't bother to try. She was distantly aware of Evan groaning her name, felt his hot cum spurt inside her, but she couldn't manage more than looping her arms around his neck and pulling him close as they rode the wave together.

He collapsed on top of her and kissed her, his tongue darting into her mouth before he rolled to his side and pulled her against him.

She wanted to say something to him, to thank him for the amazing sex—and what felt like a million explosive orgasms—but she couldn't. She'd already started to drift off to sleep.

Chapter Nine

Evan rolled onto his back, his eyelids fluttering open. He took in the darkened room around him. Unfamiliar surroundings. Lily's room. Where was she? Did he smell something cooking?

No. It was a little past midnight. Lily wouldn't be cooking right now, would she? She probably went to the bathroom. He tried to go back to sleep, sure it was just a dream — the result of skipping dinner and engaging in a bit of rigorous sex — but his growling stomach wouldn't let him rest. He climbed out of bed, rubbed his sleep-filled eyes, and wandered down the hall toward the kitchen. As he got closer, the scent of onions and garlic filled the air along with the scrape of clanging pots and pans. She *was* cooking. Why now?

He rounded the corner and drew up short in the kitchen door. Lily stood at the sink, draining pasta into a colander. His mouth watered as he took in the sight of her lithe-but-curvy body, the pink panties and matching tank top leaving most of her ivory skin exposed. His cock stirred to life, though after last night she probably wouldn't want him touching her for at least a week. He put his hand to his crotch to quell his rising cock, but it only made the problem worse. He cleared his throat when she set the big pasta pan down on the sideboard. "What are you doing?"

She jumped and spun around, her hand to her chest and her eyes flashing. "Oh, hi. You scared me."

"Sorry. I was just wondering why you weren't in bed." He walked over to where she stood and wrapped his arms around her waist. He dropped his head to kiss her shoulder, feeling the strange need to punch his fist into the air when she gave a soft sigh and leaned into him.

"Couldn't sleep. Too hungry," she mumbled.

"Yeah, me too." But he was suddenly hungry for other things. Things not involving food. Or, at least, not pasta. Chocolate sauce and whipped cream, maybe.

Lily gave his hair a tug and he brought his gaze up to hers. She shook her head, amusement glinting in those incredible eyes. "Not right now, mister. You just about killed me last night. Sit down. This is ready. I'll feed you, if you're interested. *Food*, Evan, not sex."

Who was he to argue when a beautiful woman offered to feed him what he knew would be a delicious meal? He walked the few steps to the table and flopped into a chair, watching Lily as she moved around the kitchen. Even this late at night, she still moved with a fluid grace that captivated him. Her muscles were long and lean, reminding him of a ballet dancer's. Her waist was nipped, its smallness accentuated by the swell of her breasts and the curve of her full hips. She had an ass that would make even J-Lo jealous. She had her hair pulled into a messy ponytail that draped down her back in long, silken waves his fingers itched to tangle in.

And a small tattoo — a pink and yellow butterfly — rode high on her left hip, just above the waistband of her bikini panties. He smiled. "Nice butterfly."

She turned, a plate heaping with pasta in her small hands, and gave him a sheepish smile. "Thanks. Another impulsive act. I got it the day I turned eighteen."

He laughed. It suited her somehow, that tiny butterfly hidden from the view of most people in her life. They'd had sex twice, and he'd just seen the thing now. If she'd worn one of the T-shirts she told him she slept in, he would have been deprived of its view.

She padded over to the table, her bare feet whispering across the hardwood floor, and set the plate and a fork in front of him. She returned to the stove long enough to make up a smaller plate for herself before she sat across from him, her gaze glued to the food in front of her.

"This smells incredible. What is it?" he asked, trying to draw her eyes back to him.

"Honestly, nothing special. Just pasta with a sauce made with garlic, olive oil, onions, and plum tomatoes. It took as long to reheat it as it did to make it."

"Why didn't you wake me?" he asked. *That* got her attention. She snapped her gaze up to his, uncertainty flashing in her eyes.

"I wasn't sure what was going on."

He frowned. "What do you mean?"

"Well..." She set her fork down, pulling one knee up to her chest. She sighed. "What was earlier all about? You've got me a little confused here."

"What do you mean?"

She snorted a laugh. "All those orgasms. You wouldn't let up. Not that I'm complaining or anything, mind you, but I'd like to know what brought it on. It seemed to me like you were trying to prove something to somebody. Or yourself."

Busted. "I wasn't..."

She put her leg down as she held up her hand to stop him, waving it in the air before she reached down and picked up her fork and dug into her meal. "Don't start. Yes, you were. I don't mind being the center of that kind of attention, but I know something motivated you to come over out of the blue and attack me like that." She glanced at him in between bites, her gaze challenging. "At least be honest with me."

He heaved a sigh and set down his fork. Should he tell her the truth? Would she get upset if he confessed the motivations behind the visit? It didn't matter. If he *didn't* tell her the truth, she'd send him packing. And, knowing what he knew about her, he didn't think the truth would bother her. It might help to talk to someone about his feelings—he hadn't admitted them to anyone since he'd moved out of his condo. "Okay. I got a letter from my ex-wife. She and her fiancé, Scott, are getting married next month."

"Would Scott be the ex-best friend, or has she moved on to someone else?"

He tapped his finger on the table. "The first one."

Lily wrinkled her nose. "That sucks."

He couldn't have said it better himself. "Yeah." He shook his head. "That's not even the part that gets me the maddest. She told me in the letter that we had no passion in our lives, and she gets so much more from Scott."

Lily's eyes went wide. She blinked at him a few times, her mouth gaping, before she shook her head. "You've got to be kidding me. I know you're one hell of a passionate man."

"Maybe last night was just a fluke."

"What about that kiss after the bar? Or time in your pool? Neither of those were flukes."

He shrugged. "Yeah, that would be the logical way to look at this, but I wasn't feeling very logical last night. Maybe it was just a matter of finding the right—" He clamped his mouth shut before he could finish a sentence he had no business saying out loud. If he'd confessed how right she felt to him, she'd misconstrue his words and think he was looking for a commitment. Nothing could be further from the truth. Things hadn't changed since that night in the bar. No matter how much his mind screamed that he'd finally found someone that meant something. He shook his head. "Finding a *responsive* woman." Yeah, that was it. No commitment for this guy. At least not for another fifty or so years.

"Funny, Toby used to say I wasn't."

"Responsive?" He found that a little hard to believe. After last night, a *lot* hard to believe.

She nodded. "Course, that could have been because he never bothered to touch me in a place that might make me respond."

"That bad, huh?" He laughed as he took a bite of pasta. The intense flavor of the garlic laced with fresh tomatoes burst to life on his tongue. He moaned in appreciation. Maybe he should offer to pay her to stock his freezer with her home-cooked meals. "This is damned amazing, Lily."

She rolled her eyes. "Thanks. It's nothing. *Really.* And, yes, it was that bad. I'd prefer to block the whole sordid incident from my memory, if you don't mind."

She met his gaze with another challenging stare, but when he raised an eyebrow, she broke down laughing.

"What about the other men?" He'd hesitated to ask the question, not sure if he really wanted to know the answer. But he wanted to get to know her better—bad idea, but he couldn't help it—so he asked anyway. She met the question with a frown.

"What other men?"

"There was only Toby?" He found that hard to believe. Although, maybe not, if he judged by her curious perusal of his cock in the pool. He sat forward, waiting for her answer.

"Well, there was one other guy in high school—a boy, really—who knew even less about pleasing a woman than Toby. He lasted one night." She laughed. "Don't think I'm some naïve little girl, though, because I'm not."

"Oh, believe me, I know that."

"But I'm not anything special, either." She sighed and pushed her plate away. "Don't spread this around, but I think that's the reason I posed for the magazine. I signed on just after my breakup with Toby, and I needed some reassurance that I wasn't a hideous beast."

A beast? Had she not glanced in a mirror lately? "Yeah, and you got the centerfold."

"It was a slow month. You should have seen the other girls. They were complete dogs." She winked at him despite the sliver of uncertainty in her eyes.

He laughed at her sudden lack of self-confidence. "I hate to point this out, but I *did* see them, and they *weren't* dogs."

"Airbrushing is an amazing thing, isn't it?" She swatted his shin with her toes. "I feel compelled to tell you, though, Mr. Big City, that you're reading me wrong. You thought I was a naïve small town girl until you saw the centerfold, and then you probably expected some kind of wild woman. Sorry to disappoint, buddy, but I'm neither."

"Actually, I think you're both, and that's what has me so intrigued."

She narrowed her eyes at him. "How do you figure?"

"A naïve, inexperienced woman wouldn't have had the courage to stroke me the way you did in the pool. But I knew, by the way you *explored*, that it was a fairly new experience for you. You didn't shy away like a lot of women would do. You're very open and honest, even when it comes to enjoying yourself during sex."

"God, this is embarrassing." Her face reddened and she took a big gulp of her water from the glass she'd set on the table earlier. Some of the liquid dripped down her chin and he had the strong but absurd urge to lick it from her skin.

"Why? It's only the truth. Don't ever be afraid to say anything to me. And you can expect that I'm going to be candid with you. That's who I am." He smiled, liking the fact that, for once, Lily seemed speechless. "And that's how you are, too. Don't ever feel like you have to hold yourself back on my account. Because you don't."

She gave him a weak, somewhat uncertain smile, her fingers toying with the edge of her navy blue placemat. "Since you seem to be in the mood for honesty," she began, her tone hesitant but curious, "can I ask you a question?"

"Go ahead." He almost told her she could ask anything, but he remembered where that conversation had led to before and didn't want to go down that road again. He just prayed it wouldn't be anything that might dredge up bad memories and ruin the moment.

"Will you tell me a little about your family?"

He smiled, even though he knew the line of questioning would take them into very personal territory. Telling a lover about his family seemed more personal to Evan than talking about past relationships. Lovers came and went, but family was the one constant when it came to matters of the heart. "Sure. I have one sister, Alexis. She lives in Chicago with her husband and my six nieces and nephews."

"Six?" Her loud gulp filled the room. "Brave woman."

Yeah, he tended to think so, too. He'd spent enough time around her brood to think she ought to be nominated for sainthood. "She stays home with them. Like, all the time. I don't know how she does it."

"An endless supply of valium and chairs with ankle restraints?"

He laughed. "In all honesty, I wouldn't be surprised."

"What about your parents?" she asked after a few moments of comfortable silence.

"Out by Chicago. In the suburbs. They live about ten miles from the city. My dad has a law firm, and my mother teaches at the local high school." He leaned forward and took her hand. "What about you? Tell me about your family."

"Well, you know about my brother, Tony. My other brother Jake, the older one, lives in town with his wife Mary. They don't have any kids yet. My father married a woman six years older than me, and I have three stepbrothers age thirteen and under. Hannah, the stepco—mother, is pregnant. Due in a couple of months."

He smiled when she rolled her eyes, a frown marring her delicate features. "I take it you're not excited about it," he said softly.

"Excited?" she snorted. "I think they're all nuts. My mom owns the wellness center. She's been a little eccentric since the divorce. She's caught between who she wants to be and who she was raised to be. It's a very unusual sight to behold, let me tell you."

"I'll bet. Your mom is Anne, right?"

"Yeah. How did you know that?"

"I've been in for massages a couple of times since I moved here. I had appointments with your mom." He watched as her eyes narrowed and she pursed her lips.

"So you've met my mom and you're just choosing to mention this to me now?"

He shrugged. "I didn't think it was all that important."

Lily swatted his leg again, but instead of pulling away, this time she kept her toes against him, rubbing gently up and down his shin. "You don't need to go there for a massage, you know. No sense paying for one if you don't have to. I can give you one sometime."

"Are you certified?"

She nodded. "I can fill in doing massages if my mom or Marnie are sick."

He needed to send a huge gift basket to the real estate agent who'd talked him into buying this house. Lily cooked like a gourmet chef, fucked like a sex queen, *and* gave massages? He smiled. "Very cool."

"Oh, you *would* think so." She gave him a phony glare, her amusement evident in her eyes. "Pig."

He reached out and took her hand across the small table, bringing it to his mouth and brushing a kiss over her knuckles. "You wouldn't expect anything different."

"You don't know how true that is." She stood up and cleared the plates away, taking the dishes to the sink. *Rinse, stack, load.* He laughed, remembering how she'd told him about her system when it came to dishes.

She turned back to him once she finished, one hand perched on her hip and a smile he could only describe as wicked on her lips. "I have brownies for dessert if you want one."

"Homemade?"

Lily rolled her eyes. "Duh."

"Okay, you've convinced me."

She took a container out of a cabinet and put a couple of brownies on a plate. She set it in the middle of the table and started to walk toward her seat, but he snagged her wrist. "One favor, sweetheart?"

"What's that?"

"Sit on my lap." His cock twitched toward her as he said the words, and hardened as she ran her tongue over her lips.

"Um, okay," she said softly.

She started to sit, but he shook his head. "No, straddle me."

"Okay." She smiled as she straddled his lap, settling her cloth-covered pussy right against his groin. He bit back a moan as she wriggled against him.

Lily reached behind her to pull the plate closer. She snagged a brownie and tore off a chunk, waving it in front of his mouth. He inhaled the scent of dark, rich chocolate and parted his lips. She slipped the brownie chunk into his mouth. He chewed slowly to savor the flavor, the sweet taste incredible on his tongue. "That's sinful."

"Sure is. I use Godiva chocolate."

"Amazing."

"It's worth it." She smiled and fed him another chunk.

"I'll say." He reached out for the plate and broke off a chunk of brownie, bringing it to Lily's lips. "Open up."

She parted her lips, dragging her tongue over the lower one. His mouth went dry. He slipped the brownie into her mouth, and she caught his fingers as he was pulling them free. Her teeth nipped at him as her tongue swirled around his fingertips. His mind immediately flashed to her mouth performing those actions on another part of his body. He arched his hips against the heat of her pussy. She whimpered, and any sense of control he might have had went right out the window. His hand flew to her mound, shoving the elastic leg band of her panties out of the way and stroking her pussy. Her whimpering turned into moans as he found her clit and brushed his fingers over it. She was so hot, so wet, that he couldn't stand it anymore. He had to get inside her. *Now.*

His mind stuck on the thought of burying his hard-on deep inside Lily's hot cunt. She was as turned on as he was—he could see it plain in her eyes. The thought spurred him on. He pulled her closer, positioning his cock at her entrance, and pulled her down as he lifted his hips to plunge deep.

"Oh," Lily breathed, her gaze locking with his, hers filled with surprise. But then she smiled, and he knew everything was all right. He returned the smile as best as he could considering the state of his lust-fogged mind. She did that to him every time—made him unable to think, unable to breathe. Something good was happening here, really good. He refused to put a name to it, knowing that would be too much, too soon. But he reveled in it, the feeling of being connected to someone in such a strong way. He'd never felt anything more perfect, and doubted he would again. If he'd been looking for a woman to spend his life with, Lily would have been it. Why couldn't he have met her before he'd met Jessica?

He shook off the depressing thought, throwing his concentration into something much more important. He glanced at Lily and found her chewing on that lip again. "Kiss me, Lily."

She released her lip and leaned in, her lips touching his in the barest of kisses. Before she could pull back he put his hand on the back of her head and tugged her close. This time she met his lips with as much force and passion as he felt bottled up inside him. Her tongue darted in and out of his mouth, her teeth nibbling his lips, her fingers working their way through his hair. His cock swelled even more inside her and he pumped his hips gently a few times.

She was so hot and slick, he could spend forever just sitting there inside her. But he wanted more. He wanted her to be as hot for him as he was for her. He broke the kiss and smiled at her, panting. "You've got to move, sweetheart."

"Um, okay." She looked flustered for all of two seconds

before she lifted herself and began sliding up and down his cock. He squeezed her hips, guiding her rhythm as he thrust up into her. Heat spiraled through him, running all the way to his toes. A guy could get used to such a warm, willing woman. Too bad he wasn't looking for someone to get used to.

He brought his hand between them and circled his finger over her clit to coax a long, drawn-out moan from her lips as he continued to thrust deep inside her. She rose up and slammed down on him, her pace quickening and her rhythm growing more and more erratic with every thrust of his hips. She felt so good...he'd never get enough.

He felt the orgasm building in him, swift and strong, and knew he could do nothing to stop it. "I'm close, Lily."

"So am I," she said, panting. "Very close, Evan. I... *ah*..." Her words ended on a shuddering sob as he felt her clench around him, her muscles squeezing his cock, pulling him deeper inside her. She convulsed into a series of shudders, her nails digging into his shoulders. It was enough to send him over the edge.

He threw his head back, a primal-sounding growl escaping his lips, as his climax ripped through him. His grip tightened on her hips as he bucked, pumping his cum into her for what seemed like endless minutes. When he finally stilled, Lily leaned in and kissed him. Her warm lips felt right against his—too right. He wanted more from her than she was willing to give.

That could be a problem.

A cold chill ran through him and, seeming to sense his sudden hesitation, she pulled back. "Is something wrong?"

He shook his head, afraid to speak for fear that he'd tell her how he really felt about her. *Talk about a mood-killer.* She didn't want declarations of affection. She wanted hot, passionate sex. He could give her that. He shoved the emotions aside and smiled at her. "I'm fine. Are you okay?"

The dazed-but-satisfied look in her eyes answered his question. A tired smile spread over her lips and she stroked a lock of hair off his forehead. "That was unexpected. Again."

"But not unwanted."

"No." She winked at him and something a little too close to his heart clenched. "Definitely not. You've got the whole element of surprise thing down pat. In fact, why don't we go back to bed?"

"To sleep?"

She shook her head.

"I'm going to need a few minutes to recover. I'm not a teenager anymore."

She pushed off his lap, straightened her panties, and held her hand out to him. "That's okay. My recovery time is practically nothing. I'm sure you can find a few ways to occupy yourself until you feel...*ready* again."

He laughed as he let her lead him down the hall.

* * * * *

Lily woke up in a terrific mood. The sun shone through the sheers covering the windows, her body felt sore-but-rested, and she felt more awake than she usually did at this ungodly hour. She had Evan and a night of incredible sex to thank. She rolled over to wrap her arms around him, and got an armful of pillow instead. His side of the bed was empty. And cold. He'd been gone for a while. A chill ran through her.

She sat up in bed and glanced around the room. All his clothes were gone, right down to the tie and shoes. Well, damn. So much for her good morning. She hadn't wanted a commitment or anything—at least not that she'd admit to him—but a "goodbye" or a "see you later" would have been polite. She hadn't figured him to be the type to skip out in the middle of the night.

She'd like to consider him a friend—albeit one with some obvious benefits—and she didn't like being blown off by friends. Grumbling, she padded down the hall to the kitchen, surprised to find the dishes done and a note on the table. She picked up the small square of white paper.

Sorry to rush out on you, but I have a breakfast meeting at seven and I thought it would be best to avoid the awkward morning after thing. Last night was amazing. I think I got an hour of sleep. I'll be dreaming about you when I'm falling asleep in the meeting. Thank you. You made me feel a lot better. I'll see you around. Evan

See you around? What the fuck was that all about? If she was so goddamned amazing, why was he blowing her off? It's not like she asked him for a diamond or anything. There was nothing wrong with two consenting adults enjoying a little casual playtime. But this felt like some kind of a brush-off. If he'd really wanted to "see her around", he would have made a point to tell her he'd call, or stop by.

See you around?

Whatever.

She supposed he was right about the awkward part, though. They'd both made it clear that they wanted no more than a fling. She planned to keep it that way, despite that pesky inner voice urging her to take things a step further. The voice that tried to chime in now, yelling at her that she was acting like an idiot. She slapped a mental gag on the voice and shook her head. Did this note mean Evan didn't want to see her again? Was she that terrible in bed that he couldn't stand the sight of her? She hoped not. For the first time in her life, she knew what incredible sex was. She'd be damned if she'd give that up without a fight.

Watch out, Evan Acardi. I'm not even close to finished with you yet.

Chapter Ten

"So Evan just left?" Marnie threw a breadcrumb into the water and laughed as a duck snatched it up. "And you haven't heard from him in five days?"

The heat had abated some this week. Lily and Marnie had taken a walk in the park after work to enjoy the nice weather while they had it. The forecaster was calling for the heat and humidity to return in a few days, along with another bout of rain. Lily groaned. *There's nothing like living in a sauna.*

Lily shrugged at Marnie's question, determined to pretend his desertion didn't bother her as much as it did. "That about sums it up. I don't get it. If the sex was so excellent, why is he avoiding me? If he doesn't want it to happen again, all he has to do is say something. It's not like I'm going to chase him through town, begging for sex."

She'd given it some serious thought, but she didn't need to do anything else to make everyone in town think she was some kind of shameless hussy. So she'd called Janet, the resident sexpert, for advice. Janet was too busy at work to talk, so Lily had to settle for Marnie.

"What do you think I should do?" she asked as Marnie fed the ducks and geese another slice of bread. The birds squawked and honked as they fought for the bread chunks, some of them losing their footing and tumbling down the gentle incline toward the pond that sat in the middle of the park. "Should I call him, or let him come to me on his own?" *If* he came to her at all.

Marnie let out a little, thoughtful-sounding sigh. "Call him."

"That would make me sound needy."

Marnie glanced at her, her eyebrows raised and her lips

"Okay, so I *am* needy. But I don't have to act that way. If I call him, he's going to think I'm too forward."

"True." Marnie stretched her legs out in front of her on the grass and pulled another slice of bread from the bag she'd picked up at the store across the street. "But if you don't call, he might think you're no longer interested."

"Or he might rejoice the fact that he's gotten rid of the bitchy brunette across the street that he made a huge mistake in sleeping with."

Marnie turned her attention back to the birds in front of them, breaking tiny pieces of bread off the slice and tossing them in all directions. Lily winced, imagining a horrific scene straight out of the classic movie *The Birds*. "So you really think I should call him?" she asked, trying to ignore that one duck that kept looking at her shoelaces like they might make a tasty lunch.

Marnie turned to face Lily again, giving her a sage little nod. "You'll never know until you call, Lily."

"Yeah, you're probably right about that."

"Probably? The answer isn't going to fall out of the sky."

She looked heavenward, praying that some kind of answer to her dilemma would do just that. No such luck. The only things in the sky, besides the clouds, were pigeons. She looked back down to Marnie before she pressed her luck too far and ended up with a face full of bird poop.

She wouldn't get any sign from above. She needed to work this problem out on her own. And, despite her reluctance and downright cowardice, she would confront Evan and make him see their arrangement could be very good for both of them. She didn't want forever, but she did want a fling—with all the fun and emotions included. She wanted to eat dinner with him a few nights a week. Talk with him about everything, good and bad. Fall asleep in his arms and actually wake up beside him in the morning. Was that too much to ask? She had to find out. If he didn't want the same thing she did, then maybe his disappearing act was for the best.

The geese honking brought Lily out of her thoughts. She scooted back on the grass, not wanting to lose her shoes to a big, hungry bird. She'd settle for a short-term affair with Evan, even though in her heart she knew she wanted more. But she'd take what she could get, even if it took a little convincing to make him see her point of view. When he got home from work that night, she'd go over to his place and talk to him. But for now, she should try to think about something else. Otherwise, she'd work herself into a big ball of trembling nerves in the couple of hours before she'd see him.

"Have you come to any decision about what to do about Joe?" she asked Marnie. Talking about Marnie's messed-up love life might make Lily's seem not so bad.

"I don't think it's going to work out. He's so distant lately."

"That's too bad." *Like I haven't told you that at least a million times over the years.* "Have you tried to talk to him about your feelings?"

"Yeah. He thinks I'm being overly sensitive. He says he's just tired from work, but I don't know." Marnie pushed a blonde curl away from her eyes and sighed. "We've been together for seven years. The way I see it, either it's time for him to propose, or time for me to move on with my life."

Uh-oh. *Potential crisis alert.* "Did you give him an ultimatum?"

"Well, yeah. I need to know, once and for all, if he's as serious about us as I am."

Lily gulped. She'd be willing to bet a thousand dollars he wasn't. A million even. "Wow. So what did he say?" When would Marnie see the relationship had come to an end years ago? Marnie had been the one to convince Lily it was time to break up with Toby. Why couldn't she see her relationship with Joe was having the same problems?

Marnie plucked a violet from the grass and lifted it to her nose before twirling the stem around her fingers. She smiled, but

Lily saw the pain in her eyes. Lily's heart went out to her and she felt bad for all the questioning. She shook her head. "Have you talked to Janet lately? We've been playing phone tag for the past few days."

Marnie's dark expression lightened and she smiled. She tossed the rest of the bread to the ducks and stood up, brushing her hands down the front of her shorts. "She met someone new."

"Oh, yeah?" Like this was a surprise? Janet met someone new almost every Monday and dumped him by Saturday night.

"Some guy she works with. I think she said his name is Brick."

Brick? "Like the things you use to build walls?"

Marnie nodded.

Janet sure knew how to pick them. "What does he do?"

"Some kind of manual labor. I think she said he's a roofing contractor."

Figured. Janet had a certain type of man she liked—big, very strong, and lacking in the brain department. She didn't like a man to talk back. Lily laughed. "Think *she'll* ever meet Mr. Right?"

"Not if she keeps searching for Mr. Hot-in-Bed."

Lily would have laughed, had Marnie's words not reminded her of her situation with Evan. Isn't that who she'd been looking for when she'd slept with him? Mr. Hot-in-Bed? Why did it suddenly seem like he'd become so much more in an unnervingly short amount of time?

She stood up, gave the ducks and geese a final, wary glance, and followed Marnie back up the hill to the dirt pathway leading back to the parking lot. When they reached Marnie's car, Lily turned down her offer of a ride home.

"I have a few errands I'd like to run while the nice weather holds out," she told her. "Thanks, anyway."

Marnie placed her hand on Lily's shoulder and smiled. "You're worrying about this too much. It'll all work out. Things always do."

Lily's smile faltered. Things would work out, but she wasn't sure if she'd like the resolution.

* * * * *

Lily walked through the streets of downtown Tranquility, sidestepping small children riding skateboards and bicycles as they screamed and laughed. The sights and sounds of summer vacation brought back memories that made her smile. An ice cream truck stopped on the corner, its happy, childish music filling the street. It would be great to be a kid again, with her biggest worry being over having enough money to get an ice cream every afternoon. Now, things had changed.

Had they ever.

A few women gave her strange looks as they walked past her, and one even went out of her way to avoid bumping elbows with her. Lily bit back a bitchy reply, given the amount of children in the area, and it only made her feel worse to not be able to speak her mind. She balled her hands into fists at her sides, her teeth clenched and a knot forming I her stomach.

What the hell is this all about? I posed nude for a magazine. I'm not a leper.

She picked up a few things at the pharmacy and made a pit stop at the video store on her way home. The tall, thin teenager behind the counter gaped at her as she walked into the little, dark wood paneled store. As the son of one of her father's employees, Lily would have expected more from him. She shot him a glare as she moved toward the new release rack, biting back the urge to tell him to go wash his greasy blond hair.

She picked up a DVD she'd wanted to see for a while, something she'd missed in the theaters. Now would be the perfect time, since the man she wanted to spend her nights with apparently had other ideas. She still held to the theory that men sucked, but Evan's particular talent in that department kept her awake at night. She liked how he sucked on her lips, her tongue, her nipples, her clit…she squeezed her legs together as she felt a trickle of moisture well in her pussy. *Not here. This is* so *inappropriate.*

She passed the curtained-off adult section of the store and couldn't resist taking a peek. She'd never been inside, and she figured it wouldn't hurt just to look. She pushed past the curtains and crept into the room.

"Talk about anticlimactic," she muttered. She'd expected flashing neon lights, pictures of naked people engaged in all kinds of debauchery, maybe some tacky red vinyl decorations. What she found was a room that looked just like the rest of the video store, except the movies on the shelves weren't meant for general audiences.

She browsed the videos, lifting up a few boxes and reading the back cover copy—and trying not to be shocked at the blatant displays right on the fronts of the boxes. Okay, so maybe the room *was* a little like she'd first expected. Toby had always said porn was dirty, so he'd never watch it with her, despite how curious she was. She'd hoped watching others do it would give him a little drive to try something new. But she did pick up a few interesting ideas—if she could get Evan involved again.

In the end, she put the boxes down and started to leave the room. What was the sense of getting a porn movie if she had no one to watch it with? Evan wasn't reliable in the lover department, taking off for days at a time. And maybe he was like Toby—totally against adult movies of any kind.

That would be just her luck.

Though she doubted it. He did have a subscription to *Seduced.* And he'd asked her if she owned a vibrator. A prudish man wouldn't act like that, would he?

She sighed as she turned to walk out of the room. First, she needed to concentrate on getting him back into her bed. Then she could worry about taking a trip to the adult section of the video store with him. She had almost reached the door when someone came out of the aisle next to her and slammed into her.

"Sorry. I didn't see you there," a familiar voice said.

She looked up at a face she knew well.

And almost had a heart attack. "Toby?"

His gray eyes widened so far she thought they might pop out of his head. He sputtered and cursed, his face reddening like a cooked lobster. He shook his head in apparent disbelief, his blond hair falling over his forehead, which had started to dampen with sweat. "What are you doing in here, Lily? Looking to broaden your depraved horizons?"

She snorted. Toby considered anything past missionary depraved. Or at least she'd thought so. Now she wasn't so sure. She glanced down at the stack of videos he clutched to his chest. He held them closer to his green cotton shirt and stepped back.

"Yeah, that's exactly what I'm doing." She gave him a wink that seemed to make him even more nervous. "What about you? Adding to your closet collection of dirty films?"

He shook his head, the fear in his eyes making her laugh. "I came in here by mistake."

What had she ever seen in him? He was a good-looking guy, in that high-school-quarterback-who-refuses-to-grow-up kind of way, but his fair, bulky good looks didn't thrill her like Evan did.

"Let me guess. You were looking for the Disney section. Give it a rest, Toby. I caught you. You've been watching porn films."

His expression darkened as he shifted his stance to an obviously defensive one. "Well, it's only because you broke up with me."

"Don't give me that shit. You were walking around here like you own the place. You've probably been renting this stuff for years."

His eyes narrowed and his jaw clenched. His nostrils flared as he opened his mouth. "You want to know the truth, Lily? Fine. But don't forget, you asked for it."

Asked for *what*? What truth was he talking about? Had she missed something in the year they'd dated?

"I watch these kinds of movies. I love them. I get off on them, if you must know."

Oh. *That* truth. She gaped at him, blinking her eyes in disbelief. Apparently, she *had* missed something while they'd been dating.

"Then why did you tell me you didn't like them?"

"Because that's not the kind of thing you talk about with the woman you plan to marry."

She blinked. Wouldn't sex be a pretty important discussion in a marriage? One would think so. "What else did you choose to not discuss with me?"

She finally leaned over his arms enough to catch a glimpse of the cover of the video on top of the pile. The picture depicted a man bound in black leather straps, on his hands and knees, a woman standing over his with a whip in her hand. Her eyes widened and she held back a laugh.

Well, she tried to. When she glanced up at his face, the snort of laughter burst free, no matter how much she fought against it. The discovery was like being hit between the eyes with a sledgehammer. Why had she not noticed this side of him? That didn't say much for her observation skills. "Ohmygod! You're a closet submissive, aren't you?"

"No. Of course not," Toby blustered, his face so deep red it started to appear purple. "What I watch and what I am are two separate things."

Yeah, right. Things started to make a lot more sense now. He didn't want to do anything else with her sexually because it didn't interest him. *She* hadn't interested him, at least not in bed. "Why did you never ask me to play, Toby? Think I couldn't handle it?"

He gulped, looking at her as if he'd seen her for the first time. "I...I didn't think you'd be interested."

She wouldn't have been, but it would have been nice for him to check with her first. "So you saw a Mistress on the side?"

He blinked. "I'm sorry. I didn't think..."

"You seem to do a lot of *not* thinking lately huh?" *What a way to justify cheating on your girlfriend, Stumpy.* She patted his cheek. "No hard feelings, sweetie. Well, maybe a few. Remember that editorial you ran about me?"

He nodded as he tried to slip the videos onto a shelf—any shelf. She bit back a smile.

"How do you think the town would feel about *your* contribution to the decline of morals in society, with your little porn fetish?"

He fumed and sputtered a little more. She hoped he didn't have a stroke. Then she'd be forced to save his miserable, cheating hide by calling 9-1-1.

He took a step closer to her, teetering on his feet. "At least my," *cough,* "hobby is private. It's not out there in the open for the whole world to see."

She reached around and patted his ass, chuckling when he jumped back as if her touch burned him. "Not yet it's not. Just watch what you say about me from now on, okay? Or else you might find yourself in a bit of trouble. See you around."

She left him standing there, gaping at her from the parted curtains of the adult section, and she added an extra swing to her hips.

Check out what you won't be getting, babe. Ever again.

She paid for the movie and left the video store, feeling strangely better than she had in months. Digging up a little dirt on an ex had a wonderful effect on a girl.

She laughed the whole way home. Poor Toby would probably be waiting for her revenge for weeks. Months. Years, even, because she had no revenge planned.

Just the scared look on his face had been enough.

And knowing he'd probably be ready to pee his pants every time he saw her around town helped ease her *troubled* mind.

Chapter Eleven

Evan sat on his front steps, soaking in the last rays of the fading sun, his gaze stuck on Lily's darkened windows. He'd been acting in a way that would give his mother fits, a way she raised him to never treat a woman. He'd become a first class jerk. He hadn't called Lily in days—five, to be exact. And he'd done all he could to avoid her. Why? He had a hot, willing woman ready for him every time he touched her. A woman who didn't ask for a ring or a mortgage or a bunch of children. A woman who wanted the same thing out of their time together that he did—zero commitment. What man in his right mind would give that up?

One afraid of falling in love.

He pushed a hand through his hair as the answer and the accompanying fear smacked him upside the head and stole the breath from his lungs. It would be so easy to sink into those big blue eyes and lose himself. Easier than it had been to lose himself in her body. A cold, tight knot formed in his stomach, growing larger by the second. He didn't want to fall in love, because he knew it couldn't last. They'd grow apart. And the pain from his divorce and Jessica's betrayal, though faded to a dull ache, hadn't completely gone away. It had become more of a warning—a warning to keep his heart to himself or risk getting it broken again.

But Lily made him want to forget every valuable lesson he'd learned.

She was a sex kitten and a domestic goddess all rolled into one perfect woman—the woman he thought he'd found in Jessica. But he'd been wrong then. Very wrong. He didn't know if he dared to risk it all again.

Something in his mind kept telling him that Lily would be different, but he didn't want to take the chance. She might be everything he'd ever wanted, but she was also many things he didn't want. Love. Commitment. The loss of control. He couldn't deal with it without feeling like his head would explode, but at the same time, it pained him to be away from her.

So, he hadn't called.

She probably hated him now, probably wouldn't ever want to talk to him again. He wouldn't be surprised if she'd had some kind of curse put on his sorry hide. And he deserved it, too. All of her anger, all of her wrath. Because she deserved so much more than he'd give her.

She deserved better than *him*.

A shrill ringing from inside the house brought him out of his melancholy thoughts. The telephone. He ran inside and yanked the receiver off the base. "Hello?"

"Hey, sexy."

Lily. Her husky voice and light tone made the knot in his stomach intensify. He gulped. "Hey, yourself."

"What are you doing, sitting out there all alone? You look lost."

Wasn't that the truth? "I am." So she'd been watching him watch her house. Quite a turn of events.

"Anything I can do to help?" she asked, her tone laced with sexual innuendo. He should hang up. He needed to tell her things wouldn't work out between them. He needed to be strong, and stick to his resolution to stay away from the woman who could turn his world upside down and twist his heart into a heap of useless flesh.

But he couldn't. "Depends. What do you have in mind?" *Oh, Evan, you are so weak.*

"Well, I was thinking a mind-blowing orgasm or two, but if you have other plans…" Her voice trailed off in a seductive laugh that dried his throat and sent shivers all the way down his spine.

He made a snap decision, despite knowing it only added one more nail to the coffin of his bachelorhood. "I think I can manage to free a few minutes of my busy day. Why don't you come over and make good on that suggestion?"

His doorbell rang a second later. When he pulled the door open, he wasn't surprised to find Lily standing there, a cell phone to her ear. She gave him a smile that did things to his insides as she turned off the phone and stepped inside.

She closed the door behind her with a small, private smile on her face. Her hair hung down in long, loose waves over the skin-tight, stretchy pink dress she wore. Her feet were bare—her legs, too, except for the delicate gold anklet that surrounded her right ankle. The dress fell to about her mid-thigh and his tongue seemed to swell in his mouth. "Nice outfit," he managed. Barely.

She laughed, her eyes twinkling. "It's not the dress that's important. It's what I have on under it."

His breath caught in his lungs as he took an involuntary step back. *Oh God.* He needed to sit down. All the blood in his body rushed to his crotch and his stomach bottomed out. "Wha-what are you wearing under it?"

"Not a single thing." She stood up on her tiptoes and kissed him soundly on the lips. "And I promise to forgive you for not calling for five days, if you make it up to me."

He tried to draw a breath, but his lungs had turned to stone. "What do you want?" *Anything. Anything at all. Just please put an end to my misery.*

"I want you to make me come at least three times tonight." She ran her finger down his chest, her tongue, tracing the fullness of her lower lip.

He forced a laugh despite the fact that he was getting dizzy from oxygen depravation. "Done. In fact, I'll double that as soon as I get you upstairs into my bed."

She touched her fingers to his lips, sending an electrical jolt through him. He reached for her hand, but she batted him away.

"Not yet." She gave him a coy smile. "It's your turn first

tonight, babe."

* * * * *

Lily smiled at him—hoping it looked bold and brazen but thinking she didn't make it much past dumb and naive—and knelt down in front of him.

"What are you doing?" he asked, his voice cracking. He backed up against the foyer wall, his hands clenched into fists at his sides and his erection straining against the front of his pants.

He'd apparently taken off his dress shirt after work, but still wore the olive green pants. The white undershirt he had on was a stark contrast to his dark skin. It made her fingers itch to bury under the soft cotton and run her fingers through the springy hair on his chest. He had no idea how beautiful he was.

"What I would have done in your pool if you weren't chest deep in the water," she told him, not taking her eyes off his lean, chiseled body. His clothing did nothing to hide his utter perfection.

She unbuckled his belt and unzipped his pants, slipping her hand inside his briefs. She circled his cock with her fingers, stroking in just the way he'd shown her he liked. He rewarded her efforts with a sharp hiss of breath. "This is quite a surprise."

Well, somebody had to do something about your little hesitation problem. "You don't like it?"

"It's definitely a good surprise." His breathing escalated into panting when she circled her thumb over the head of his cock, spreading the drop of moisture at the tip over the sensitive skin. "What brought this on?"

She stopped and glanced up at him. The uncertainty in his eyes mirrored what she felt inside. She pushed it away, choosing to concentrate on the present and all she planned to do to him. "I missed the way you touch me."

He groaned when she wrapped her hand around his length and stroked. "I missed touching you."

"So why didn't you call?"

"I'm not looking for a commitment. I didn't want you to get the wrong idea."

She laughed. As if. "Neither am I. Why are you so hung up on that?"

His cock twitched against her palm and she leaned in to blow a warm, slow breath over it. Evan shook his head, his legs shaking. "I just want to make sure we're on the same page here."

"Do you want me to make you come?"

He nodded. His eyes drifted closed, a pained look on his face. When he opened his eyes he looked down at her, his gaze even more uncertain than before. *What is it you're not telling me, Evan?* Did he want more than he seemed willing to admit?

She shook her head. There would be time for those thoughts later. Now, she had more important things on her mind. She wanted to taste him—so much her mouth watered. "We're most definitely on the same page, Evan. No need to worry."

She leaned in, her lips parted, but he put his hand on her forehead to stop her from getting any closer. "Wait a second. We should talk a little more about this. What exactly do you expect from…this?"

She let out a long sigh as frustration tightened her belly into a knot. Obviously he had to be crazy. Why else would he pass up the offer of a spectacular blowjob? At least she hoped it would be spectacular. She couldn't say, since she'd never given one before. But how would she learn if he wouldn't let her get close enough to touch? How much plainer could she make this? She rocked back on her heels and looked up at him, shaking her head. "What's wrong with two consenting adults consenting to a little fun?"

"But—"

"No buts." She gave his thigh a light swat. "I told you I'm not looking for any kind of a commitment."

Evan dropped his hand back to his side. He nodded slowly, almost imperceptibly. "I like you, Lily. Don't get me wrong. But my divorce...it wasn't a pleasant thing. I can't handle another relationship like that right now."

Well, duh. Did he not hear a word she'd just said to him? "Listen, Don Juan. As tempting as you seem to think it might be, I'm *not* going to fall in love with you. You're not the only one with issues. I just found out my ex cheated on me, too, and I did nothing to please him in bed. What do you think that does for a girl's ego? You don't see me running away from sex because I'm afraid of another attachment."

"True, but—"

Hello! The tension radiating through him filled the room and his cock bobbed in her face. If he'd stop being so damned stubborn, she could make him a very happy man. *She hoped.* "No buts, remember? When I am finally ready to settle down, I know what kind of man I want. You are definitely *not* him. Feel better?" She bit her lip as the harsh words left her mouth. Lies, all of them. But she wasn't in the position to beg him for more than he was willing to give.

Evan blinked down at her, a confused expression on his handsome face. "I don't know. I think so...though now you've got me wondering if there's something wrong with me."

"Well, yeah there is. I'm on my knees here, wanting to give you the blowjob of your life, and all you want to talk about is your aversion to commitment."

"I just don't know... You want to *what*?"

"Like you didn't know." She rolled her eyes before shifting her gaze to his cock. Their conversation had done nothing to wither his arousal. His cock jutted out from his body, blushed red and throbbing, another fat drop of precum glistening on the tip. She licked her lips. "Are you going to shut up now so I can have some fun?"

The back of Evan's head hit the wall with a thump. "By all means."

"Thank you."

Lily leaned in and dragged her tongue over the droplet of

moisture. He tasted salty and sweet, the essence of masculinity — and just like the sex she knew they'd have if he could let go of his issues long enough to enjoy himself again. He hissed a sharp breath when she swirled her tongue over the head of his cock. She laughed and blew a hot breath over the damp skin.

Evan groaned. "You're torturing me."

"You don't like to be tortured?"

"It's a very good kind of torture, Lily." He smiled down at her, his eyes glazing over. If the past five days had been as unfulfilling for him as they had for her, he had to be ready to explode. She smiled at the thought.

"Well, since you put it that way…" She trailed her tongue down the length of his cock and back up, licking and stroking every inch of him until he moaned her name. She cupped his balls in her palm, the weight of them heavy and hot even through his pants. He arched his hips against her mouth, urging her to take his cock inside. His hands came to her hair, tangling there to hold her head in place. Needing no further encouragement, she slipped his length into her mouth.

He hissed and groaned, his hold on her head tightening in her hair to the point of pain. She lifted her mouth almost completely off him, and slid back down again, setting a slow, maddening pace she knew drove him nuts by the way he pumped his hips toward her as she stroked. He tasted amazing, like nothing she'd ever known, and the way he responded to her mouth filled her with a sense of power. She controlled his arousal, and would control when he came. She controlled the pace, and could tease and pleasure him at will. She loved every second of it.

Evan used his hands in her hair to guide her, showing her without words what pleased him. Her pussy grew soaked as she sucked and licked and kissed. A trickle of moisture ran down her leg. She squeezed her thighs together against the sudden rush of lust. She fought the urge to touch her clit and bring herself to orgasm. This was Evan's moment. The last time they'd been together, he'd given her so much. She wanted to return the favor.

Evan's grip on her hair tightened even more, his fingertips digging into her scalp as the muscles of his thighs clenched. "Lily, maybe you'd better stop."

Not in this lifetime. Call her selfish, but she wanted the whole experience, not just part of it. She sucked harder, took him deeper, urging him to let go and empty himself into her mouth. He fought it for only a little longer before he gave in to his climax, a long, low groan escaping his parted lips, his semen spurting against the back of her throat. He bucked against her, holding her head in place while he spent himself inside her. She swallowed down every drop. The whole experience left her weak and wanting. She slipped his softening cock out of her mouth, placing a gentle kiss on his thigh. He slid down to the floor and pulled her between his open legs.

He closed his eyes, his face flushed and his chest heaving. "Fuck, Lily. Are you trying to kill me?"

She laughed, her fingers stroking his chest. "I hope you're not too close to dying yet. I was hoping we could have a little more fun."

He popped an eye open, and then the other, and smiled at her. "Gee, I don't know. I think I'm kinda tired."

She reached between them and circled her fingers around his flaccid cock. After a few strokes of her hand, it started to come to life again. She winked at him. "Ya think? You feel pretty awake to me."

" *Shit.* That confirms it. You are trying to kill me." He laughed, his voice husky and tired. "Wanna chance floor burn on your pretty ass, or do you want to move this upstairs to my bedroom?"

"Who says you get to be on top?"

"Me." He moved her away and stood up, offering her his hand. When she took it, he pulled her off the ground and against his chest in one swift motion, sealing his lips to hers. His tongue slid into her mouth in a possessive gesture before he pulled away. "Bedroom, Lily. Before we don't make it there at all."

* * * * *

The second Evan slammed the bedroom door shut behind them, he was all over her. His hands were everywhere, his lips on her mouth, her cheeks, her neck. He yanked her dress over her head and tossed it across the room. He backed her into the door and brought his mouth to her breasts.

She arched into him and moaned, already halfway gone as his tongue flicked over her beaded nipples. His lips sealed over her skin and he sucked one nipple fully into his mouth, rolling it gently back and forth with his teeth. She cried out at the exquisite torture.

He cupped her breast in his palm, squeezing as he lifted it higher, angling his mouth to suckle her even harder. Little spasms ran through her cunt, soaking her with her own moisture. By the time he pulled his mouth away and moved on to her other breast, she couldn't catch her breath.

He lifted his head and flicked his thumb over her stiff nipple. She cried out, her orgasm looming just out of reach. She'd been so turned on from her first foray into oral sex that any little touch made her feel ready to tumble over the edge. He seemed to sense this, though, and held her back from where she wanted to be. "Please, Evan."

"Not yet. I want to enjoy this for a little while." He shoved his hips against hers, roughly thrusting against her. His hard cock pushed against her bare belly. She wanted him inside her, didn't want to wait another second. She reached a hand between them to touch him again, but he moved out of her grasp. "Your turn right now."

He seemed wild, out of control—even more than he'd been the last time they'd had sex. The thought thrilled her more than it should, and she gave herself over to him. He could do whatever he wanted. He pulled her away from the door and brought her over to the bed. He pushed her down on her stomach on the mattress, her legs hanging over the edge, and knelt behind her. She whimpered as he moved her legs apart and licked the length of her throbbing pussy. She arched into him, but he did nothing more than lick her, up and down, still holding her back by ignoring her clit completely.

"Stop it, Evan," she ground out. "I didn't tease you."

"Your memory teased me for days." He spread her lips and swirled his tongue over her clit, at the same time thrusting what had to be at least two fingers into her cunt. She whimpered, trying to squirm back against him, but he held her in place with a hand on her ass. Every time she got close to coming, he pulled back. He kept her hovering there for what seemed like an eternity, until she choked out a sob and begged him for release.

He thrust his fingers in and out of her cunt in time with the flicks of his tongue across her clit, and she came with a loud moan. She buried her face in the navy blue comforter, inhaling his scent as tears leaked from her eyes. Her body shuddered with the force of her climax, drawing another shaky sob from her. When Evan moved away, she felt strangely empty. Every cell in her being cried for him to come back.

When she felt his hand on her back, she glanced over her shoulder. He stood behind her, his huge erection jutting out from his body, a look in his eyes she'd almost describe as dangerous. *Uh-oh.* What had she gotten herself into?

She started to move away, but he didn't give her a chance to escape. He flipped her to her back, looming over her in a way that excited her, and made her just the tiniest bit nervous. He locked his arms under her knees and set his hands by her hips on the bed, spreading her legs wide. "Just how flexible are you, Lily?"

Oh God. She opened her mouth to answer, but only a wanton whisper came out. His gaze dropped to her pussy and he licked his lips. "You taste so good. I can't get enough of you. But I want something else now."

He slid his arms higher up the mattress, bringing her knees

level with her breasts. The position left her feeling open and exposed. Allowing him to take such liberties with her made her even wetter. He fit his cock against her entrance, staring down into her eyes as he held himself back. A quiver ran through her cunt as she waited for his thrust. "Evan, please. *Now.*"

He locked his gaze with hers as he sank into her. *All* the way into her. He pulled back and stroked in again, this time faster and harder than the first. The depth of his thrusts shocked the breath out of her. She could swear she felt him nudging against the back of her womb. She brought her hands up to his shoulders, hanging on to steady the dizzy feeling spiraling inside her. His shoulders heaved under her touch, his hot gasping breaths fanning her face as he pumped into her. He felt so amazing, and, at least for now, he was all hers.

He pushed her legs up a little higher, angling his hips to deepen the thrusts. The new position dragged a shuddering moan from her lips. She felt the orgasm begin low in her belly, spurred on by the sensation of being filled to completion by Evan's cock.

His thrusts grew even more erratic, more powerful, as his own orgasm approached. "I can't wait much longer," he told her, his voice not more than a whisper.

"So don't." As soon as she said the words, her orgasm exploded around her. She held tight to his shoulders to avoid being swept away as shudders shook her body and the world faded to sound and light. She gave in to the sensations, letting them flow over her, surround her, drown her in all she felt for him. She could never tell him how she felt, so she let it pour out in energy from her fingertips, hoping some of her emotions would meld with something deep inside of him and he'd see the truth. They couldn't be more perfect for each other. If he'd let go of his hang-ups, he'd see that.

"Let go, Evan," she whispered, meaning so much more than in the physical sense. As he convulsed above her, spurting his cum into her in hot waves, she hoped he'd started to let go of his emotions as well. She saw the truth in his eyes just before he snapped them closed and threw his head back, and it filled her with joy. He cared. He might deny it and pretend it didn't exist, but she'd seen it in his eyes. He couldn't hide it from her anymore. She smiled to herself as she ran her hand over the back of his neck.

Hold on to your denials while you still can, Evan. I don't intend to let you keep them for too much longer.

Chapter Twelve

Lily pried her eyes open as the sun spilled into the room. She yawned as things started to come into focus. Evan had woken her up three times during the night, his cock hard and ready for her. Her pussy had responded every time. She wasn't complaining, not really, but she dreaded having to work on very little sleep. Again. She stretched her hand across the bed, reaching out for him. Her heart skidded to a stop when she found his side of the bed empty again.

What the hell?

Hadn't they moved past all his stupid insecurities about what he thought she wanted last night? She'd thought so. So why was she here, all alone again, in Evan's bed…?

Wait a second. *Evan's bed?* She glanced around the room. Navy blue sheet set, matching comforter and curtains, dark-stained dresser, massive sleigh bed. Arousing masculine scent hanging in the air. Yep. Definitely Evan's bedroom. So if he wasn't in bed, where was he? The scent of something cooking— or was that burning?— caught her attention. She got up, pulled on the white T-shirt she found on the end of the bed, and wandered down the stairs and into the kitchen. She giggled when she saw Evan, wearing nothing but a pair of gray sweatpants, drop a pan into the sink while he cursed up a storm.

He froze, his shoulders hunched and his head down. "What's so funny?"

"Good morning to you, too." Her fingers itched to run down his back, to trace the line of every defined muscle.

"Is it now?" He spun around, his expression dark under a pair of thin, black metal-framed glasses. She'd never found glasses particularly sexy, but the slim, stylish frames looked good on him. They made him appear even more serious and intelligent, adding a depth to him she hadn't noticed before. *Definitely sexy.* Her mouth went dry as his expression brought back memories of the night before.

"Having problems?" She forced a light tone into her voice when she spoke, knowing he wouldn't appreciate being burdened with her emotions.

She stepped further into the room and leaned against the center island. The heat from the six-burner cook top in the middle of the island warmed her back. As sleep receded, she took in the spacious kitchen. Jealousy spiked in her stomach. She'd give anything for a kitchen like this. The room had to be at least twenty feet by twenty feet, with light oak cabinets along three of the walls. The countertops were blue granite—real granite, not the cheap veneer she had in her own kitchen—and the appliances were all top-of-the-line, brushed stainless steel. The back wall of the kitchen, free of cabinets and appliances, had several huge windows overlooking the back yard and the wooded area beyond the fence.

Evan cleared his throat. "I think you might be looking at my kitchen with more lust in your eyes than when you look at me."

"Does that offend you?" She chuckled when he narrowed his eyes at her. "I'm just kidding, Evan. Relax. But I have to say this is the most amazing kitchen I've ever seen. From the state of the pans stacked in the sink, though, I have to wonder if this place isn't going to waste on you." She ran her fingers over the shiny, smooth surface of the counter with envy.

Evan grabbed her hand, brought it to his mouth and kissed her fingers. "I ran into a slight problem trying to impress you with my cooking skills."

Oh, *really*? "What's that?"

"I don't have any." He smiled at her sheepishly, spreading his hands out in front of him. "I don't suppose you'd settle for a bowl of cereal?"

She wrinkled her nose and shuddered at the thought. "I never touch the stuff. Do you want me to cook breakfast?"

"I couldn't ask you to do that." He shook his head, a smile spreading across his face. "What am I saying? It isn't often that I have someone offer to cook for me. Especially a beautiful woman standing in my kitchen wearing my clothes."

She blinked up at him, a sliver of guilt running through her. Maybe she should have tried to find her dress before putting his on. "You don't mind, do you? I found it on the end of the bed."

"No. I put it there for you. I thought you might be more comfortable in this than the dress you had on last night. Which, by the way, looked absolutely *phenomenal*. Did I mention that I really like you in skirts?"

"I think you may have said that before." She stood on her tiptoes and gave him a quick kiss before moving to the fridge. "I'm working under the assumption that everything in here is fit to eat. Is there anything I should avoid?"

"Everything's fine."

Everything being a carton of milk, a small bag of shredded jack cheese, eggs, a pint container of strawberries, a quart of orange juice, and a plastic bag that held a piece of grilled steak. She laughed. "It looks like you haven't been shopping in weeks."

"I do take-out most of the time." He gave her an uncertain smile. "And I had a lot more in there, but I used most of it trying to fix you something edible."

Poor guy. She would have felt sorry for him, if the emotion hadn't been overcome by the humor of the situation.

And why did he feel the need to impress her, when he claimed to be interested in only her body? *Very curious.* Did he realize his actions broadcast his emotions a lot louder than his words ever did?

"You should come over for dinner once in a while." She took out omelet fixings as well as the steak and put the ingredients on the counter. "I don't mind having guests from time to time."

She bit her lip as she realized how her words must sound to him. Given his fear of commitment, he'd probably run in the other direction. But he didn't. He walked up behind her and pinched her ass. She jumped. "I seem to recall you telling me the last time how rude it was to invite myself to dinner."

"You were ogling nude pictures of me then."

He laughed and kissed the side of her neck, sending a shiver through her. "And it's better to have me ogling the real thing?"

"Much, now that I know what you can do with your hands." She smiled when a mock-insulted look passed over his face. "And your tongue."

"Watch it, or I might have to drag you back upstairs." He growled playfully against her hair, but when he ground his hips against her ass, she felt the beginnings of a very real erection.

"Not yet. I need food." She turned around and pushed him away when he started to wrap his arms around her. "I cannot cook with you hanging all over me. Can't you control your hormonal impulses for twenty minutes?"

"Okay, slave driver. Get on with it then." He pinched her ass again before he backed away to give her room to work.

She shook her head when he started to move toward the table. He might not be doing the cooking, but she wouldn't let him off the hook that easy. "Don't you dare go anywhere. You're going to have to work for your meal. Get me a bowl, a whisk, a frying pan that doesn't have something unrecognizable burnt to the inside, and a spatula. Do you have any cooking spray?"

"Cooking spray? What's that?" He blinked his eyes at her, his expression amusingly blank. "Would it be in the cabinet or the fridge?"

"Never mind. You obviously don't have any. Get some butter instead. Put a little in the pan—the clean one—put the pan on the stove, and turn the heat to medium. Let the butter melt while we get the eggs ready, but don't let it burn."

He grabbed a bowl out of the cabinet next to the fridge, and rummaged around in a lower cabinet until he found a clean frying pan. He set the pan on the stove and started melting the butter while he searched around in a drawer in the center island, finally pulling out a spatula. "Um, I don't think I have a whisk."

When it came to kitchen skills, the man was hopeless. If she was going to teach him how to cook, she would have to take him shopping first. "Okay. Get a fork instead."

"They're right there." He gestured to the drawer under the spot of counter where she got the ingredients ready.

"Thanks." She got what she needed and carried everything over to the center island, where Evan had the butter melting nicely in the pan. "You're off to a good start."

He raised an eyebrow at her. "I'm melting *butter*. This isn't exactly rocket science."

"Well, good. I'm glad you feel that way." She pushed the bowl and carton of eggs in his direction. "Crack these for me."

"And what are you going to do while I do all the work?" he asked, his eyes glinting with amusement.

"I'll crack the whip."

"Geez, you're bossy this morning." He shook his head, but did as she asked him to do. Once he had the eggs all cracked into the bowl, she added a little water and whipped them up with the fork while he disposed of the shells.

She jumped and squealed when he came up behind her and wrapped his arms around her waist. He licked the shell of her ear. "Have I mentioned how sexy you are when you take charge like this?"

Her pussy dampened as his breath brushed the side of her throat. She turned and wrapped her arms around his neck. "Why don't you show me instead?"

She closed her eyes and waited for his kiss, frowning when it didn't come.

"I would," he told her, "but you told me not to burn the

butter."

She sighed as he stepped away and turned his attention to the pan on the stove.

"Pour the eggs in," she told him. She sucked her lower lip into her mouth as she watched him cook. She studied his every move carefully, wanting to memorize it all. Her heart ached as she thought about their arrangement and its temporary status. She didn't want temporary, damn it. She wanted more. But whether or not he agreed remained to be seen.

A little while later they sat at his metal and glass table, the breakfast Evan had cooked on plates in front of them. She hadn't had to lift a finger with the meal. She'd only given him instructions, and he'd followed them without complaint. Part of her protested teaching him any more cooking skills. If he learned to cook on his own, that would be one more reason for him to stay away from her.

She brushed her hair behind her ears and let out a small sigh. It would be in her best interests to push those thoughts away for now and just enjoy the morning. She could think of ways to entice him to stay later, but she couldn't let it become an obsession. That would most definitely frighten him away.

"Did I tell you I ran into Toby at the video store?" she asked him in between bites.

He froze with the fork halfway to his mouth, his expression darkening. "Oh, really? What happened?" he asked slowly, his tone wary.

"He was in the adult section."

Evan sat back in his chair, his eyes wide. A laugh escaped him. "Really?"

"Yep. All that preaching about me causing the morality decline in town was just a front for his own issues." She set her fork down and picked up her glass to take a sip of orange juice. "And that's not all. Apparently he's a submissive and was too afraid to tell me, so he'd been seeing someone else on the side to get his needs taken care of."

Evan stayed silent for a few seconds, his gaze searching her face. His lips drew into a grim line and his jaw muscles ticked. "How do you feel about that?"

Was that jealousy she detected in his eyes as she talked about Toby? She almost smiled. "I feel a little hurt, obviously, because he lied to me and cheated on me. I'm angry because he didn't have the guts to come clean and tell me how he felt. But it all worked out for the best. I don't need a man who can't talk to me about anything and everything."

Would Evan have trusted her with a secret like that? She had a feeling he would.

He nodded, picking up his own glass and gulping half the juice. He set the glass down on the table with a thump and heaved a sigh. "If things had been different, if he'd told you the truth from the beginning, would you have stayed with him?"

She didn't even have to think about it before she answered. "No. I could never have provided for him what he needed. Like I said, it's better this way." She smiled. "But I don't think he's going to be giving me any more problems about the pictures. I've taken care of that quite nicely."

Evan's eyes narrowed. "What did you do?"

"Absolutely nothing, and I plan to keep it that way. But he doesn't have to know that." She lifted her glass and polished off her juice before she stood up from the table. "I really hate to cut this short, but I have to be at work in an hour. Let me help you get the dishes done before I leave."

She started to pick her plate up from the table, but Evan put his hand over hers. "I'll deal with the dishes. You go home and get ready. I'll give you a ride downtown if you want."

She started to say no, that she could manage the short walk to work just fine on her own, but for some reason—probably morning-after temporary insanity—she found herself nodding in agreement. That couldn't be a good sign.

Don't get used to this, girl. It isn't going to last forever. But she wanted it to. With all her heart.

Pretty sad, considering she barely knew the guy.

* * * * *

A half-hour later Lily stood propped against the passenger-side door of Evan's car inside his open garage. When he walked out the door and stood in front of her, her stomach fell to her knees. The sight of him in black pants and a charcoal gray shirt had her heart skipping a beat or two. Okay, a few hundred. The man was just too sexy for his own good. He was lucky they were in public, or she might have done something embarrassing like tear his clothes off and taken him on the cement floor. The more she thought about it, though, the more it seemed to be not such a bad idea. Maybe after work...she shook off the thought when she realized he was speaking to her. "What did you say?"

He kissed her cheek. "You're hopeless sometimes, you know that? I said, go around to the driver's side and get in."

"Why? Is this door broken?" She tried the handle. It opened fine. She wrinkled her nose. "What's going on? Is this some kind of kinky sex thing? Do you get off on watching women climb across the console?"

He laughed. "No. It's not a kinky sex thing. It's a learning to drive thing. Get behind the wheel."

A cold chill swept through her at his words. Learning to drive? Was he kidding? Or did he have a death wish he conveniently forgot to mention? She stood there, gaping up at him, her eyes stuck on rapid-blink mode.

"Lily?" He took her hand, turned it palm up, and pressed the keys into it before closing her fingers around the cold metal ring with the small, shiny instruments of death attached. "Go ahead and get in, okay?"

She shook her head as he moved her out of the way and climbed into the passenger seat. He shut the door and rolled down the window. "Earth to Lily. You're going to be late for work if you stand in the garage much longer. Stop the freaking out and get in please."

Spurred into action at the thought of being late, she hurried around the car and climbed into the driver's seat. She could barely see over the steering wheel.

"You'd better adjust the seat," he told her. "Pull it closer. You can't drive if you can't reach the pedals."

He didn't *really* expect her to drive his classic car, did he? She slid him a nervous glance out of the corner of her eye. Uh-oh. That's exactly what he had planned. "Evan?"

"Yes, Lily?"

She could see him just barely hanging on to his patience. Not a good thing since they hadn't even made it out onto the road yet. "You don't really want me to drive this through town, do you? On actual roads?"

"Roads would be preferable to back yards or sidewalks."

Oh, he had no idea what he was getting himself into. "Um, okay."

"Relax. It will be fine. Put the key in the ignition and start the car."

Breathe, Lily. If you pass out, you'll get the both of you killed for sure. She did as he instructed, her hands shaking so badly she feared she'd snap the key off in the ignition.

"Excellent. You're doing great."

"Oh, shut up." She shot him a dirty look at the patronizing tone in his voice. *No shit. Even a monkey can start a car.*

He chuckled. "Buckle your seatbelt."

"Good idea." Especially since she tended to cause... *problems* when she drove. She seemed to have a little trouble staying on the road.

She fastened the seatbelt around her and wiped her sweaty palms down her pants before gripping the wheel. "Okay. I think I'm ready."

"You think? You don't know?" Evan laughed again. "You've done this before. You're going to be just fine."

She rolled her eyes. He had *way* too much faith in her. "It's been ten years since I've driven anything more than the antique cars at the amusement park. I don't want to ruin your car."

"You won't. You're too careful for that."

She repressed a snort, knowing there was only one way to convince him of her horrific driving skills. She had to show him. She just hoped she didn't wrap his pretty car around a tree trunk in the process.

But he gave her the sweetest, most caring look as he leaned across the console and kissed her cheek. She melted. Maybe it wouldn't be so bad. He guided her to pull the car out of the driveway, and her hands barely shook as she did so. She should have taken that as a sign—a bad one—and stopped right then. She was too caught up in the way he looked at her to think about how horribly wrong she knew things could go from there to pay attention to omens.

Once clear of the driveway she put the car in drive and stepped on the gas. The car pitched forward so fast her face almost smacked the steering wheel. She stepped on the brake and the car screeched to a stop. Her head bounced off the headrest and Evan murmured a curse. She glanced over at him, expecting to find him praying. He just shook his head and motioned for her to continue.

"Take it slow. Nice and easy," he told her, his hand gripping his thigh so hard his knuckles turned white. She would have laughed had she not been the current cause of the white knuckles. Seeing him like that didn't do much for restoring her faith in her ability to drive. She let up on the brake and let the car glide down the street. Yeah. This was much more like it. Ten miles per hour might not get her to work in time, but it would get her there with all her body parts intact.

"Not *that* easy," Evan mumbled. "You've got to find a happy medium, or it's going to take us a month to get into town. Press down on the gas a little."

She growled in frustration. *Take it easy, Lily. You can do this. Evan is right here. He's not going to let anything happen to you. Just tap on the gas pedal…there you go. Good girl. Now keep the car on the* *road, keep the pressure on the pedal constant...*she looked down at the speedometer. Fifteen miles per hour. *Oo-kay.* Maybe she could give it just a little more gas. She pressed a little harder on the gas pedal and watched the speedometer needle move up to the twenty-five mark. *Good girl! You've got it.*

"Mailbox!" Evan's voice broke into her thoughts. She snapped her eyes back to the road just in time to yank the wheel to the left and avoid taking out Mrs. Parker's mailbox.

"How long did you say it's been since you've driven a car?" Evan asked, his breathing jagged and his face a pale, ghostly white. Well, she *had* warned him, hadn't she?

"Ten years."

"Yeah, it shows. You're a little rusty."

She choked on a laugh at his huge understatement. "No, this has nothing to do with being out of practice. I was pretty much this bad before." She managed a smile, despite feeling like she might pass out at any time. "At least I didn't drive *this* car through someone's house."

Evan coughed and smacked his chest with his fist. "Tell me you're joking."

"Of course I am." She laughed, starting to feel a little more relaxed. "It wasn't a house. More of a shed, really."

Evan leaned forward and banged his forehead on the dashboard, muttering something that sounded suspiciously like "Stupid idea, really stupid." *Huh.* She'd warned him, but he, like a typical pig-headed man, had chosen to ignore her repeated warnings.

He reached across the console and patted her thigh. "Slow down and stop at the stop sign at the end of the road."

She shook her head. She might be a terrible driver, but that didn't make her a complete idiot. "Ya think? I thought I might just drive right through and hope I don't hit something."

His fingers dug into her leg and she yelped. "Lily, this isn't funny. This is my car we're talking about. My *car*."

She frowned. He said the word car like a new mother would say baby. Shouldn't he be a little more worried about his *life*? "I get it. Your *car*. I promise I won't dent the thing."

I will not dent the car. I will not dent the car. She wondered how he'd feel if she caught it on fire. Probably he wouldn't like it very much.

Probably? He'd kill you, girl. Forget how you think he feels about you. The car is his baby. You hurt the baby, you die.

She had a feeling she wouldn't make it to work alive.

She was doing fine—great, even—until her palms got sweaty again. She tried to wipe them on her pants, one after the other, but she still couldn't hold her grip on the steering wheel. The car jerked left and right as she tried to remedy the clammy palm problem.

"What the hell are you doing?" Evan asked—*screeched*.

His outburst shook her even more and she dropped her hands from the wheel. She wheezed, unable to draw a full breath, as panic coursed through her.

"Hands on the wheel! Hands on the wheel!" Evan shouted.

Gasping for breath, he grabbed the wheel as the wind blew an empty trash barrel from the end of someone's driveway into the street. Directly in her path. What was this, some kind of sadistic video game?

She swerved to avoid the trash barrel, putting them right in the path of a small—but very sturdy-looking—tree. With a gasp from her and what sounded suspiciously like a whimper from Evan, she yanked the wheel away from the tree.

And stomped on the brakes just in time to keep from slamming into a chain-link fence.

With shaky hands, she slammed the car into park. "*Holy shit!*"

Evan, gasping for breath beside her, nodded. "Okay, you were right. No offense or anything, but you suck at driving. I think I saw my life flash before my eyes for a second there.

Maybe we should have practiced in a parking lot first. Next time, I'll have to remember that."

Did he hit his head on the windshield when she'd braked so hard? "Next time? Are you *high*? There will be no next time. There shouldn't have been a *this* time. I can't drive. Get over it."

He let out a deep breath and she could practically hear him counting to ten in his mind. After an endless second, he turned to her and smiled, despite the tension she still saw on his face. "Are you going to give up on teaching me how to cook?"

"No," she said softly, suspiciously, not liking his tone. "But that's different."

"Not so much." He put his shaky hand to her chin and managed a weak laugh. "If you won't give up on me, I'm not going to give up on you."

He'd change his tune damned quick the first time she hit something in his *car*. She wrinkled her nose. The next time, it would serve him right if she did total the damned thing.

Men.

She'd just have to figure out a way to convince the guy that another driving lesson would be a very bad idea.

Evan patted her shoulder, adding to her insecurity. "It's okay, you know."

No, it really wasn't.

She leaned forward and hit her head on the steering wheel.

Chapter Thirteen

Lily sat at the wellness center's front desk, sipping water from a blue plastic bottle and leafing through a magazine, when Marnie walked into the lobby. She smiled as she took a seat next to Lily.

"How's it going?"

"It's going. Been busy." Lily answered noncommittally. She yawned, her sleeping habits having gone downhill since she'd started seeing Evan. The past week and a half they'd seen each other when they could, but he'd been finishing a time-consuming project until late most nights. Their time together had consisted of a late-night romp in bed every few days followed by a rushed breakfast as they both hurried to get out the door. She smiled, thinking they sounded like a married couple.

Now where had that thought come from?

She didn't want to be *married* to Evan. She wanted him in her life, true, but marriage? Just the thought gave her hives. She was too impulsive to settle down with just one man. Not yet.

"How's the hunk across the street?" Marnie asked, yanking Lily from the unpleasant turn her thoughts had taken.

"Evan?"

"As if you have a whole street full of them. Yes, of course Evan."

"He's good." As good as can be for a man she was supposed to be having a fling with — a fling that had turned into so much more when she hadn't been looking. This was *so* not fair. She didn't have the time or the energy to deal with unwanted love.

Oh, no. She was so not in love with the guy.

Marnie tapped her fingernails on the white lacquer surface of the counter. "You don't look so happy anymore. I thought you and Evan had worked everything out."

"I'm fine."

"No, you're not." Marnie stepped around the counter and put her arm around Lily's shoulder. "You look like you need to talk. What's going on that has you so down?"

Lily heaved a sigh and dropped the empty water bottle in the bag she'd left sitting on the floor next to the chair. She did want to talk, and Marnie was a good listener. "Do you remember when I said after Toby and I broke up I'd never get serious with another man again?"

Marnie flopped into the chair next to her and propped her feet up on the counter. "Yep. Sure do."

"Well, I lied."

Marnie laughed and patted Lily's leg. "Well, I'd hope so. You've been seeing Evan for a few weeks now, right?"

Seeing? Not exactly the right choice of words. Screwing his brains out might fit better, but she'd ruined her so-called reputation enough with the pictures. "Yeah, so?"

"Generally, if you're seeing someone for more than a couple of dates, things start to get more serious."

Either that or the sex is so good, a person doesn't want to give it up. It was that good for her. Was it for Evan? He had a lot more experience in that area than she did, but he seemed to enjoy himself immensely every time. "Okay, I'm still with you."

"You'd be a very cold woman not to get attached to a guy like Evan," Marnie concluded, again patting Lily's knee again. Warped déjà vu of the birds-and-bees talk she'd had at twelve with her mother floated through Lily's mind. Talk about glossing over the important parts.

"But I don't want to get involved. Not in anything serious. Neither does Evan."

"Yeah, okay. Sure."

Lily snapped her head up at the sarcastic tone in Marnie's voice. "What do you mean by that?"

"You're not the casual fling type, Lily. You never have been. Look at how long you stuck it out with Toby the Cold Fish."

Toby the Lying, Cheating Asshole was more like it. Too bad he couldn't have been a little more honest in their relationship. "I've changed." Take that, Marnie. Take that Evan. Take that, self. She smiled with her new resolve, but didn't really feel it inside. Marnie's words rang a little too true.

"No, you haven't. You think you have, but you're really still the same sweet, brutally honest, impulsive Lily I've known forever." Marnie smiled. "You posed for the pictures after your breakup with Toby. I know you don't want to hear this, but do you think part of it had to do with revenge?"

"Of course not," she huffed. "I posed for them because I wanted to."

"I know you did. I'm not saying that you wouldn't have done them anyway, but I do think part of your decision came down to what happened between you and Toby. He wasn't very nice to you. He made you feel like less of a person—less of a woman—and you lashed out in a way that showed him how wrong he was."

She nearly had to sit on her hands to control the shaking. An icy ball of cold anxiety settled in the pit of her stomach. Marnie was right. Why had she not seen the reason before? Yes, she'd chosen to pose for the pictures as an impulse. At the time, she'd called it a way to liven up her stagnating life. But had she really done it, in part, to prove to Toby that she was more of a woman than he'd treated her? The answer hit her hard, practically knocking the wind out of her.

Yes.

Well, damn. What had she gotten herself into?

Lily checked her watch and let out a dramatic sigh. She

wouldn't let Marnie see how her astute observations had rattled her. "Okay, session's up, Dr. Marnie. Who do I write the check out to?"

"You can laugh about it all you want, Lily, but the truth still remains the same. Toby hurt you. You got your revenge." She gave Lily a wicked smile. "But it's not all bad. You also got a very hunky guy in the process."

When had Marnie turned into such a relationship guru? Marnie listened well, but Janet could be counted on for good advice and observations. Marnie couldn't even get her own love life straight, hanging around for seven years waiting for Joe to propose or get out of her life. But her words sounded so true, so well-thought-out. Lily was about a second away from calling the National Enquirer. Aliens had obviously abducted her sweet-but-just-a-little-bit-clueless friend and left a genius in her place. "You're right. About the revenge part. I never saw it that way before."

Marnie shrugged a shoulder. "What are friends for?"

"Support and the occasional psychoanalysis." Lily laughed.

"So, about Evan..."

"What about him?" Lily braced herself, not looking forward to Marnie's answer. What did Marnie think about her relationship—or lack of one—with Evan, and what would she suggest Lily do about it?

"He's not part of your revenge, is he?" Marnie asked, her voice hesitant.

Lily rolled her eyes despite the shock of fear that ran through her. Was that possible? Had she been using Evan to get back at Toby for turning into such a scumbag? Her mind said maybe, but her heart answered with a definite no. Having been told all her life to stop following her heart and to think before she acted, she chose her words accordingly. "Probably. He just got divorced, like, a few months ago. He's not looking for anything. I left Toby a couple of months ago, and I'm just looking for a little fun. What could be more convenient?"

"Falling in love with the guy isn't convenient."

"Who said anything about love?" As if she'd let herself do something stupid like that.

"Your eyes. When I first mentioned his name."

"Yeah, okay. Whatever." Lily shook off the uneasy feeling as she stood up and went to collect her things. She needed to go home, soak in a hot bath, and pretend Marnie didn't know what she was talking about. Love? That didn't even enter the picture. She couldn't love Evan. It didn't matter how smart, sexy, and incredibly handsome he was. It didn't matter that he could make her come six times in one night without breaking a sweat. Well, okay, not *much* of a sweat, anyway. It didn't matter that he made her heart stop with just a look, a touch, a sound. Or that she didn't want to be away from him long, and when she was, her heart felt empty. It didn't matter that—

Uh-oh.

Could Marnie possibly be *right*?

No way. Not a chance in hell.

But you—she kicked the little voice in the back of her head before it could start any problems.

Marnie followed Lily into the staff room. "Are you seeing Evan tonight?"

Lily shook her head, collecting her bag and heading toward the door. "He's working on a project. He'll be working late, so I'm all alone again." She didn't relish spending the night alone, but he promised her an evening out once he'd wrapped up what he was working on.

"Why don't you come to dinner with Joe and I, and Janet and Brick?"

Lily fought the urge to roll her eyes. The last thing she wanted to do was be reminded that her friends enjoyed normal relationships. At least closer to normal than what she had. "I don't think that's a good idea."

"Come on. We're going to Angela's," Marnie mentioned the

name of Lily's favorite restaurant, one of the few in town that didn't serve fast food or worse—health food.

Lily paused in the middle of packing her towel in her bag. It had been a long time since she'd had a good meal someone else cooked, and it had been nearly as long since she'd been out with friends and had a good time. And spending the evening with people would be a way to keep her mind off Evan and the ever-present gnawing in her stomach when she thought about him. "Okay, fine. I guess going out with two couples would be better than staying home."

Marnie beamed. "Meet us there at five. We're having an early dinner because Janet and Brick have plans afterward."

"Sounds good."

* * * * *

Standing in line at the bank, waiting to cash her paycheck, Lily started to have second thoughts. What had she agreed to? Why had she thought being the fifth wheel would help get her mind off Evan? Ha! It would make her think of him. Wish he was there with her, sitting next to her at the table. Waiting until he could take her home and make love—er, *have sex* with her.

She groaned in frustration, tugging on the end of her ponytail. Maybe it would be best to break it off with Evan before she got even more involved. And then she thought about the way he touched her, the way his deep voice stroked her like a caress, the way his touch seared straight to her soul.

Maybe not.

Maybe she should stick it out a little longer. Something like this was bound to fizzle out on its own, right? She shook her head. She'd begun to have serious doubts.

A man behind her snickered, and for the first time Lily noticed the unnatural silence surrounding her. Pulled from her thoughts by the stares of the men and the glares of the women standing in the long lunchtime line, she frowned. Would those pictures ever go away?

Doubtful.

She'd apparently been branded for life.

Women wouldn't meet her eyes, but the men were just the opposite. Most of them stared openly, a few of them having the courage to leer. She laughed to herself. When would these freaks get over it already? It wasn't like most of them hadn't seen a woman naked before.

The stares and leers she tried to push aside as jokes took a different turn once she'd cashed her check and gotten ready to leave the bank. A youngish-looking man sauntered up to her, his mouth twisted into an exaggerated smile and a glazed look in his blue eyes. His brown hair was slicked back from his face, looking greasy to the touch. She wrinkled her nose.

"Hey, baby, aren't you the one who was in *Seduced* magazine?" he asked a little too loudly. She resisted the urge to kick him in the shins.

What was this, Hollywood? Did she suddenly have to watch out for paparazzi? "No. You must be thinking of someone else."

He smelled like alcohol, which had her a little worried. She tried to step around him, but he put his big body in between her and the door and wouldn't let her pass. "What's the matter, sweetheart? I've seen everything you have. Don't get all shy on me now. Why don't you let me take you out to dinner?"

Because standing near him for more than two seconds made her want to throw up? "No, thanks. I have to go now. If you'll excuse me."

She tried to step around him again, but he caught her arm and pulled her closer to him. She did the only thing a girl could do in a situation like that. She kneed him in the nuts.

He groaned hard and leaned against the wall, but didn't go down. Instead, he turned his dark, glaring eyes on her. *Shit.* He must have been too drunk to notice the pain. She lifted her knee to do it again, but he was surprisingly quick for a drunken asshole. He put his hand out to grab for her, lost his balance, and knocked her on her ass.

Okay, that did it. No more playing around. This jerk was going down. Using her speed to her advantage, she jumped up from the ground and would have gone after him again—had her father not stepped between her and the drunken moron.

"Do you have a problem with my daughter, Stuart?" Frank boomed, his shoulders squared and his huge hands clenched into fists at his sides.

"No, Mr. Baxter. Of course not. I'm sorry."

Stuart Chambers. She'd thought he looked familiar. The freak was a friend of her brother Jake. Didn't these guys have anything better to do than chase her around? Why did they assume that, just because she'd posed nude in a magazine, that she'd automatically bare it all for them in private?

"You owe Lily an apology," Frank continued. He took a step toward Stuart and the smaller man shrunk back against the wall.

"I'm sorry, Lily," Stuart whispered, his gaze darting around the room. All eyes had turned to them, the movement and noise had come to a standstill. Lily's face flamed as she took in each and every gaze turned her way. She really should look into online banking.

"Go home and sleep it off, Stuart." Frank waved his hand toward the door and Stuart slunk away. If he'd had a tail, it would have been between his legs. Lily stifled an embarrassed laugh as she turned her attention to her father.

"Thanks, Dad," she said tentatively.

"Anytime, sweetie." For the first time in weeks, Frank Baxter actually smiled at his daughter.

"Huh?"

He put his arms around her and hugged her tight, not letting go for what seemed like an eternity. When he stepped back, a strange understanding filled his gaze. "Anthony and I had a good talk last week at dinner. He explained to me that you didn't do anything wrong."

"Oh, really? Tony said that, huh?"

He laughed. "Well, actually, he told me it could have been a lot worse. With as strict as your mother and I were when you children grew up, rebellion could have turned into a crack-addicted, pregnant hooker."

She blinked. Well, that was one way to get Frank's attention. "Oh, yeah. You guys are so lucky we turned out the way we did."

"In the long run, I have to agree that the pictures were...tastefully done."

Translation—they pissed him off in a major way, but he'd accept them as long as he wasn't forcefully reminded of them at every turn.

What was going on in this town? Had somebody spiked the drinking supply with Xanax? First Marnie's bump in intelligence, then her father's acceptance of her as a person? What was next? Would Janet start dating an astrophysicist?

Fat chance.

"Just do me a favor, Lily Jane."

Change my name and move out of state? "What do you need?"

"Don't do something like those pictures again, okay? I'm not a young man anymore, and I don't think my heart could take it."

She smiled. "Done."

She left the bank feeling better, though she doubted Frank's amnesty would last long. But it would be nice while it lasted.

* * * * *

Lily sat squashed in the corner of a little booth in Angela's, stuck between Janet's bony ass and the wood-paneled wall. Soft music played in the background, the low murmurs of diners at tables around them filling the air. The scents of garlic and tomatoes hung heavy in the room, making Lily's stomach knot. Watching Janet and Brick make kissy faces at each other all

193

night—and listening to all the juvenile sounds that accompanied the faces—had made her lose her appetite. Poor Brick. He seemed to think he and Janet had something special. Didn't he know Janet was a serial dater?

She almost felt bad for the guy. He wasn't typical of the type Janet usually dated. Yes, he was big—well over six feet with the shoulders of a linebacker. She understood where he'd gotten the nickname. If it was a nickname. No one's parents would be cruel enough to name their child after building materials, would they? All in all, he wasn't a bad looking guy. Lily might have been envious of Janet, if Evan didn't make every man she met pale in comparison. Brick had the same fair-haired, blue eyes, Scandinavian good looks as Janet. She laughed at the idea of the two of them having children. With Brick's height and Janet's beauty, they'd be giving birth to the next generation of supermodels.

He leaned his muscular arms on the table, engrossed in conversation about work with Joe. Janet had her arm around his shoulder, hanging on his every word. Lily shook her head. She gave their relationship another week, maybe two, before Janet got bored and walked away.

She glanced at the plate of spaghetti and meatballs in front of her. She pushed the food around on her plate with her fork, her stomach churning. Sitting here with Janet and Brick acting so publicly affectionate turned her inside out. It only served to remind her that what she had with Evan meant nothing in the grand scheme of things. She wanted romantic dinners, and flowers, and candy. She got a few nights of incredible sex, but it wasn't the same.

Her gaze snapped up to Marnie and Joe. Every once in a while Marnie shot him a dirty look out of the corner of her eye, and neither of them looked happy to be together. Why did they continue to hang on to something that had so obviously died a long time ago? Either it was time to make The Big Commitment, or time to move on to bigger and better things.

She blew out a breath. Wouldn't that advice work for what

she had with Evan?

In her heart, she knew it would, no matter how much she hated to admit it. Her heart had moved past the fling stage into some very dangerous territory. She should pull away before she damaged the delicate organ irreparably. But could she walk away from him now that she'd gotten so close?

What was wrong with her? She didn't want to be attached to him. She didn't *want* to feel anything for him but lust. He talked about friendship, but she couldn't even handle that. When their affair was over, they would have to make a clean break. There was no way she'd be able to see him, hang out with him, and not feel her heart break every time. A tear welled in her eye, but she batted it away. Crying over the situation would be stupid. She'd known what she was getting into from moment one. He'd been very honest about his feelings, and she doubted he'd change.

"Where's Mr. Fi—um, Evan tonight?" Janet asked in between breaks from the guy she apparently considered a human respirator. "He couldn't make it?"

"I didn't ask him," Lily mumbled. Yeah, that would have gone over well. *Hey, Evan? Do you want to go out to dinner with two of my friends and their significant others so we can watch them show each other how in love they are?* Like that would ever happen. "He's been busy."

Janet rolled her eyes. "So have you. That doesn't mean he needs to ignore you."

All eyes at the table turned in Lily's direction. She got a bad feeling in the pit of her stomach. Joe, the Mafioso in training, shook his head. "Do you want me to talk some sense into the guy?"

Um, no! "No, I think I'm really fine. We're not exclusive or anything."

Brick looked around Janet, his eyes widened with interest. "Oh, really? So you're not seeing anyone seriously, then?" He laughed.

Janet poked him in the ribs. "Don't even start."

Oh, this was such a mistake. She should get out of there before the room turned into a three-ring circus.

A teenaged busboy came by the table to refill their water glasses. He reached for Lily's glass across the table and his eyes widened. He caught one look at her, turned beet red, and dumped the whole pitcher of ice water into her lap. She gasped as the cold liquid seeped through her clothes and chilled her to the bone.

The busboy dropped the plastic pitcher onto the table with a thunk and picked up Janet's cloth napkin. "I'm so sorry. I don't know what got into me. Let me help you clean up."

Lily glanced down at the water puddling in her lap. *As if.* "If you even think about touching me, I'm going to break every bone in your hand."

The kid yanked his hand back as if she'd burned him. He stood there blinking at her, his expression frightened and uncertain. She dismissed him with a wave of her hand. "Get out of here before you dump my pasta over my head next."

She pursed her lips, watching him scurry away across the dark laminate floor, disappearing through the swinging doors into the kitchen before she grabbed her purse and gave Janet a shove. "Let me out."

Brick moved off the bench and Janet followed. She put her hand on Lily's shoulder, a pitying look on her face. "Lily, wait. Don't leave yet."

Did she want her to sit through the rest of the meal with her cold nipples beaded against her lavender T-shirt—now so soaked that it displayed every flower on her white lace bra? *Yeah, right.* "I have to get home and change. Thank you for inviting me."

She gave Brick, the leering bastard, a dirty look as she dug through her purse for the money to cover her meal. She pulled a damp ten out of her wallet and handed it to Janet. "I'll talk to you later, okay?"

"Yeah, sure," Janet said softly. Marnie mumbled a goodbye, which Lily ignored.

She left without a second look, storming out of the restaurant and down the street. She made it home in record time, stripped out of her wet clothes, and dropped them into the hamper. So much for a fun night out with friends. Why did she feel the need to put herself through the torture?

She pulled on one of her old T-shirts and climbed into bed, thinking if she slept the night from hell off, she'd forget about it by morning. The cool satin sheets felt good against her skin and she started to relax. Maybe she was making too big a deal out of the whole situation. She settled her head against the pillow and closed her eyes, belly breathing to relax herself. Amazingly enough, it worked. Soon she felt like she was floating on a cloud high above the world and all her troubles, soaring through the clouds.

She came crashing back down to earth—and her bad mood—when someone pounded on her door.

Who the hell would show up and bug her at bedtime?

She laughed when she caught a glimpse of the glowing red numbers on her alarm clock. Five past seven. When had she turned into an old lady?

She threw on a pair of shorts—didn't want a repeat of the Jake-at-six-am-episode—and walked to the door, expecting to find Janet or Marnie, or hope of all hopes, Evan. But when she swung the door open, she found out her visitor wasn't any of them, or anyone she wanted to see.

Toby stood on her front steps, a big, goofy, *stupid* smile on his face.

Chapter Fourteen

"Hello, Lily." Toby shuffled his feet on the cement steps, his hands clasped behind his back. He gulped audibly as she glared at him. "How are you doing?"

"What do you want?" she snapped, in no mood for pleasantries after the day she'd had. Hadn't she made it clear the last time they'd spoken that she was through with him?

He blinked and his idiotically happy expression faltered. "I was hoping we could talk."

"About what?" She crossed her arms over her chest and stared him down, trying to put a lid on her aggravation. It was a losing battle. "Should we start with your closet porn fetish? Or maybe the fact that you saw fit to get your sexual needs met outside the relationship? Or maybe, and this is my favorite, the fact that you couldn't manage to please me in bed because you faked being such a goddamned prude?"

Toby's expression went from uncertain to angry and his hands came up to his hips. He glared at her as he shook his head. "Knock it off, Lily. I just want to talk, not fight. Think you can be adult enough to handle that?"

After the evening she'd had? Doubtful. "I'm not in the mood for any of your peaceful crap. I've had a long couple of days. A fight sounds like a good stress reliever right about now. What do you think? Care to do a little verbal sparring?" She raised an eyebrow at him, knowing her words would irritate him. Toby preferred to be sweet and kind to someone's face and thrust a knife between their shoulder blades when they'd turned their back. The open confrontation would make him uncomfortable. She smiled at the thought.

Toby's eyebrows knit together in a frown. "Lily, this is

serious."

His expression—and the worried tone of his voice—made her wonder if he truly did have a problem. "What happened? Is everything okay?"

"No, not really." He slumped against the doorframe. "I've missed you so much."

What the hell? Okay, now she was certain. The whole world had gone crazy. "No, you haven't. I'd say you missed the sex, but since I wasn't what you were looking for, I wouldn't even go that far."

"But I have!" Toby whined, making her want to punch him in the nose. Didn't he realize whining made him look like a wimp? She hated wimpy guys. "Lily, I want to know if you'll consider taking me back."

"Why?"

"Because I love you."

What brought this on? Fear of spending his life alone? A latent brain tumor? "Okay. Whatever you say. Do you feel faint? Does your head hurt? Need me to call a doctor?"

"No. I'm trying to be serious, Lily. Why can't you understand that?"

"I'm being serious, Toby. I think you're *seriously* out of your mind. Can you please leave now before my head explodes from all this weirdness?"

She tried to shut the door, but he wouldn't budge from the doorframe. He looked down at her with big, sad puppy-dog eyes that made her sick to her stomach. Any second now, she'd wake up from this too-real and very strange dream and everything in her life would be back to normal.

Toby, apparently, hadn't yet figured out that he was a product of her overtaxed imagination. He tried to smile at her. "Just give me five minutes of your time."

Not likely.

She opened her mouth to tell him to do something obscene

to himself when she saw Evan coming up the steps. He gave her a questioning look and gestured to Toby. She shook her head and he smiled.

"Sorry I'm late, baby. I got caught up at work." He walked past Toby and planted a smacking kiss on her lips. When he pulled back, Toby glared at both of them.

"Who the hell are you?" He jabbed his finger at Evan when he spoke, his eyes shooting fire.

"Evan." He smiled and draped his arm over her shoulder. "Lily's boyfriend. Who the hell are *you*?"

"Toby. Her fiancé."

"*Former* fiancé." Lily rolled her eyes at the proprietary tone in Toby's voice. "We broke up, remember?"

Toby's face took on an almost desperate expression as his gaze darted from Lily to Evan and back again. "We wouldn't have, if you hadn't gotten scared and dumped me. I think we deserve another chance."

"And I think you deserve a punch in the gut. What a scumbag."

"Why don't you go watch your videos?" Evan stepped inside and waved the bag in his hand in Toby's face. A black plastic bag with the name of an adult toy store she recognized printed in gold letters on the side. A little thrill coursed through her at the sight. "We have more important things to attend to."

He slammed the door in Toby's face.

"Thanks. What a stroke of genius," Lily told him, trying to keep her breathing under control. Evan smelled so good and looked even better and that bag…he didn't really buy something from that store, did he? She shook her head, reminding herself not to get her hopes up. It had just been a diversion to get Toby out of the house.

"I only spoke the truth." Evan handed her the bag. "This is for you."

Her mouth went dry and her heart thumped against her

chest. "What's really inside it? Candy or something?"

"Something I thought you might enjoy." A sly smile formed on Evan's face and he gave the bag a poke with his index finger. "Open it up and find out."

Suspicion raised the hair on the back of her neck. What the hell had he done? The look in his eyes told her it was something naughty. Very naughty. Her knees went weak.

She reached into the bag pulled out a long box with a half-naked woman on it. She narrowed her eyes at him. Was he trying to tell her something? "A dildo, Evan?"

He winked at her and her knees went weak. "Yeah. I thought you might enjoy it on the nights I have to work late. On the ones I don't, like tonight, I'd like to help you enjoy it."

Her heart pounded in her chest at the heat she saw in his eyes, but she almost laughed when she looked back down at the box in her hands. "You've got to be kidding. Playing together? I don't really see that as sexy. I'm feeling more than a little embarrassed right now."

His deep laugh rumbled through every nerve in her body. He tucked his finger under her chin and brought her gaze back up to his. The intensity in his eyes made her want to melt into a puddle at his feet. "Believe me, sweetheart, a little play can be very erotic."

* * * * *

Lily had no idea how sexy she looked, spread naked before him on her bed, her legs parted and her eyes closed. The light of the setting sun that filtered in through the open shades caressed her skin, giving it a golden hue and brushing her light brown hair with golden blonde streaks. Her nipples stood up in firm peaks and her cunt was already dripping with moisture.

Evan's throat felt like he'd swallowed cotton, and his heart threatened to burst out of his chest it beat so hard. His tongue itched to catch the trickle of moisture seeping from her cunt, but he held himself back. She had to be the most perfect thing he'd ever seen, lying there trembling, her pussy swollen and glistening, her breasts heaving with each deep, uncertain, aroused breath she took. The fake cock had been a stroke of genius—just what he'd been looking for. He'd missed her for the past couple of nights, when he'd slept alone in his big, cold bed. He bet she'd missed him, too, and he wanted to make it up to her. He planned to make her come more times tonight than he ever had. That was an ambition worth aiming for.

"Evan?" she asked softly, gazing at him through half-lidded eyes.

Her whisper rippled through him, his cock hardening even more against his pants. "Yes?"

"What the hell are you waiting for? I'm starting to get cold."

He laughed. "Can't have that," he mumbled, stripping out of his clothes. When he'd removed everything, freeing his painfully erect cock, he joined her on the bed. She arched toward him and his mouth watered just thinking about sinking into all that wet heat. "Why so impatient tonight?"

"It's been days," she moaned dramatically. "I might explode from want if you don't touch me soon." She looked up at him as he leaned over her, a sly smile on her face.

Once she'd gotten past the unease at what he wanted to do to her, she'd gotten right into it. He couldn't wait to play, to show his woman another facet of the relationship they could share.

His woman?

No.

He shook off the funny feeling saying it in his mind gave him. Lily didn't belong to him, and he didn't belong to her. They were just having a little fun. If he'd been serious about her, he would have brought her jewelry. Or flowers. *Not* a six-inch purple plastic cock—which, he made sure, was an inch smaller than his own length. He just wanted to add a sense of adventure to their play. He didn't want her replacing him with a sex toy.

Stop thinking so much, he warned himself. It could be dangerous to his current state of mind. If he let himself get attached to Lily...well, he couldn't.

That's final.

"What do you want, Lily?" he asked, fighting to get control of the onslaught of emotions welling inside him. "What would you like me to do to you?"

Her breath caught in her throat when he bent down and captured a nipple in his mouth, swirling his tongue over the stiff peak before popping it out of his mouth.

"Whatever you want to do is fine."

He froze at her words. She had no idea the permission she'd just granted him. He bit back the satisfied smile threatening to break free and brushed his fingers over her cheek. "There are so many things I want to do to you. We'll start slow."

He picked the dildo up from the comforter and held it up for her to see. "Do you want this?"

Her eyes flared. "I want you to stop teasing me. I'm going out of my mind."

He trailed the tip of the toy up the inside of her leg. "You want this?"

She let out a soft moan that made his heart skip a beat. Either she really enjoyed his idea for light play, or she would do anything to please him. He didn't know which idea shook him more. The play turned him on, too, more than he could ever explain to her, but he'd bought the toy for another reason. He'd wanted to make her happy. Admitting it made him feel needy. He wasn't. Wouldn't let himself need her in any way.

He leaned in and whispered in her ear. "Do you know how much I want to fuck you right now, Lily? I can barely hold myself back."

Her whimper of arousal should have pleased him. But it left an empty, hollow feeling inside him instead. He couldn't tell her how much it killed him to pretend he felt nothing for her beyond sexual desire. It got harder and harder every day—and caused him to avoid her more and more. They wouldn't be able to continue the affair much longer, so he wanted to make it the best for her as he could while it lasted.

When he brought the dildo to her wet pussy and trailed it along her outer lips, she shivered. He liked that. He moved her lips apart with his fingers and traced the tip of the cock over her clit. Her lips parted on a low moan and she ground her hips up to meet his hand. He slid it back down to her entrance and pushed just the first few inches of the cock into her cunt. She moaned.

"Do you like this, Lily?"

She nodded as she drew a deep, gasping breath.

"Still think it isn't sexy?"

"No." She tried to smile, but barely managed it. She shook her head as a shudder racked her beautiful body. "It's very sexy. Very arousing. But if you don't stop teasing me I'm going to have to beat you."

"Sounds like fun." He laughed. "Another night, though. Tonight, it's my turn to have all the fun."

Her glare melted into a lust-filled gaze as he stroked the cock into her. She spread her legs further, giving him better access, while he thrust the toy in and out of her with as much slowness as his shaking hands could manage. He circled her clit with his thumb, slowly stroking her, bringing her to the very edge of madness before pulling back. She whimpered and arched her hips as he pulled the toy out of her, but he shook his head.

"Patience. You're going to come when I'm inside you, and not a second before."

He trailed the dildo up her body, leaving a path of her moisture on her abdomen, and brought it up to her lips. "Open your mouth."

He thrust it into her mouth a few times, his cock twitching as she got into the play. She swirled her tongue around the purple head, sucking it deep with every thrust. And then she opened her eyes and winked at him. He froze. She was deliberately teasing him, turning him on as she pretended to be lost in the throes of lust. He'd been trying to work her up, and he had, but she'd managed to bring him to the edge of control right along with her. He laughed. She thought she was so funny? He'd show her.

He pulled the dildo out of her mouth, dragging the tip down her chin, across her collarbone, and to her breasts. Alternating between heavy and light pressure, teasing strokes and circles, he played with her nipples until she cried out. She arched into the touch, gasping for breath, her lips parted in an "O". A ragged moan escaped her and she dug her nails into his thigh. "Stop teasing, Evan."

He smiled down at her as he shook his head slowly, dropping the toy to her navel and circling around the sensitive skin of her abdomen. She grabbed his wrist and dragged his hand lower, stopping as he rested the toy against her pussy.

"Show me what you want me to do," he told her. Irritation warred with lust in her gaze and he thought he'd taken the game a step too far. But she surprised him. With her hand over his, she helped him guide the cock into her cunt, pumping in and out in leisurely strokes.

"Do you want more than that?" he asked, not able to take his eyes off her pussy as they worked together to pleasure her.

"Yes," she whispered, her voice thready with need. "Touch my clit."

He brought the fingers of his free hand to the bundle of nerves, stroking lightly. "Like this?"

"Don't be an idiot. Harder."

He smiled as he increased the pressure and pace. She dropped her hand from his as she bucked against his fingers and the thrusting toy, rewarding him with a powerful, nearly instant orgasm that shook his world as much as hers. Her cunt muscles clenched around the dildo as he continued to thrust it in and out of her. He stopped stroking her clit and pressed his finger down on the pulsing flesh, milking the last of her shudders from her. She reached for his cock, but he moved out of her way. One stroke and he'd be done for. He wanted to be inside her, soaking up the last shudders of her orgasm, when he came.

He couldn't wait another second. He dropped Lily's new toy to the floor, fit himself between her legs, and thrust his cock into her cunt in one long, complete stroke. She wrapped her legs around his waist, digging her heels into his ass, spurring him on as he pounded into her. His pace was frantic, growing more erratic by the second, and he could do nothing to stop it. He finally let go and groaned as he came into her, collapsing on top of her, his lust sated. He kissed her softly as he rolled to his back and pulled her on top of him.

"Well?" he asked when they could breathe again. "What do you think? Silly, still?"

She shook her head, her eyes cloudy with sleep. "Not even close."

He pulled her into his arms and let himself wrap around her as they fell asleep.

Chapter Fifteen

Lily stood at the stove at six the next morning, stirring the scrambled eggs and bacon sizzling in the frying pan. The scent of French toast mingled with the scent of bacon in the air to create an enticing aroma. If Evan didn't wake up soon, there had to be something wrong with his nasal passages.

She took a sip from her coffee mug—her third refill since climbing out of bed an hour ago. The caffeine did nothing for the fatigue slowly creeping up on her after a fitful night of tossing and turning. Evan hadn't kept her awake. He must have been tired from his workweek, because he slept soundly through the whole night. She, however, hadn't been able to get her eyes to close. The playful bout of sex coupled with the feelings for him she could no longer deny, shook her right to her core. She'd needed to get out of bed before she'd do something stupid.

Like waking Evan up and telling him how much she loved him.

She laughed at herself despite the seriousness of her sudden situation. *That* would have sent him running in the other direction for sure.

But it was the complete and utter truth, as much as it pained her to admit it. She loved him. Probably had for a while, despite denying it for so long. Marnie had been right—she hadn't changed. She really couldn't do casual sex. But in this instance, she didn't have a choice. Evan didn't want a relationship and she'd promised not to push him. She had to find some way to get over him before she slipped and told him how she felt.

She sensed his presence more than heard him walk into the room. Not a good sign. When a woman started to feel her lover behind her without needing to turn around, she'd gotten a little too attached. She pretended she didn't notice him as she scooped the eggs onto a plate.

He came up behind her and wrapped his arms around her, his breath tickling her ear. "Do you need any help?"

"No, thanks. I'd rather not make a run to the emergency room on my day off."

"You have the day off? I thought you taught on Saturdays?"

"I did. The class was cancelled due to low enrollment." She sighed and shook her head. "I swear, those stupid pictures are going to ruin my mother's business."

"I wouldn't count on it. They'll get over it." He kissed her ear and she fought the shiver that ran through her at his touch. A tear welled in her eye, but she ignored it. This was not a time to cry. She'd known all along their fling would end someday. *Someday* had come sooner than expected, but she had to learn to deal with it.

"I hope they get over it sooner rather than later. It isn't fair that the wellness center should suffer for something I did." She shrugged, her mood taking a turn for the worse. Those pictures...she didn't want to regret them, but everything in her life seemed to deem that she should.

"Don't feel bad about it," Evan said, seeming to read her mind. "You looked incredible. I'm very proud of you."

"Um, thanks." Why did he have to pick now to be proud of her? She couldn't dump him after what he'd said. He was the only one who made her feel good about herself, and at the moment, she needed the moral booster.

"You're welcome."

She heard the tension in his voice and suspicion kicked in. Was he trying to make her feel good about herself, or did he have an ulterior motive? She turned around and stared at him. The troubled look in his eyes told her he hadn't been completely honest with her. She frowned. "Tell me what's up or I'm going to dump these eggs over your head."

Evan sighed and ran a hand through his hair. She thought he might lie to her, but he walked across the kitchen and slumped into a chair, his gaze pained. "I got the wedding invitation from Jessica and Scott."

Oh, great. Lovely. She didn't need his emotional pain, or to hear about his ex, when she had so many things on her mind. Hearing the man she loved pine away for his ex wasn't her ideal way to spend a Saturday morning. Still, she couldn't turn him away, not when he needed her. Even if he'd never love her back.

"What are you going to do?" she asked. "You aren't going, are you?"

He snorted. "No way. I couldn't put myself through that. I think, too, that I'm ready to move on."

A tiny spark of hope flared inside her. She waited for him to say that he wanted to move on with her, but of course, he didn't. Because it wasn't true. The only place he wanted to move on with her was in her dreams. And maybe his nightmares. "Well, good for you." *Then I guess you have no use for me anymore, do you?*

The truth of the matter struck her then, as she stared at him staring at her. She'd been his transition woman. He'd told her he hadn't been with anyone since his divorce. Lily had been just the convenient woman across the street, good for a lay.

Disposable.

Her heart clenched into a painful ball and she fought back a fresh onslaught of tears. What was with her? She never cried. Ever. But it seemed to be commonplace around Evan.

He was *so* bad for her.

Get a hold of yourself, Lily. He wants to talk. He considers you a friend. If you play your cards right, you might just get to keep him, after all.

She forced herself to sit across from him at the table, fold her hands demurely in front of her, and listen to what he had to say.

"I still want to send a gift, though," he continued, giving her a funny look that made her more than a little suspicious. "You know, for old time's sake?"

Old time's sake, my ass. He was up to something, and she could just about guarantee she wouldn't like it. "Okay, I give. Tell me about the gift."

"I was kinda hoping I could talk you into giving me that autograph."

Shit. She should have seen this coming. She'd been too blinded by her own idiocy—and her love for a selfish jerk who thought of her as something no better than last week's trash—to notice. "You've got to be kidding. Why?"

But she knew why. He wanted to show off the woman he'd been screwing—or at least how that woman looked all made up and airbrushed to kingdom come. What had she been thinking? The guy was scum, like all men. An icy blast of anger froze her blood, effectively cooling any stirrings of lust she might have felt. What a stupid fool she'd been, buying into all his talk of friendship.

Shut up, Lil. You're overreacting. This is what you wanted from the beginning, remember?

She didn't love him. She just wanted a roll in the hay—just like he did.

Obviously.

She was lying to herself, but she just couldn't help it. She needed to stop clinging to a man who had no interest in anything she had to offer in the long term. She needed to get it through her thick skull what she was to him.

A trophy.

He just wanted to say he'd screwed a nude model.

Well, fine. She could play at this, too. She didn't need him, or any other man for that matter. She was better off alone, just like she'd said all along. She shrugged, trying to seal off the part of her heart that wanted to scream out at the unfairness of it all. She finally found a man who didn't bore her to death after the first few dates, and he wanted nothing more from her than an autograph across her breasts so he could send it to his ex-wife. *Scumbag.* "Sure. Fine. Whatever. Bring me the magazine and I'll sign it for you."

She kept her expression impassive as he leaned over and kissed her on the cheek. "Thanks, babe. You're the best."

And you deserve to get hit by an eighteen-wheeler on your way across the street. "No problem."

She smiled sweetly, her anger too fresh to feel her heart breaking. She brushed aside the pain as a new resolve formed a lump of stone in her chest. He wanted an affair? Fine. He could have it. But he could forget the friendship they'd started to form. She'd be what he wanted her to be when they'd first agreed to the fling.

A warm body in his bed. Nothing more.

"Hey, are you busy today?" he asked as he pushed himself up from the chair and went to the counter to pour a cup of coffee. "I want to run home and take a shower after breakfast, but I thought maybe we could go out for another driving lesson, since you don't have to work."

What a saint, the wonderful man trying to teach the poor dumb slut how to drive.

Not.

She gritted her teeth. "How about later this afternoon? I have a few things I want to do first." *Like climb back into bed and bawl my eyes out like some kind of little kid before I plot my revenge against you, jerk. How does taking you apart piece by piece sound?*

She took out a plastic container and piled the entire pan of eggs and bacon into it. She slapped the cover on it and dropped the container on the countertop next to his mug. "Here. Enjoy. I'll catch up with you later."

"Are you kicking me out?" He blinked at her, confusion spreading across those dark-chocolate eyes. She almost felt bad for him. Almost.

She shrugged. "Yeah. I didn't sleep well and I'm really

tired. I want to catch a nap, and then I have a few errands to run."

"Oh. Okay. I guess I'll see you later. Come by around noon?"

No way. Her face would still be red and puffy. Besides, she wouldn't be able to spend the entire day with him without strangling him or breaking down in tears every time he looked at her. "Better make it four o'clock. That will give me plenty of time to get everything done."

"Sure. Fine. Whatever you say," he agreed, but didn't look happy about it. He leaned in to kiss her, but she turned and he only got her cheek. He frowned. "Are you mad at me about something?"

The autograph, you friggin' moron. In one sentence, he'd managed to make her feel like what she'd been trying to convince everyone she wasn't. A tramp. "I don't mean to be snippy. I'm just tired, okay?"

"Yeah. Great. I'll see you at four?" He stared at her for a few seconds too long, a pained look in his eyes. It killed her to stand there, keeping her expression impassive, when she really wanted to jump into his arms and never let him go.

"Four it is. I'll meet you at your house."

He nodded and turned to leave, giving her one final shake of his head as he walked down the hall toward the front door. As soon as the door closed behind him, she slumped back into her chair and put her head on the table, refusing to let herself cry.

He's not worth it, Lily.

That stupid little voice inside her took that moment to chime in its own opinion.

Oh, yes he is.

* * * * *

"I think you're finally getting the hang of this," Evan praised as Lily drove his car through the quiet side streets.

"Keep going. You're doing great."

"Thanks." She shrugged, apparently doing her best to ignore him, like she had been all afternoon. What the hell was up with her, anyway? If this was about the autograph, why didn't she just say so? If she'd changed her mind, fine. He'd forget about it. It didn't mean that much to him. He didn't like the silent treatment. And he'd come to find out he didn't like Lily mad at him, either. *Not even a little bit.*

Did that say something for the way he felt about her?

Don't be stupid. She doesn't want you for anything more than a fling. But what if she did want more? What if she'd gone into this expecting him to change his mind? He glanced at her, taking in the grim set of her jaw, the sparks of fire in her eyes, the lips drawn into a scowl. Something had her in a tizzy this afternoon, but she wouldn't tell him what. Her anger ate at him, turning him inside out.

And if he didn't start paying attention to the road, she was going to run his car into someone's house. He shook his head and focused his gaze on the road ahead and on her driving. It seemed the lady worked very well under pressure.

"What do you say to a celebration dinner?" he asked, crossing his fingers that she'd say yes. He'd do anything to put the smile back on her face.

But she didn't smile. She rolled her eyes. "To celebrate what? The fact that I'm not going to be convicted of vehicular homicide, or assault of a chain link fence?"

He laughed, though he didn't see much humor in the situation. "Sure. Why not?"

"Are you paying?" She slowed the car to a stop for a stop sign.

"Yep."

She shrugged, never taking her eyes from the road. "Okay, then. I guess dinner won't kill me."

He frowned. That didn't sound very promising. "Lily, are you okay?"

"Why wouldn't I be?"

"You seem a little distant. If this is about the autograph, forget it. It was a stupid idea, and I'm sorry."

She pulled the car over to the side of the road and shifted into park. When she turned to look at him, he thought he saw sadness mixed with the humor in her eyes, but it flashed away before he could be sure. "It's not about the autograph. It's not about *you* at all. I just want to enjoy this time we have together, okay, because you and I both know that it's not going to last forever."

His breath caught in his throat and his heart stopped. Why did that sound like the most horrible thing in the world?

He shook off the bad feeling her attitude gave him and patted her knee. They'd work this out. Everything would be fine. "Where do you want to go for dinner?"

"Do you like Italian? How about Angela's?"

"Sounds good." He nodded, though he didn't care where they went. He just wanted to get her somewhere public, where she didn't have to concentrate on driving but wouldn't make a scene, and have a discussion with her about their future. He had to find out if she wanted more.

"Excellent. I'm starved. I don't feel like driving anymore. Why don't we get out and walk from here."

He got out of the car and met her on the sidewalk. She placed his keys in his hand.

"Do you think you'll be ready to get your license soon?"

She shook her head. "I don't know if I want to. I'll have to think about that."

"Well, why the hell not?"

She turned to glare at him. "Because it's my life, okay? I don't need you or anyone else telling me what to do."

Okay. *Fine.*

He could see this was going to be a fun evening.

She sped down the sidewalk toward the restaurant and he

had trouble keeping up. He finally had to run to catch up with her. He grabbed her arm and hauled her back against him, stilling her movements. "What's the hurry?"

"I told you. I'm starved."

She was such a liar. He saw it in her face. What was her problem? He smiled despite the cold lump that had settled in his stomach. This night was going to end very badly if he didn't do something to change the direction they were headed.

He shoved aside his need for serious conversation and brushed a soft kiss over the shell of her ear. "Me, too. But food isn't the first thing on my mind. You are."

Her eyes darkened as she looked up at him. He smiled in triumph. So that's what this was all about. She was uncomfortable with the new direction their fling had taken in the recent days. Well, good. He felt uneasy about it, too. Maybe it was time to get things back on track and get back to the sex they'd first agreed upon when starting out in this...affair. If he couldn't convince her with his words to let things develop into something more serious, he might still have a chance at convincing her using other methods. Orgasms. Lots of them. Repeatedly until she realized they should at least give a real relationship a chance.

And if that didn't work, he'd have to kidnap her and tie her to his bed until she caved.

He hoped it wouldn't come to that. He didn't need to be brought up on charges, but he refused to let his woman go without a fight. And she was his. He could admit it to himself now with only a small sliver of discomfort.

"Really?" she asked, her voice small and deceptively meek. He nearly laughed. Lily didn't have a meek bone in her body.

He leaned in and ran his tongue along the skin just below her ear. "Really. I can't wait to get you into bed tonight."

"Who says you'll be getting me into bed?"

The tremble in your legs does. "Me."

She closed her eyes and let out a sigh. "We'll see."

He shook his head, brushing his lips back and forth against her neck until she whimpered. "We both know what's going to happen when we leave here. But maybe I still have a few surprises for you."

"Surprises?" She ducked out of his grasp and stepped under the restaurant's awning, spinning on her heels with her hands on her hips. "What kind of surprises? Like last night?"

He shook his head, though the idea held more than a little appeal. "Nothing like that. You'll see."

He took her arm and steered her through the restaurant door, not willing to answer any more of her questions. In truth, he had no plans for the night. He just knew he wanted her under him, around him, naked and screaming his name.

And if he didn't stop thinking such lascivious thoughts, he'd probably burst right out the zipper of his jeans. *Down, boy.*

The hostess showed them to their table—unfortunately right in the middle of the room under an enormous globe light, leaving no chance for play. At least not any play he knew Lily would accept. He decided to go the verbal route instead and see where that led them.

"What are you having?" she asked him, glancing at her menu with a frown on her face.

"You."

"Stop. Now. I'm talking about dinner. This was your idea, remember?" She kicked his shin under the table. He winced as the toe of her shoe struck the center of the bone.

Oh, he remembered. Why hadn't he suggested takeout? Something he could have eaten right off her body? He shivered at the thought. Next time…next time he would definitely have to try that. And he knew Lily—she'd be more than willing to try anything he suggested.

Another thought that made him shiver. Right down to his toes.

"Yes. My idea. I know. Bad idea, I'm thinking."

She glanced over the top of her menu at him, her eyebrows raised. "Why is that?"

"Because everyone is staring at you. I think I'm getting jealous."

She frowned. "What? No. No one is staring at me. I would have..." her voice trailed off as she set her menu down and looked around the restaurant.

Many eyes rested on her incredible body, and Evan resisted the urge to growl "mine". That would have been a huge mistake, considering it probably would have earned him Lily's running shoe up his ass.

Her eyes narrowed and her face reddened. He put his hand on her forearm to keep her from standing up. She didn't get it yet, but making a scene would only make matters worse when it came to wanting everyone to forget about those stupid pictures. He had the strange urge to yell. All these men wanted her, some probably went home and made love to their wives and girlfriends thinking about her, but only Evan got to take the real Lily to bed at the end of the night.

He shook his head at the glare in her eyes as she looked around the room. The real Lily, he'd come to learn, was about so much more than a few naked pictures. Pictures that really didn't look all that much like her, if he had to admit the truth. Compared to the siren in the magazine, Lily was fresh, young, and innocent. He loved all of that about her.

But he absolutely, positively, did *not* love Lily.

Because that would be wrong.

They'd gone into this fling looking for a little affair, some satisfaction between friends that could end at any time and they'd walk away, their budding friendship still intact. But—

No buts, Evan. Lily didn't want more from this relationship. Any time things started to get serious, she got angry. He'd be better off forgetting his plan and walking away before he got too serious.

Keep on lying to yourself, buddy. One of these days you might actually believe some of that shit.

He pushed a hand through his hair and took a big gulp of his water. What would it take to make that stupid voice in his head clamp its annoying little mouth shut? He cared about Lily, yes, and he wanted to see what the future held for their relationship, but love most certainly did not enter the picture.

"Are you okay staying here?" he asked her, half hoping she said no. He could use any excuse to get away from the very public restaurant dining room—so he could take her to bed and show both of them that his hands were shaking for some other reason than falling in love. It was lust. Plain and excruciatingly simple.

That. Was. *All.*

He needed to prove it to her, as well as himself.

"I'm fine." Lily pulled her hand out from under his and picked up her menu again. "What about you? Are you sick? You don't look very good."

He let out a small, shaky laugh. She had no idea. "I'm fine." *Just head over heels in an emotion I refuse to name, with no hope of breaking free. Ever.* "I must be tired. We had kind of a long night last night."

She blushed, a rarity for Lily. He liked it.

"Yeah, I guess we were a little busy." She buried her face further into her menu so that only the top of her head showed over the green cardboard. "It was interesting."

"And a hell of a lot of fun."

She snapped her gaze up to his. "You think so?"

He nodded. "Next time I go to that store, I want to take you with me." He took her hand away from the menu and cupped it between his. He leaned forward and continued speaking in a whisper. "There are so many things I want to try with you. Do you remember that night on the phone, when I told you I wanted to fuck your ass?"

Her eyes widened and she let out a little squeak. Her hand

shot out from between his so fast she knocked her water glass over. It hit the table with a thunk followed by the clink of ice cubes as they scattered on the smooth wooden surface. She swiped her napkin off the table and mopped up what little water had been in the glass, her hands shaking, refusing to meet his gaze. "Sorry. I didn't mean to be such a ditz."

"That just comes naturally to you, doesn't it?"

That got her attention. She snapped her gaze to his and stuck her tongue out at him. Her toes connected with his shin again, a little harder this time.

"Hey! Cut that out!"

"Why? I'm having so much fun." She smiled sweetly just as the waiter stopped next to their table. She glanced at the guy and her face clouded over. She let out a breath and rolled her eyes.

What was that all about?

"What can I get for you tonight?" the kid asked. His eyes widened with abject fear when he saw Lily. Did Evan need to beat the crap out of this kid?

Lily caught his gaze and shook her head. "I'll have the fettuccine alfredo and more water to drink." She gave the waiter a gentle smile and Evan felt a pang of jealously. "And make sure this time the water is in a glass, not on my lap."

The boy blinked. "Yes, ma'am," he said, nodding vigorously, before turning his attention to Evan. "What can I get for you?"

"The same."

Evan glanced at Lily after the waiter had left them to deliver their orders to the kitchen. "What was that all about? Do you know him or something?"

"I came in last night with some friends. He got a little nervous and dumped a whole pitcher of water in my lap."

Evan would have laughed, if he hadn't been stuck on the "friends" part of her story. "With Marnie and Janet?" he asked, hoping like hell they'd had a girls' night out and she hadn't been seeing someone else on the side.

"Yep, those two, and their boyfriends."

"Oh." His voice sounded as flat as he felt inside. "That's nice. And you were on a date, too?"

"Nope. I went solo. I would have called," she told him, her hand resting on his, "but you said you had to work late. Plus, I thought you might be uncomfortable spending time with them, since we're not dating or anything."

What the hell did she call what they were doing right now? It sure the fuck seemed like a date to him. He shook his head. "Yeah. Whatever."

"Evan?"

He didn't even look up. Instead, he concentrated on a nonexistent spot on the table. What was it going to take for him to get the point? She'd told him, in many ways, that she wanted nothing to do with a long-term relationship. He needed to let go of that hope before it destroyed him.

"Evan, come on. Don't be like this. We agreed from the beginning to keep this casual."

Yeah, and if he'd known from the beginning how much casual *sucked*, he never would have agreed to it. But he had, and now he had to live with it. "I know. I just think…" He looked up at her, into eyes filled with denial as she slowly shook her head. *Shit.* He couldn't do this to her. She wanted casual, fine, but he didn't think he could take it anymore. It would be better if, after tonight, they went back to being just neighbors like they'd been before this whole stupid thing even started.

He'd miss her touch, the way she felt around him when he made love to her, but it would be better to break away now, before things got out of hand, than to wait until he couldn't breathe without her and acted like some lovesick fool when she left.

"So, are we okay here?" Lily asked, her fingers wrapping around his.

"Yep." No way in hell. He was so not okay that he wanted

to get up and leave before she had a chance to do any more damage to his ego. Or his heart.

She kicked his shin again, but this time it was more of a tap to get his attention than a kick meant to cause pain. He looked up at her and she smiled, her eyes sad. "It's for the best, Evan. All of it."

Didn't he know it. Lily looked down at the table, refusing to meet his eyes until the waiter came back to the table with their food. They ate in silence for a while, Evan's mind stuck on Lily and what he could do to turn things in his favor. It all came back to that one thing they had in common—their explosive chemistry in the bedroom. He had to give it one more shot. But if, after tonight, she still wanted to keep things casual, he'd have to walk away for good.

"Hurry up and eat," he told her. "I need you so bad I can't even breathe."

Her eyes widened and she gaped at him. "What? Why the sudden turn of events?"

"I want you. Tonight. All night, Lily." Because it would have to last him the rest of his life.

She dropped her fork to the table with a clatter. The creamy white sauce from the pasta twirled on the fork splattered in all directions. And all over his black shirt. *Better work on that timing, buddy.*

She scooped up her already-soaked napkin and leaned over the table, trying to wipe the sauce from his shirt. "God, Evan, I am so sorry. I don't know what my problem is. I'll buy you a new shirt if this doesn't come out."

"Nothing a little laundry detergent won't take care of." He grabbed her hand and stilled her movements before she soaked him right through to his skin. He brought her fingers to his mouth and sucked her index finger inside. She let out a small whimper and her eyes sparked with sudden lust, fueling his own desire to have her. He needed one last time before it all blew up in his face, and he wanted to make it something he'd remember for a long time to come.

She'd remember, too. He'd make sure of it. Lily's natural curiosity of sex fascinated him. He knew, despite her willingness, she hadn't had the opportunity to try new things. He liked how open she was to suggestions, and how she never tried to hide her enjoyment. Tonight, he had to do something that would break down all her walls. He had to show her everything he felt. This was his last shot, and he intended to make it a good one. Even if he couldn't say the words, he could still show her the emotions that ran deep inside him. It sounded simple. But was it really?

He didn't know. Nothing seemed clear anymore. He ran his fingers along the inside of her wrist, delighting in the gasp that escaped her lips. He needed to get her out of there before he really pissed her off by ripping off her clothes and fucking her on the table in front of everyone in the restaurant.

* * * * *

"Do you want me to drive?" Lily asked as Evan hurried her down the street toward his car. Her whole body hummed with electricity, her nerves tingling and her panties well past damp. Something had changed between them. The awareness between them had become stronger, more intense. Like a living, breathing thing threatening to squeeze the life out of her if he didn't get inside her soon.

"No." Evan stopped by his car, kissed her hard and fast, and let her go. He had a primal, untamed look in his eyes that sent a jolt of heat straight to her pussy. "Get in the car, Lily."

She smiled. After torturing her last night did he really think she'd make this easy for him? "What's the hurry?"

He took her hand and pressed it to the front of his jeans. His erection throbbed against her palm. "Oh. That."

"Yeah, *that*." He nipped at her lower lip, his hands shaking as he gave her a push toward the passenger side of the car. "Get in the car so I can get you home and get in you."

"When you put it that way…" She climbed into the car and put her seatbelt on just as Evan pulled away from the curb and sped down the road to their street.

When he got to his driveway, he slammed the car in park and got out. She followed, pulling her house keys from her purse. He grabbed her hand and led her toward her house.

"What's wrong with your bed tonight?" she asked.

"Yours is better."

Was he nuts? She had a double bed. His was a king. Was he planning to play some kind of kinky camp counselor role-playing game? "Why is mine better?"

"You'll see."

"Does this have anything to do with the dildo you bought me?"

He stopped walking and sucked in a sharp breath. "Not tonight."

"Then what's going on?"

"Tonight, I think you need to see how beautiful you are, despite what you seem to think."

"What do you mean? I never said I was a hideous cow."

"No, but you keep telling me that you look nothing like the woman in the pictures. You're wrong about that, Lily." He pulled her close for a long, scorching kiss that fried a good portion of her brain cells before started walking again, making it to her front door in record time. He pulled the keys from her hand and let them inside.

However it happened, she couldn't recall, but she soon stood before him in her bedroom naked and very willing. He'd stripped off his own clothes and taken a seat on her mattress, his heated gaze locked with hers and sending shivers through her. Her pussy throbbed, her nipples ached, but she felt nervous about what he wanted to do. What was he up to? He usually talked candidly about exactly what he wanted them to do—what he wanted to do to her, but something about this encounter—

everything about it—was different than the times before.

Evan sat on the edge of the bed, his legs spread slightly, his cock thrusting up into the air. "Come here," he told her.

Thinking he wanted her to suck him, she licked her lips as she approached. But when she tried to get down on her knees to take him in her mouth, he shook his head. "No. Straddle my lap. Face away from me. Don't sit down yet."

Um, okay. Frowning, she did as told. And then she saw his reasoning.

He had them positioned across from her full-length mirror.

She gulped. "Evan, I don't know—"

"Hush." His arms came around her, his hands resting on her belly, his fingers splayed across her hips. A ripple of anxiety joined the curls of arousal in her belly and she closed her eyes.

"Lily, open your eyes. You need to watch this."

She shook her head, squeezing her eyes even more tightly shut.

"Lily," his silky voice held a warning tone, one she chose to ignore. She couldn't even look at pictures of herself in a magazine. No way was she going to watch while he...while they...

"No," she told him, uncertainty building in her by the second.

His palm came down on her upper thigh with a smack. She yelped and tried to jump away even as a rush of moisture trailed down her thigh. *Omigod.* Evan held her in place with one hand as a sharp quiver ran from her clit straight to her cunt. Her thigh tingled, the twinge of pain morphing into arousal as he rubbed the spot he'd spanked. "Open your eyes, Lily," he whispered, his breath hot and moist against her hip. She dared to open one eye, and then the other, just in time to watch his tongue dart out of his mouth. He licked the skin of her hip. She shivered and let out a little sigh.

She brought her hand over his, holding him to her stomach

while she rocked on her feet. "I need to sit down."

Through the reflection, she watched surprise flicker in Evan's gaze. "Did you like that?"

"Yes. A little too much." And if he did it again she might come right on the spot.

He searched her gaze for what felt like an eternity before he nodded slowly. "Then by all means. Sit."

He lowered her to his lap, positioning her on his thighs. His rigid cock rested against her back, the weeping head dampening the skin over her spine. She couldn't help but wriggle back against him. He rewarded her efforts with a groan.

"Keep watching," he told her. He draped her legs over his thighs and moved his legs apart, revealing her glistening pussy. Her breathing hitched as her gaze locked with his in the mirror and she saw the intensity in his eyes.

His hands stroked her breasts, pulling and plucking at her nipples, cupping the full weight of the globes in his palms. He leaned forward and kissed her shoulder—and then he bit her there, his white teeth locking onto the skin as his lips curled in a feral smile. His teeth didn't sink into her skin and he didn't cause her any pain, but she recognized his act for what it was—a possession. She shivered down to her toes.

He dropped his hands lower, smoothing his palms over her belly, his fingers stretching down to her mound. She had an unimpeded view of his fingers slipping lower still, dipping into the moisture welling in her cunt. She arched her hips toward his touch, swallowing to wet her Sahara-dry throat. The crinkly hairs of his arms abraded her nipples as he stroked two fingers in and out of her, his fingers disappearing into her pussy. She couldn't pull her eyes away from the sight.

His thumb came up to circle her clit, the pace of his strokes within her increasing by small increments. Her breaths came in panting gasps, her body a spring being wound to the breaking point.

And then his movements stopped.

She blinked at him, uttering small sounds of protest. He laughed.

"Trust me, Lily. I'll make it good for you."

His light tone made her smile, despite the tension throbbing through her. "You always do."

"And I always will." He didn't give her time to contemplate his words. He gripped her hips and lifted her, lowering her down onto his waiting cock.

She hissed out a breath as he brought her all the way down, completely impaling her on his rigid flesh. She leaned forward and dug her fingers into the hard muscles of his thighs, her hips rocking back and forth in a swaying motion she couldn't control. He used his hands to guide her into a steady rhythm, lifting up and dropping down on his erection.

She'd never seen such an arousing sight as Evan's cock sliding in and out of her. Seeing her cunt entrance stretched taut, filled with Evan, made her go weak everywhere. His fingers brushed her clit, stroking her softly, and she quivered.

"Do you see how beautiful you are?" he asked, kissing the side of her neck.

"No. I see how beautiful *you* are." She smiled at his touch. "And how beautiful we are together."

With a shake of his head and a reprimanding smile, he increased the pace of her strokes and started pumping his hips. The position made his cock bump the entrance of her womb with every down-stroke, leaving her aching and panting and practically screaming for release. One final stroke of his finger on her clit gave her what she wanted.

Her world exploded around her, everything disappearing as her vision grayed. She pitched forward, digging her nails harder into his thighs, vaguely aware of his hand coming around her belly to keep her from falling to the floor.

He shifted, pulling out of her spasming cunt, pushing her legs to the floor, and her hands to the floor in front of her. He stood behind her, his hand rubbing the round globes of her ass, while she fought to keep her arms and legs from giving out after such intense pleasure. His hand came down on her ass, a little harder than the time before, but not intolerable. It sent a series of quivers through her cunt. She moaned when he rubbed the warm, wet head of his cock up and down along her slit. His thumb pressed against the rosebud of her anus.

"Next time, Lily. Next time that's where I'll be."

She lifted her head to see him staring at her reflection—not her face, but her ass. She gulped at the heated, almost reverent look in his eyes. Would she really let him do what he'd hinted at more than once?

Yes. She trusted him. She'd let him do just about anything.

She watched as his hand came back, then forward, connecting with the soft flesh of her ass again. This was the hardest one yet—and it sent her into a long, shimmering orgasm. Light burst behind her eyes, her whole body tingled pleasantly, her cunt muscles clenching and unclenching. A ripple ran through her belly as he caressed what must be a red spot on her ass.

He gave her no warning when he fit his cock against her entrance and slammed into her, filling her in one thrust. A small scream erupted from her throat at the harsh, unexpected claiming. She shivered, every nerve from the tip of her toes to the top of her head tingling. His thrusts were hard, unforgiving, pumping into her with short stabs. Her arms threatened to give out, her legs, too, as his fingers dug into her hips to pull her back to him with every thrust. The look on his face told her he was close to release—very close. She squeezed her cunt muscles tight around him, hoping to coax the orgasm from him. It worked.

Evan bucked against her before he stilled, his hot cum shooting into her in spurts, his head thrown back, his mouth open in a soundless moan. After one final, sharp thrust, he pulled out of her and dragged her to her feet. His mouth descended on hers, his lips heavy, his tongue seeking, and she wrapped her arms around his neck.

He collapsed backward on the bed, taking her with him, before he rolled her to her back and came up on his side, stroking the skin of her mid-section lightly.

"That was amazing," she whispered, leaning in to kiss his temple.

He smiled. "But did I accomplish my goal? Did you see what I see when I look at you?"

A wanton idiot who couldn't control her facial expressions? "Sure."

He leaned in and kissed her softly. When he pulled back, she saw a definite, unmistakable emotion in his dark eyes—one that echoed inside her and made her giddy all over.

Love.

She opened her mouth, but clamped it shut as the emotion in his eyes dimmed and died away, replaced by supreme satisfaction. Had she imagined the whole thing? She must have. Evan didn't love her. He never would.

Sex, Lily. It's all about the sex. How many times do I have to repeat that before you get the picture?

She couldn't do this anymore. She turned her back to him as tears welled in her eyes. Why did it have to hurt this much? She wanted to ask him to stay the night, but she couldn't speak past the softball-sized lump clogging her throat. She knew he wouldn't, just as she knew why this time had been different than all the other times.

Because he wouldn't be back.

She let out a shaky sigh as he wrapped his arm around her waist. At least she'd have the memories. She wouldn't beg him to change his mind about their future. She wouldn't even beg him to spend the night. She'd take what little time they had left like an adult, and she wouldn't look back.

Well, okay, she would. She'd probably regret the whole affair—especially how quickly it ended—for the rest of her life. But she'd never let him know.

"Are you okay?" he asked, his breath fanning through her hair.

She inched away, burying her face into her pillow. "I'm fine."

At least she would be.

In about a hundred years.

Chapter Sixteen

Evan woke with a start, his gaze scanning the dark, quiet room. The only sounds he heard were crickets chirping in the darkness of the night, and Lily breathing evenly and deeply beside him. He glanced at her, his heart swelling as he took in the sight of her hair fanned over the pillowcase, her lips full and pink even in sleep. His heart pounded, his lungs constricted, and his stomach churned. The worst that could possibly happen had happened.

He'd fallen in love with her.

He sat up and blew out a couple of sharp breaths. She lay in bed, curled in the covers, looking like the most beautiful thing he'd ever seen with her hair mussed and the sheet pulled up to her shoulders. He loved everything about her, right down to the dusting of freckles on her nose that had been airbrushed out in the magazine photos.

But he couldn't love her!

Hadn't he learned his lesson? Didn't he know better than to get involved with the wrong woman?

He should, but apparently what he'd learned with Jessica hadn't been enough. He'd gone and done something stupid yet again. Now he had to find a way out of it. Lily had made it quite clear many times. She only wanted sex from him, nothing more. If he begged for more, he'd look like a fool. He refused to beg. For *anything*. Jessica had been the first woman to make a fool out of him.

And the last.

He slid out of bed, careful not to wake Lily, and pulled on his clothes, leaving his shoes off until he got to the front door. He slipped out the door and into the humid air of the very early morning. The leaves of the trees rustled in the breeze, the faint scent of roses from the garden of a neighboring house wafting through the air as he hurried across the street.

What had he been thinking?

Not much, at least not with his mind. He'd been thinking with his dick, and his heart had followed. His mind hadn't even entered the equation. Now he was in too deep. So much for keeping things casual between them. He'd never had that problem before. What had happened this time?

You fell in love, moron. You should have known from the start that she wouldn't be right for you.

He *had* known, something inside had told him to steer clear of her, but he'd pursued her anyway. If it hadn't been for those damned pictures, maybe he would have left her alone. But he hadn't, and he'd done the unthinkable.

He let himself into his house, closed and locked the door behind him, and strode into the kitchen. He rummaged through the cabinets until he found what he was looking for — the bottle of aged whiskey his brother-in-law had sent him for his last birthday. Not bothering with a glass, he brought the bottle to his lips and took a couple of swigs. It burned going down, but he welcomed the feeling. It got his mind off his stupidity. He set the bottle on the counter with a thump. Even drinking himself into oblivion held no appeal tonight. He wanted to go back, climb into bed with Lily, and pretend he wasn't so head over heels he couldn't keep his thoughts straight. But he couldn't do that. He'd promised her a casual fling, and that's exactly what she would get.

What *both* of them would get.

Lily would probably curse a blue streak when she woke up and found him gone again. Being a woman, she'd no doubt want some kind of closure. She'd get over it, though. And this time, he had no intentions of letting her back into his life. Despite what he'd told her in the bar that first night, he now knew they could never be friends. Why had he ever thought they could go back to being acquaintances after the amazing sex they'd had? It just wouldn't be possible.

He walked up the stairs to the bathroom and turned the shower on cold. He stripped and got in, slumping down on the cool tile bench with his head in his hands. He let the cold water run over his back, seep into his skin all the way to his bones, and hoped it would rid him of the terrible ache he felt from the prospect of not seeing Lily again.

It didn't do a damned thing.

* * * * *

At first, when Lily woke up and stretched, she thought Evan might be down the hall in the kitchen trying to make her breakfast. She smiled at the thought, even though she knew she'd have to redo the entire meal. At least he tried, unlike some men she knew. She drew in a deep breath. The room still smelled of sex and Evan, but she noticed no sign of food, or even coffee. The hair on the back of her neck rose as dread pooled in her stomach. She got out of bed—and then noticed even his shoes were gone. She gulped. That couldn't be a good thing.

She slipped a T-shirt over her head and hurried down the hall. The house was quiet, silent. Empty.

Evan was gone.

She checked all over the house for a note, but he hadn't left one. The jerk had gone and done it. He'd walked out on her without even saying goodbye. This time, she wouldn't go after him. He had made his choice, chosen to end the affair, and she'd have to live with it. Whether she liked it—or wanted to kill him for it.

She tried not to cry, she really did, but she couldn't seem to hold back the tears that streamed from her eyes. They soaked her cheeks and dampened her T-shirt, running in hot rivers down her skin. She knew he'd only wanted one thing from her—and it had nothing to do with a ring—but it still hurt now that the end had finally come. Last night, he'd been different. More gentle, more caring, more thorough in his lovemaking. She'd hoped he'd been trying to tell her with actions what he couldn't voice. He'd been telling her something, all right, but not what she'd hoped to hear.

He'd been telling her goodbye.

She'd known that, admitted it to herself just before she'd fallen asleep in his arms. But the knowledge did nothing to ease the ache building inside her.

And then she got mad.

Who the hell did he think he was, walking out on her like some teenager in the middle of the night? Didn't he realize she knew where to find him — and if she chose, how much of a living hell she could make his life? The thought of rounding up Tony and Jake and maybe even Joe made her chuckle. Wouldn't it serve him right to wake up to three big, angry guys pounding on his door?

She shook her head as the visual lost its appeal. She had no right to be mad at him. He'd never promised her anything. His words last night about always making it good for her had been lies. She'd known that, and if she'd believed them, she had no one to blame but herself.

She was a complete idiot if she sat around crying over a guy she'd never be able to keep. Yes, it hurt. Yes, she wanted to go over to his house and strangle the life out of him. But, homicidal tendencies aside, they'd agreed upon one thing when they'd started their affair. Sex. Nothing more, nothing less. She couldn't fault the guy for sticking to the original plan — but she *could* fault herself for deviating from it. The pain she felt, the misery at the thought of never holding him again — it was all her fault. No one else's. As much as she loathed admitting she was wrong, she was.

See. That wasn't so bad, Lily. You're wrong! Wrong, wrong, wrong.

She gave the little voice a mental kick, sending it squealing into the corner of her mind. *Enough, already.*

She tried to laugh the whole thing off. It would be yet another interesting story to share with the man she'd eventually marry—the story where she had her heart broken by a man she'd been on a total of one date with. That thought brought a fresh batch of tears. She hadn't wanted to *marry* Evan, but the thought of marrying someone else left her cold. The thought of *him* marrying someone else made her want to break the windshield of his car with a baseball bat. Did she have one of those hanging around? Probably not, but she did have a hammer somewhere in the basement.

The telephone rang, saving Evan's car from eminent destruction. Was that him calling? If so, she planned to give him a piece of her mind. She yanked the receiver off the cradle and brought it to her ear. "Hello?"

"Hey, hon."

She blew out an annoyed, yet relieved, breath. Not Evan. "Hi, Janet."

"Gee, don't sound so happy to hear from me."

"Sorry."

"I just wanted to make sure you were okay. You know. After the other night."

"It was just water, Janet. I think I'll survive." She slumped into a kitchen chair, her stomach knotting as thoughts of Evan invaded her mind. She pushed them aside before they choked her, trying to put her focus back on the conversation.

"Hey, do you want to meet up this afternoon?" Janet asked. "Marnie and I are going to go shopping in Concord."

She almost said no, but in the end decided shopping might be just what she needed to get her mind off Evan. It had been a long time since she'd indulged in a shopping spree, and her credit card had an obscenely high limit.

She started to feel better already. "Sure. Sounds great."

"Excellent. I'll pick you up in a couple of hours."

* * * * *

Two hours later Lily sat on her front steps, waiting for

Janet. She'd spent an unusual amount of time on her hair and makeup, put aside her usual yoga pants and comfortable shirts for a pair of hip-hugging jean shorts and a cropped tank top, and dug a pair of strappy, wedge-heeled sandals she hadn't worn in forever out of her closet. The final effect reminded her more of the woman in the magazine than the real Lily, but playing dress-up had an amazing effect on her mood. She felt good. Well, almost good. At least she hadn't burst into tears in over a half-hour.

Janet's little red hatchback pulled into Lily's driveway just as the front door of Evan's house opened and he walked outside. She hurried down the walkway, almost spraining her ankle twice in an attempt to get into the car before he noticed her. She was determined not to let him see how much he'd upset her.

He upset her more when he didn't even try to get her attention.

Scum.

She climbed into the passenger seat of Janet's car, muttering curses under her breath as she slammed the door and turned to Janet, a hundred-watt and completely phony smile plastered on her face. "Hey. How are you?"

"What's up with you and Mr. Fine Ass?" Janet asked as she backed out of the driveway. "Trouble in paradise?"

Lily gave a shaky laugh. "Paradise? It's more like Atlantis."

Janet frowned. "How so?"

"It sank to the bottom of the ocean, drowning all inhabitants."

Janet laughed, but Lily failed to see the humor in her world, as she knew it, coming to an abrupt and total halt.

Chapter Seventeen

Two weeks.

Lily glanced at the calendar hanging from her kitchen wall and shook her head. Evan had walked out on her two weeks ago. She thought the pain would have faded by now, but it still held strong. She'd peeked out the window a few minutes ago and seen him washing his car in his driveway. It broke her heart to even look at the guy. But that hadn't stopped her from ogling his bare, wet back as he stretched over the hood, caressing the car like his used to caress her body. What woman wouldn't watch such perfection in motion? Her mouth watered, bringing back memories of watching him after his early morning runs.

She might be heartbroken, but she wasn't dead.

How was he doing? Was he seeing someone else?

She didn't doubt it for a second. Men like that rarely stayed single for long. Figured, since she couldn't seem to find anyone to take her mind off Mr. Fine Ass across the street. Not that she'd really tried, because she hadn't. Not this soon. She didn't have the heart. Plus, finding someone for anonymous sex to help her forget about the fling with Evan didn't work in a small town. Especially when one had posed sans clothing for a national magazine.

She heaved a sigh and walked away from the window. Why did she torture herself this way? She didn't need a man in her life, especially one who didn't want her. She could wish for him to change his mind all she wanted, but it wouldn't happen.

Someone knocking on her door brought her out of her reverie—just in time, too. The whole self-pity thing had started to get annoying as the days passed. She'd spent the better part of the past two weeks hoping it would just go away.

She ran down the hall to answer the door, knowing it wouldn't be Evan but unable to stop the hope that flared inside her every time the phone rang, or someone knocked on her door.

She found her brother, Jake—the jerk who hadn't spoken to her in weeks—standing on her front steps, his hands clasped in front of him and a contrite expression on his face that somehow annoyed her. She glared at him. "What do you want?"

"I came to apologize, as much as you might not believe that."

She raised an eyebrow. Sure, he did. Mr. High and Mighty always had an ulterior motive. It had been that way since they were kids. She crossed her arms over her chest. "I'll accept the apology, but you can forget even starting the accompanying lecture. I don't need to hear it."

Jake gave her an uneasy smile and shifted from foot to foot. "No lecture, honey. I'm really and truly sorry I blew up at you like that."

She shook her head. "So I take it none of your friends saw the magazine, so you no longer have anything to be angry about?"

"My friends? You wish. They all saw it, Lil, and they've been bugging me for your phone number ever since."

"That doesn't say a lot for their collective intelligence, since my number is in the phone book and most of them know where I live." When had her class valedictorian brother started hanging out with morons?

"That's not the point. The point is I had no right to get so angry over something that didn't really cause any harm. You have a right to express yourself in any way fit—well, any way within reason—and I have no right to butt into your life and try to tell you otherwise. You're old enough to make your own decisions, and I re-respect that."

She glanced up at the sky, ready to duck behind the door at the first sign of bad weather. Jake frowned at her. "What are you doing?"

"Looking for lightning." She smiled at him. "I'm sure you're going to be struck dead after those remarks. Honestly, I'm surprised your heart didn't stop beating when you said you respect my decisions."

Jake blinked at her, his expression hovering between anger, annoyance, and humor. He shoved his hands into his pants pockets and walked the length of the small front porch before coming back to her, a wary smile on his face. He finally broke down and laughed, pulling her in for a hug and nearly squeezing the breath out of her.

"Are you really sorry?" she asked him when he pulled back.

"Yes. And I'm proud of you, too. You went against convention, and that takes guts."

She frowned. That sounded familiar. Come to think of it, Jake's entire speech rang of familiarity. "You've been talking to Tony."

Jake gave her a sheepish grin. "Yeah."

She'd have to remember to thank Tony for talking some sense into their family members.

"Have you told your wife about the magazine subscription yet?"

Jake shook his head.

"Go home and tell her." She smiled as a thought hit her. Jake would be shocked, but as boring as he was, a little shock might not be such a bad thing. He wouldn't need to hide things like that magazine if he had a little more fun in the bedroom with his wife. She'd heard that marriages went stale after a few years, and if you didn't do something to keep things interesting, people strayed. In the interest of helping Jake hold together his marriage, she said, "Better yet, go to the adult store and buy some toys. Give your marriage a little more spice."

Jake's eyes widened until she thought they'd pop out of his head. He gaped at her, his mouth opening and closing rapidly, before he finally cleared his throat. "What did you just say? I think I need to have my hearing checked."

"No, you heard me right. There's a neat store in Concord that—"

Jake covered his ears and spoke loudly. "I am *not* hearing this."

She lifted his hands from his ears, shaking her head. "I'm serious, Jake. Learn to have a little fun. Not just in that aspect, but in everything."

Jake shrugged. "If you say so."

He could deny it all he wanted, but she saw the curiosity in his eyes. She smiled to herself. It was about time the guy tried lightening up.

Jake started to go when she saw Evan come up the steps behind him. "Hi, Lily," he said, his glare on Jake. Lily bit back a laugh. She knew what Evan was thinking, she'd experienced his jealousy on more than one occasion, but she wasn't about to stop him. It would be fun to watch him make a fool out of himself. He deserved to suffer a little before she kicked him to the curb. She leaned back against the doorframe and watched Jake eye Evan.

"Who are you?" Jake asked, his shoulders squaring as his eyes narrowed.

Evan crossed his arms over his chest. "I should be asking you the same thing."

"I think I asked you first."

"I'm Lily's boyfriend," Evan practically growled. "How does that sound?"

Jake frowned. "It sounds fine. I just hope you realize the whole control freak thing just gets her mad. Trust me. I know firsthand."

"Oh, really?" Evan took a step toward Jake.

Before things got too out of hand, Lily stepped in to separate them. A little torture never hurt, but she didn't need a bloody brawl in her front yard. She grabbed Evan's arm and pulled him back. "Evan, this is my older brother, Jake. Jake, this is Evan, my neighbor across the street. Now play nice."

"I thought he said he was your boyfriend." Jake threw Evan a wary glare.

Lily shook her head. "He's delusional."

"Do you want me to beat him up for you?"

Sometimes she swore she was surrounded by muscle-bound meatheads. A fight between Jake and Evan would be a toss-up, and she didn't want her brother getting hurt.

"He's not dangerous, Jake. At least not to me." Lily smiled and patted her brother's shoulder.

"Oh, I get it. Lover's spat." Jake kissed Lily on the cheek before he turned to Evan. "If you hurt her, I'll kill you. Although, she'd probably do you in before I could get a chance, so good luck. You'll need it. She's a handful."

"I know she is. That's what I love about her," Evan said softly, his expression serious.

Lily watched Jake walk down the driveway, get into his car, and—

Hold on a second.

Did Evan say he loved her? "Evan, did you just say what I think you did?" Maybe she was the one who was delusional.

He let out a deep sigh, his gaze falling everywhere but on hers. He ran a hand through his thick hair, his tongue moistening his lips. When he finally glanced down at her, his lips lifted into a shaky half smile. "Yes, I did."

She narrowed her eyes at him, not ready to accept his words at face value just yet. "Did you mean it, or were you just trying to get rid of my brother?"

"I mean it, Lily. I love you. I thought I could walk away, but I can't." He stepped closer, his scent invading her personal space in a big way, overpowering weeks' worth of anger and resentment. He crushed her against him, his lips seeking hers, his tongue plunging into her mouth when she parted her lips in surprise.

She clung to him as he deepened the kiss, backing her into the doorframe and pressing his body to hers. His incredible body. She gulped. He was hard everywhere. Her fingers tangled in his hair, holding him close, afraid he might pull away and tell her this was all a big joke. That thought cooled her enough for her to see reason.

She pulled back from him, looked into his handsome, loving face, and smacked him upside the head. "What were you thinking, walking out on me like that? Do you know how much you hurt me, you scumbag?"

He backed up a step in time to avoid another swat, looking like he didn't know whether to laugh or get mad. He caught her hands in his. "I'm sorry. I really am."

"Well, goody for you." She pursed her lips and narrowed her eyes at him, ducking away when he made a grab for her. She stepped into the house and stood behind the half-open door. "I'm sorry, too. Sorry I ever got involved with you in the first place."

He froze, his expression taking a chilly turn. "You don't mean that."

"Don't tell me what I mean, Evan. You're not my keeper."

He let out a small laugh and shook his head. "No shit. You don't need a keeper, Lily, and that's not what I want."

She stopped halfway through slamming the door in his face. As satisfying as that would have been, she had the sudden urge to hear him out. "And what exactly is it you *do* want?"

In answer, he pushed into the house, slammed the door, and had her back against it before she could utter a single protest. She gasped at the feel of his bare chest pressed against her thin T-shirt, his rigid cock hard against her belly. He kissed her roughly, letting her feel all his wants and emotions from just the touch of his lips and tongue. When he broke the kiss he didn't move away. He stood there against her, pressing her body into the cool metal door. It was a good thing, too, considering the consistency of her leg muscles now resembled mashed potatoes.

"Can you ever forgive me?" he asked.

The expression on his face—a cross between sad puppy-dog eyes and extremely aroused male—had her nodding. "Okay. I think I can manage that. One thing, though."

"What's that?"

"We're going to take this slowly." She took a breath, trying to ignore the way his closeness made her tingle all over and dampened her panties. "I want it all—romance, flowers, and chocolate, fancy dinners."

He was nodding before she even finished. "Done."

"I also want you to know that, if you sneak out of bed in the middle of the night again, it had better be to buy me an extravagantly expensive present."

"Yes, ma'am."

The words sounded so ridiculous coming from his mouth she couldn't help but laugh.

"What do we do about our houses?" he asked her after another quick kiss. "I hate to be a pain about this and all, but I'm not giving up my shower."

"We'll deal with who gets to keep what when the time comes," she told him, kissing his jaw. "Slow and easy, remember? It's going to be a very long time before that time comes."

"If you insist." Evan let out a dramatic sigh. "I'll get you to cave, though."

She smiled as she shook her head. "Doubtful."

"Whatever you say." He nipped her jaw, her earlobe, sending a jolt straight down to her pussy. "But don't think I'm going to give up on trying. In fact, I'm going to start now."

A shudder racked her body. "How do you plan to do that?"

He gave her an exaggerated wink. "With orgasms. How else?" He picked her up in his arms and carried her to the bedroom.

* * * * *

"You'd tell me if I did anything that hurt you, or made you uncomfortable, right?" Evan asked as he kissed his way down Lily's naked body.

She whimpered as he dipped his tongue into her navel. "Of course I would."

"Good." He grinned up at her, but his smile quickly faltered. "What about that last time? When I…"

His gaze locked with hers, and the intensity she found there would have knocked her off her feet if she hadn't been lying back against her sheets. "When you spanked me?"

"Yeah." He shrugged a shoulder in a move she knew he'd meant to look disarming, but it only increased the tension between them. "I didn't take it too far, did I?"

"Did you enjoy it?"

"Hell, yes. But I've never done anything like that before." He dropped lower until she felt his breath blow against her drenched pussy with every word he spoke. "I just want to make sure you enjoyed it, too."

"I did enjoy it, more than you could ever know. I'll tell you if you've gone too far." She laughed as his tongue tickled the inside of her thigh. "I trust you, Evan. Don't feel like you have to hold anything back for me."

The look in his eyes as he glanced up to meet her gaze could only be described as primal. He gave her a slow, smoldering smile that set her body on fire. "Remember you said that."

"Okay, but…" The rest of her sentence trailed off as he ran his tongue down the length of her slit.

He parted her pussy lips with his thumbs, his tongue drawing circles over her clit. Her sex-deprived body responded immediately, a current so strong running through her that it sucked the breath from her lungs and made her heart pound against the wall of her chest.

With his tongue busy, he stroked his fingers up and down the sensitive skin before finally plunging them inside her waiting cunt. She let out a breath on a hiss as his fingers curled, finding her G-spot and massaging. It was all too much. She could barely stand the pleasure running through her, turning her blood to fire in her veins.

He stroked and thrust and circled until she felt like she'd come out of her skin. Her body exploded into a thousand points of gold and silver light, her vision yellowing at the edges and her hearing fading in and out as her orgasm carried her away on the tide of sensation. She grabbed fistfuls of cotton, pulling the corners of the sheet from the bed as her body bowed and her arms clenched. She screamed his name as he continued to touch her, to make love to her with his hands and mouth until she'd come two more times. He finally let her go and came up beside her, covering her mouth with his for a quick kiss before flopping onto his back on the mattress. Her body floated for an eternity before she drifted back to the ground enough to roll onto her side and meet his eyes. He smiled.

And then it hit her.

He loved her.

Just saying the words in her head made her feel giddy. Powerful. Like she could do anything. Even let go of herself to let him know how she felt. "Evan?"

"Yeah?" he cupped her cheek in his palm, stroking his thumb along her jaw.

"I love you." She gave a shaky laugh when his smile grew. "I just thought you should know that."

"Don't feel like you have to say it just because I did," he said softly. "Slow and easy, remember."

She shook her head as her heart hitched. "No. I want to say it. I can say I love you without us having to jump into marriage."

The second the words were out of her mouth, she wanted to bite them back. His eyes widened, taking on a slightly horrified expression at just the mention of the word. He swallowed hard, three times, and ran a hand down his face.

"I see you still have that pesky allergy to words relating to matrimony." She tried to laugh it off, but couldn't quite manage much more than a grimace.

He stared at her, his expression anxious, before he shook his head. "No, I don't think I do. You threw me for a minute there, but I think I'm over it. It's safe to assume that if you say the word again, I won't go into anaphylactic shock."

She raised an eyebrow at him. "Really?"

He shrugged, the casual move belying the intensity in his eyes. "Why don't I test it? Marry me, Lily."

She felt like she was the one going into shock. Her breath rushed from her lungs with a *whoosh*, her heart pounded hard against her ribcage before stopping completely. She felt like she was underwater—she couldn't see well, couldn't hear, and couldn't breathe. Evan patted her on the back.

"Should I call 9-1-1?"

"Very funny," she told him, her voice not much more than a squeak. She closed her eyes and sucked in a couple of deep breaths, not snapping her eyelids open until Evan pulled her closer and she felt his warm breath on her skin.

"Should I take that as a no?" With his hand behind her hip, he pulled her closer still, until she felt the heat of his rigid cock pressing into her naked flesh. She shivered.

"No. I mean, don't take it as a no. It's not. A no, I mean." She bit her lip to quell her babbling before he got the wrong idea. "Yes. My answer is yes."

He let out a harsh breath. "Thank God. You had me worried there for a second."

"We're not going to rush this, though. We're going to take it slowly until we get to know each other better. For now, I have other plans for you." She reached between them and grasped his cock, stroking the velvety hard length of him before she rolled on top of him and straddled his hips. "Any objections I should know about before we let this get any further?"

He shook his head. "Never."

Taking that as her cue to continue, she positioned the head of his cock at the entrance of her cunt and lowered herself down until her ass rested on his thighs. Evan let out a hiss of air as his fingers gripped her hips. "You feel so good, Lily."

"So do you." She rose up, lifting until she'd nearly pulled him out of her completely, before she slid down again. She ground her clit against his pubic bone every time she lowered herself. It sent little jolts of pleasure through her entire body.

"Come here," he told her. "Lean over and let me suck your nipples."

She did as he asked, bracing her hands on either side of his head and leaning in to his mouth. He sucked a nipple between his lips, flicking his tongue slowly across the hardened peak, rolling the flesh gently between his teeth. He moved to the other breast, affording the nipple the same treatment. The sensation of his hot, wet mouth made her come again, her body convulsing over his as shudders and shocks raced through her. He popped her nipple out of his mouth and rolled her to her back, pumping into her in short, thrusting strokes that kept her body clinging to the remnants of her orgasm. Her cunt muscles sucked him deeper, clenching and unclenching around him as he took his own release. She felt his hot seed spurt inside her in bursts, filling her full.

He collapsed on top of her and raised himself up on his elbows, staring down into her eyes. "You are the most beautiful woman in the whole world."

She nearly cried at the sincerity in his gaze. Her life couldn't get any more perfect than this.

* * * * *

Evan stood in the bathroom doorway, watching Lily splash water on her face. When she bent over to scoop water from the tap, he had a nice view of her fabulous ass, covered only in a pair of sheer white bikini panties. They were made out of some kind of slippery, silky material that looked fragile. He smiled as he imagined tearing them off her.

He stifled a yawn, not wanting her to know yet that he'd woken up. He wanted to spend a few more minutes watching her before he alerted her to his presence. His life had taken a dramatic turn in the last eight hours. He'd started out the evening like he had every evening in the weeks since he'd walked out of her bedroom. He'd done his best to avoid her. But when he'd seen her hugging some other guy, something inside him had snapped. The thought of her with anyone else brought out a very bad side of him. He'd realized at that moment with absolute clarity — he wanted her all to himself. Forever.

But she said she wanted to take it slow.

He nearly growled in frustration. He wanted her in his bed every night, and at his kitchen table for breakfast the next morning. He didn't want to wait for the time it took to plan a wedding in order to get those things. But he'd do what she asked. She deserved it and more, after what he'd put her through. And he'd do whatever it took to prove to her that he was good for her, even if it entitled waiting weeks, or months, or…he gulped…years like his last wedding.

Lily grabbed a plush peach hand towel and rubbed it vigorously over her face before she raised her head and looked in the mirror. When her gaze locked with his, her eyes widened and she let out a squeal as she jumped back. "How long have you been standing there?"

She glared at him, but it dissolved into a smile when he stuck his tongue out at her. "Long enough to want to drag you back to bed and have my way with you."

She rolled her eyes, a dramatic sigh escaping her lips. "You've had your way with me so many times in the past few hours I'm surprised you're able to um… *rise* to the occasion."

He glanced down at his cock, bare and already semi-erect. It swelled when her gaze followed his. "I don't think that will be a problem."

She blinked at him before she burst into laughter. "You're nuts, do you know that?"

Just the sound of her laughter, husky and sensual, made him hard. He stepped toward her and wrapped his arms around her waist, dragging her back against him. "If I'm nuts, it's all your fault."

She frowned. "How do you figure?"

"I was perfectly happy with my life the way it was. I didn't want another relationship, figured it wasn't worth the trouble it might cause in the end." He brushed a kiss across her cheek and watched her reflection as her face pinkened. "I thought I'd known lasting love before, and when I lost it, I said I'd never make that kind of a commitment again. But when I got to know you, I realized I'd been wrong about Jessica, and what I thought she'd meant."

She narrowed her eyes, but the corners of her mouth twitched up into a small smile. "Oh, really? So you rushed into marriage?"

He shook his head. "No, I didn't. I'd been dragging my feet about it for months, and Jessica finally talked me into it. Now I have to wonder what her motivations were. She didn't want me. She just wanted to be married. When something better came along, she didn't hesitate to grab it."

She opened her mouth to speak, but he hushed her with his hand over her mouth. "Wait a second. Just hear me out. I do have a point to this." He winced when she bit his palm, and dropped his hand. "What we have is different. I knew it from day one, even if I wouldn't let myself admit it. It's stronger. It's lasting. And I know you're not going to run off with the first guy who makes you a better offer."

She spun in his arms and wrapped her arms around his neck. "Says who?"

He leaned in and sucked her lower lip into his mouth, tugging on it gently with his teeth before he let it go. "Deny it all you want, sweetheart, but what we have is special."

She pulled back and looked at him, her expression taking a serious turn. "I know it is, and I know how hard this must be for you, after what happened with your marriage."

"Actually, it's not hard at all. With you, everything comes naturally. I don't know why I tried to fight it for so long."

She snorted a laugh. "That's simple. Because you're a man. By nature, pig-headed and stubborn."

"Oh, very funny." He reached for her, but she ducked away and ran to the bathroom door. "Hey! Where are you going?"

She gave him an exaggerated wink and glanced down at his cock. "Back to bed. Care to join me?"

In a heartbeat.

Epilogue
A note from Lily:

I bet you're wondering what happened to Evan and me, huh?

Tough. I'm not one to kiss and tell.

Just kidding. Had you going for a second there, didn't I?

Well, we didn't take it slowly, but did you really expect we would? We've been over the whole impulsive thing. That's how I am. Get over it. Evan, apparently, has an impulsive streak in him as well. When he proposed for the second time, a whopping two months after we got back together, he did it so right I couldn't resist. Flowers, candlelight, a fancy dinner, a basket full of sex toys…what girl in her right mind would have turned him down? I'm impulsive, not stupid.

Evan insisted we get married right away. To avoid making a big fuss out of it all, he'd said. But I know the real reason. He was afraid I'd change my mind. *As if.* He's stuck with me for life. Whether or not that makes him happy remains to be seen. I'll try my best, though. I always do.

We eloped. Last night. We took advantage of my father's distracted state helping Hannah and her boys care for my new baby sister. I almost feel bad for the little cutie. She's the baby of the family now. She has no idea what she's in for, living with Frank Baxter. When she gets a little older, I'll have to give her a few pointers.

Did Jake ever take my advice? I don't know, and I really don't want to. But he's been *a lot* happier lately. So has his wife.

Janet and Brick, believe it or not, are moving in together. Surprisingly, the guy's not as dumb as he seems. He knows how to keep Janet in line.

Marnie and Joe didn't fare as well. She finally saw him for the jerk he is and dumped his sorry ass. She's dating a great guy now, and with any luck, she's found what she's looking for.

The whole "dirty pictures" crap has started to die down, partly thanks to the public apology Toby printed in the paper. At least I don't feel like a pariah walking down the streets anymore.

I moved into Evan's house last month. When we sat down and really talked about it, there wasn't really much choice. His house is twice the size of mine, with the pool and *the kitchen*. I'm in absolute heaven. I still work for my mom, but now I drive my new car in every day. By myself. Evan was eventually able to talk me into getting my license. No, I haven't killed anyone—or taken out any unsuspecting fences. Evan still can't cook without me having to go out and buy a new set of pans, but I'm working on it. He'll get there. Eventually.

As for Evan, I don't plan to let him out of my sight. We're on our honeymoon—in Jamaica of all places. The women on the beach are all staring at him, and I've got to protect what's mine. I don't plan to let the passion run out of this relationship for a long, long time. Like *never*.

Oh, and the shower he spent so much time bragging about? I have one word for it.

Fabulous.

About the author:

Born in Gloucester, Massachusetts, Elisa Adams has lived most of her life on the east coast. Formerly a nursing assistant and phlebotomist, writing has been a longtime hobby. Now a full time writer, she lives on the New Hampshire border with her husband and three children.

Elisa welcomes mail from readers. You can write to her c/o Ellora's Cave Publishing at 1337 Commerce Drive, Suite 13, Stow OH 44224.

Why an electronic book?

We live in the Information Age—an exciting time in the history of human civilization in which technology rules supreme and continues to progress in leaps and bounds every minute of every hour of every day. For a multitude of reasons, more and more avid literary fans are opting to purchase e-books instead of paperbacks. The question to those not yet initiated to the world of electronic reading is simply: *why?*

1. *Price.* An electronic title at Ellora's Cave Publishing runs anywhere from 40-75% less than the cover price of the <u>exact same title</u> in paperback format. Why? Cold mathematics. It is less expensive to publish an e-book than it is to publish a paperback, so the savings are passed along to the consumer.

2. *Space.* Running out of room to house your paperback books? That is one worry you will never have with electronic novels. For a low one-time cost, you can purchase a handheld computer designed specifically for e-reading purposes. Many e-readers are larger than the average handheld, giving you plenty of screen room. Better yet, hundreds of titles can be stored within your new library—a single microchip. (Please note that Ellora's Cave does not endorse any specific brands. You can check our website at www.ellorascave.com for customer recommendations we make available to new consumers.)

3. *Mobility*. Because your new library now consists of only a microchip, your entire cache of books can be taken with you wherever you go.

4. *Personal preferences are accounted for*. Are the words you are currently reading too small? Too large? Too…**ANNOYING**? Paperback books cannot be modified according to personal preferences, but e-books can.

5. *Innovation*. The way you read a book is not the only advancement the Information Age has gifted the literary community with. There is also the factor of what you can read. Ellora's Cave Publishing will be introducing a new line of interactive titles that are available in e-book format only.

6. *Instant gratification*. Is it the middle of the night and all the bookstores are closed? Are you tired of waiting days—sometimes weeks—for online and offline bookstores to ship the novels you bought? Ellora's Cave Publishing sells instantaneous downloads 24 hours a day, 7 days a week, 365 days a year. Our e-book delivery system is 100% automated, meaning your order is filled as soon as you pay for it.

Those are a few of the top reasons why electronic novels are displacing paperbacks for many an avid reader. As always, Ellora's Cave Publishing welcomes your questions and comments. We invite you to email us at service@ellorascave.com or write to us directly at: 1337 Commerce Drive, Suite 13, Stow OH 44224.

Discover for yourself why readers can't get enough of the multiple award-winning publisher Ellora's Cave. Whether you prefer e-books or paperbacks, be sure to visit EC on the web at www.ellorascave.com for an erotic reading experience that will leave you breathless.

Printed in the United States
30416LVS00007B/133-183

9 781419 951855